SILKEN SLAVERY

His heart hammering against his delicately feminised chest, Chris is then helped to sit down on the bed by Helen. As he does so, the tight panels of the corset bite deep into his sides and he gasps in pain.

'The corset will be rather uncomfortable for a while,' she says, her splendid eyes filled with a cruel amusement, her own substantial breasts rising and falling rapidly with an obvious excitement through the fine fabric of the expensive silk blouse. 'But a strict exercise regime should reduce your waist to a less problematic size quite quickly.'

By the same author:

THE LAST STRAW

SILKEN SLAVERY

Christina Shelly

This book is a work of fiction.
In real life, make sure you practise safe sex.

First published in 2002 by
Nexus
Thames Wharf Studios
Rainville Road
London W6 9HA

www.nexus-books.co.uk

Typeset by TW Typesetting, Plymouth, Devon

Printed and bound by
Mackays of Chatham

ISBN 0 352 33708 7

PART ONE
In and Out of the Closet

One

Chris wakes from a deep, troubled sleep to painfully bright morning light and the sound of distorted disco music. Still disoriented, he throws back the covers of his large, double bed and leans over to turn off the radio alarm clock. As he does so, his painfully erect cock brushes against the damp sheets and the dream explodes in his mind, a moment of precise, overwhelming clarity. Donna. Beautiful, vibrant, sexy: Donna.

The LED reads 7.10. He falls back onto the bed and closes his eyes. When he opens them again it is 7.40. Still plagued by the dream, by its awful erotic power, his hands stroke his cock, feeding it idle caresses as the dream images float across his vision. Then he sighs wearily, the guilt of his lateness distorting the dream like a virus inserted into his neurological system by the Priests of Work, and sits up. I am, he thinks, the slave of the clock and the cock.

The dream still tormenting his mind, he crawls from the bed and staggers into the toilet/bathroom. After a long, hard and deeply refreshing piss, he finds himself, as he does on so many mornings, staring into the bathroom mirror at his reflection and wondering what he is looking at. A man? A mask? A mask hiding a secret even he has trouble coming to terms with.

He steps into the shower and submerges himself beneath a jet of steaming hot water, his cock proudly upright like a totem pole raised in praise of some mysterious sex cult. He stands still and lets the water pour over his perfectly smooth, muscular body, a hairless body whose pristine contours are the result of careful diet and daily exercise, a masculine yet also feminine body. After a few minutes he takes a small plastic razor from the soap dish and begins to shave his body, as he does every morning, obsessively seeking out the tiniest speck of hair, a painstaking examination which takes in every nook and cranny, including his expertly denuded pubic region.

As he does so he fights to rid his mind of the dream, of its incredible potency, an erotic vision that has fractured the boundary between the conscious and unconscious worlds and is making rational thought about the day ahead impossible.

But here it is: unyielding. Donna. In her sexiest dress, in her sheer black nylons, in her high, high heels. Her teasingly petite form before him like a miracle manifestation. Her strawberry lips curved into a tense, aroused half-smile, her lovely sky-blue eyes filled with a simple, powerful sexual need, her breasts, so deliberately displayed by the tight-fitting dress, rising and falling with her short, hard breaths. Perhaps only five feet four inches, but quite perfect in his hungry, desperate eyes. Donna pulling him into a dark alley, or a room, maybe even a closet. Taking his hands in hers, pulling them beneath her short dress as she presses her breasts into his chest and he brings his mouth down to meet hers. Letting him explore her nylon-sheathed thighs, feeling the womanly warmth turning to an intense, fundamental heat as his hands move up into the moisture between her hosed legs, a moisture that quickly turns to hot, wet sex, the rain forest of a brutal desire. Then their lips meet. The longest, hardest kiss, a kiss he screams his pleasure into. A kiss which turns into a molten white light as his fingers swim deep into her stormy abyss.

'You're mine,' she whispers. 'All mine.'

He washes his body with scented soap. He washes his very short, jet-black hair with a feminine shampoo. He steps from the shower with an elegance and grace unusual in most men and carefully dries himself. He covers his body in a powerful feminine body spray and then weakens its effect with a relatively neutral male deodorant. He brushes his hair without looking in the mirror and then walks back to the bedroom.

The bed is a large wooden frame upon which rests a very firm double mattress. Built into the bottom of the frame are four drawers, two on either side. He sits on the bed, leans over and pulls out one of the drawers. It is filled with carefully ordered piles of women's undergarments. From the drawer he takes a pair of white silk panties and a pair of very sheer black nylon tights. His hot, nearly shaking hands fondle these items of lingerie as if they are holy relics and with a fetishist's helpless devotion he carefully lays them out on the bed. His erection grows even stronger as he stands and takes up the panties. Momentarily he is seized by the need to masturbate, but a discipline born of experience allows him to push this need to one side and step gingerly into the soft, forgiving panties.

As he draws the panties up his smooth, long, very shapely legs, he sighs with a pleasure that has never weakened over ten years. As he stretches the panties over his rigid cock and pulls them into position around his hard, flat waist, he remembers the weekend spent as Christina, the weekend lost in his passion for all things feminine. A weekend spent in this small, expensive city flat, cut off from reality, submerged in a powerful, addictive fantasy, his only contact with other human beings the internet and the virtual community of transvestites that inhabit it, a community of which he is an eager but paradoxically shy member.

The panties are followed by the tights, the sheer black nylon tights, the most delirious fetish item in his

5

extensive feminine wardrobe. At any one time he has up to fifty pairs of tights and stockings. The feel, the look, the effect – he cannot sum up the power of his fascination with hose. He is helplessly and continually addicted, and as he expertly draws the fine, soft intense fabric over his legs he moans with an intense animal pleasure.

Once the tights have been carefully pulled into place, he admires his legs in the full-length mirror that stands next to the wardrobe and almost immediately hungers to complete the transformation into Christina. But instead of beginning the complex ritual of complete feminisation, he takes a simple white cotton shirt from the wardrobe and pulls it reluctantly over his shoulders. The shirt is followed by a suitably neutral blue tie and a disappointingly drab black wool suit. Very thin nylon socks are then slid over his hosed feet and a pair of black brogues laced into place.

Suitably attired in his office uniform, he eats his cornflake breakfast whilst watching the television news in the living room. Still half-watching the television, he then sits down at his personal computer and logs onto the internet. As expected, there is new mail from Annette, a response to his message sent late the previous evening. He had sent her a scan of a particularly erotic drawing from a new collection of erotica, a picture of an artfully petticoated youth kissing the leather-booted feet of his mistress, a very intricate pencil drawing from the early 1920s. Annette, his closest virtual 'sister', a beautiful cross-dresser who shares his sadomasochistic leanings, is full of praise for the picture, yet makes a point of wondering why he has sent her this picture rather than the picture of Christina she had originally asked for. Chris smiles and logs off, yet doesn't move from the chair. Instead, he calls up the picture of Annette, stored in a coded file on his hard drive, the picture she had sent him three weeks before, the picture that he had stared at in amazement for over an hour when it first arrived. The picture that now inspires his hand to slip between his legs and gently caress his rock hard cock through the trousers, the tights and the panties.

Annette: a twenty-five-year-old transvestite from London, a tall, blue-eyed redhead whom Chris met through a cross-dresser chat group and who had, to his surprise, sent him a picture as a file attachment with only her second e-mail. A picture of her in a very short, tight black dress, sitting cross-legged on a stool staring with a brazen sensuality into the camera's eye, her long, sexy legs wrapped in sheer black nylon, her feet erotically imprisoned in the highest of black patent leather high heels. A strikingly convincing TV who filled him with both longing and jealousy, a she-male whose friendship he has retained with constant promises of a reciprocal picture, promises which he doesn't have the courage to fulfil.

He turns from the computer and stares at the bookcase taking up most of the opposite wall. A bookcase resting on a long wooden cupboard filled to bursting point with the books that have come to define his life. He looks at these books and wonders if he has wasted all the hours spent reading them. He knows the answer to that question is a resounding *no*: without their wisdom he would be little more than a robot, a pathetic subject of wage slavery. But he recognises that the books have too often replaced life, because life, at least for Chris, has always been a problem. He stands, moves closer to the bookcase, runs his eyes along the four packed shelves, seeing, as he sees every day, the names that have helped him survive: Freud, de Sade, Masoch, Miller, Bataille, Réage. Then there are the magazines, the hundreds of neatly stacked fetish magazines locked in the cupboards beneath the bookcase. A lifetime's collection covering those dark areas of desire that have held Chris in their grasp for so long: domination and humiliation, forced feminisation, bondage.

From the bottom shelf he takes the half-read copy of a biography of Anaïs Nin and slips it into his jacket pocket, reading for the bus and the inevitably lonely lunch break. This pang of loneliness makes him think of the dream and of Donna. What would she think, he wonders, if she could see all these books and magazines, if she knew about Christina?

By the time he leaves the flat, he is already twenty minutes late.

The only seat left on the bus is next to a tall, ice-eyed blonde who regards him with blatant contempt as he attempts to sit down beside her. His face turning crimson, he avoids her gaze and stares with panic-stricken reserve into the worn cloth of the seat. Satisfied she has humiliated him, she stares angrily out of the window. Yet as soon as she looks away, his sex-addict eyes traverse the impressive contours of her black nylon sheathed and very tightly crossed legs.

His erection remains fiercely persistent as he opens his book, but the dream and Annette's e-mail make concentration impossible. So he returns to staring with aching desperation at the blonde's gorgeous legs and contemplates the strange farce that his life is in danger of becoming.

He is nearly thirty. He is single. He is a transvestite. He has worked in the planning section of the council for five years, where he is now effectively second in command. He is well paid, he is physically attractive, yet he is also painfully shy, especially with women. He is deeply bored with his work and, if he was honest with himself, desperately unhappy. Also, he is still a virgin. And as this word flashes on and off in huge red letters in his mind, he feels a familiar horror, a horror rooted in the fear that his personality problems will ensure that

8

he will never find a woman and thus never have sex. Frozen solid by eye contact, appalled by the idea of actually trying to seduce a woman, he has hidden in a hole of shy isolation for most of his adult life. What attempted intimate contacts he has made with women, mainly at university, have been disasters that have left him humiliated and scarred. Disasters compounded by the strange nature of his desires, by his helpless femininity, by his deep sadomasochism, by his constant desire to dress and act as a woman, desires which have possessed him since his very first sexual thought.

In the five years since he moved to this ugly Midlands city, and especially in the eighteen months that he has lived in the apartment building, Christina has emerged out of a morass of guilt and desire. Perhaps a positive development, most certainly an intensification of his transvestite cravings. Now he can, without too much effort, make quite a convincing woman. Now he can remove the mask for whole weekends and lose himself in her, in this delicate, ultra-feminine creature that is at the heart of every sexual thought and raw, unyielding stiffness. Yet he has been unable to move beyond the secret dressings that occupy so many evenings and weekends. The next step, getting to know other TVs in the flesh, going out and trying to pass, the whole giddying public revelation of the feminine self, has failed to materialise. He has been frozen by fear, by the fear that all sexual interaction inspires in him. He is bound in the chains of a pathological shyness, the slave of fear. Only his regular correspondence with Annette and his regular attendance at so many internet chat rooms has provided him with any true social interaction. And while it is clear Annette would like to take this tentative relationship further, Chris – Christina – remains trapped firmly in the closet.

By the time he arrives at the office, he has managed to retrieve ten minutes and avoid too many ironic looks

9

from the three women who make up the clerical staff of the Planning Records Section. Essentially an open plan office with two smaller, closed offices at each end (one for him and one for his boss, Katherine Grainger), the Planning Records Section is responsible for the computerised storage, update and renewal of every piece of planning permission data produced by the Council.

He smiles his normal shy half-smile at his staff, carefully avoiding any eye contact as he does so, and rushes into the office, collapsing into his chair behind his paper-strewn desk and turning on his computer. As the screen flickers into life, there is a knock on the door and Helen, his PA, enters the room, a file in one hand and a cup of coffee in the other.

As usual, he looks up at her and manages a genuinely warm smile of greeting, trying not to let his eyes wander over her body and confess the intense desire he feels for her and her two colleagues.

'Heavy weekend?' she asks with a slightly teasing smile, as she places the file and the cup of coffee on the desk.

A nervous laugh is the only reply as he wonders what she would think if she knew he'd spent most of the weekend dressed as a woman.

'Miss Grainger would like you to look at this,' Helen continues, 'a complaint from upstairs about missing records.'.

He nods half-heartedly: more boring donkey work. 'OK.'

As Helen turns to leave, he finally allows himself to feed on her splendid form. At 41, she is a tall, dark-featured woman with a very ample, extremely shapely figure that is today very effectively displayed by a tight black skirt reaching just above her knees and a semi-transparent white silk blouse through which the flowered pattern of her bra is clearly visible, as are the curved peaks of her tightly restrained, very large breasts. A divorcee, previously married to a wealthy businessman, she is rumoured to have secured an extremely generous settlement and have no need to work for money. As his eyes move across her long, black-hosed legs, his cock strains once more in its secret prison of nylon and satin. As she closes the office door he curses himself for not saying something, as he always does. Just some cool, relaxed remark, telling her how attractive she looks today. But he can hardly open his mouth in her presence, never mind find the courage to give her a compliment.

And so the day begins. He spends most of the morning avoiding Katherine's file and idly trying to short out the chaos of paper that remains from last week. By 11.00 a.m. he is bored stupid and decides to venture out into the main office, heart in his mouth, coffee cup in hand.

His three support staff are hard at work, but as soon as he appears they turn as one to face him, their eyes pinned firmly to his, their smiles broad, curious, vaguely teasing.

'Hello, stranger,' Donna snaps. 'Thought you'd nodded off in there.'

They laugh. He laughs. He relaxes a bit and manages to look at Donna. The youngest of the three, at thirty-five, and easily the most attractive. A beautiful, petite blonde, her hair sparkling in the late morning light and spilling over her shoulders like a honey waterfall, she is dressed in a very tight white sweater, a very short red skirt and white tights, her feet wrapped in red patent leather stilettos. Even by her somewhat brazen standards, this is a particularly sexy outfit, and poor Chris feels his knees buckle beneath him as she turns her chair to face him and crosses her legs in the process.

'Cat got your tongue?'

He laughs nervously and moans a rather pathetic, 'Seems so,' unable to pull his eyes from her legs.

'Probably spent the weekend with his secret girlfriend. She's worn him out.'

These words come from Anne, the third member of his support team. Slightly older than Helen, Anne is a tall, green-eyed redhead with a sharp, sarcastic manner. Dressed in a loose red blouse and very tight jeans, her hair tied in a bun, she makes no secret of her general indifference to the pathetic rules of office life and has already been issued a formal warning by Katherine for her abrupt manner with other staff. Chris, despite knowing that Katherine is keen to get rid of her, has failed in every way imaginable to enforce the standard disciplinary procedures.

'More coffee?' Helen asks, standing up.

Her powerful musk perfume washes over him and he nods weakly. 'Thanks.'

'What about this girlfriend then, Chris?' Donna continues. 'Why is she such a big secret?'

'I haven't got a girlfriend. I've told you before. Seriously.'

Donna smiles, her eyes seeming to fill with relief.

He wants to tell her how fantastic she looks, how much he wants her, about the terrible power of the dream and how desperately he wants it to become reality. But instead, he says nothing and fights the urge to run back to his office.

'What about a boyfriend?' Anne teases. 'Perhaps he's gay. I'm sure there are plenty of horny homos who'd go for a pretty boy like Chris.'

Donna shakes her head and slowly uncrosses her legs, her beautiful sky-blue eyes never leaving his. 'He's not gay. I can see that a mile away.'

'Well, there's something funny going on. Come on, Chris – tell us what it is.'

Anne's change of direction catches him by surprise.

'I don't know what you're rambling on about.'

'Perhaps he dresses up in women's clothes,' Anne continues, laughing loudly as poor Chris turns bright red and swallows very hard, a terrible, humiliating panic flooding over his body, his heart suddenly pounding violently. How on earth did she . . .? But then Anne is laughing in a much more sarcastic manner and Donna is smiling a blatant 'got you' smile. More teasing. Just a bizarre, horrible coincidence. No need to panic, no need to run screaming from the building.

Helen brings the coffee. Chris thanks her and returns to his office, still shocked by Anne's words. Yet he is also more excited that ever. He wonders what would have happened if he had confessed the truth, if he had pulled down his trousers and revealed the dreadful reality of his strange desire.

He is still pondering this bizarre possibility when there is a knock at the door. To his surprise, Donna enters the office, looking less confident than usual, her full, cherry-red lips curved into a slightly nervous smile.

He coughs and sits up, trying not to leer.

'There's something I want to ask you,' she says, now avoiding his already unsteady gaze.

'Fire away.' Ridiculous words, even more absurd from his mouth.

'Do you really not have a girlfriend?'

He swallows and nods, then utters a weak, desperate, 'Yes, really.'

This seems to cheer her up. Her smile broadens. 'Do you like me?'

Stunned, his heart going into overdrive and a fine sweat of nervous terror suddenly breaking out across his forehead, he can only nod weakly.

'So you do . . . like me?'

'Yes, of course. I mean –'

But he can't say it, what he has always wanted to say to her. The barrier of his terrible, unending fear rising up like a vast prison wall.

'What?'

He squirms, he swallows, he chokes. Then he looks at her, at this stunning woman. Suddenly he stares directly into her startling blue eyes and the wall collapses.

13

'You're beautiful. I think ... you're very beautiful. I've fancied you for ages.'

It is as if another being has entered his head and taken over his mouth, a confident and direct being, a real person. And as he confesses his desire, her lovely smile widens even further and she moves closer to the table. His erection swells up angrily and suddenly he feels very dizzy.

'Well, then,' she says, her voice now filled with its usual sensual confidence, 'why don't you ask me out?'

'I haven't ... I can't.'

'You can't? Why?'

'I'm too frightened.'

His pathetic reply, his all-too-true reply, brings a terrible, surprised laugh. 'Frightened? What of?'

'Of being turned down, of being laughed at. I don't know. Just frightened of making a fool of myself.'

She laughs again, this time gently, more sympathetic. 'There's no need to be frightened, Chris. Not of me. Just ask me out.'

And so he does. His voice shaking, his mind racing, his heart pounding, he asks her if she would like to go for a drink after work, and she accepts without a moment's hesitation.

As she walks from the office, his eyes eat up her gorgeous, sexy body and he nearly faints as a tidal wave of elation and desire crashes over his body.

He spends the rest of the morning remembering the dream and fighting a tremendous urge to masturbate. He replays the utterly amazing conversation, her lovely smile, her promising, hungry gaze. The dream was, it seems, a prophecy.

He spends his lunch break walking around the city centre trying to calm down. By the time he returns to the office, he feels much more relaxed and is even able to smile at his three beautiful assistants, all of whom seem deeply amused. But his good mood is quickly spoilt by the arrival of Katherine.

14

Katherine Grainger, his boss, a particularly mundane nemesis. An aggressive, career-obsessed woman. Two years younger than Chris and a year junior to him. Promoted over him when it became apparent he was merely an indifferent time-server. A tall, masculine woman who hides whatever traces of her true sex remain under what often looks like a man's business suit and the most boringly sensible of shoes, her black hair cut short, her face a no-go zone for make-up, her brown eyes always filled with grievance, her voice always a second from anger.

'We've had another complaint, Chris,' she snaps, matching into his office without knocking, standing over him like some grim harbinger of doom. 'About Anne. You really are not helping with her. It's your job to supervise her. To discipline her, if necessary. If she won't do something about her bad attitude, then you'll have to get rid of her. If you won't, I will. And if I have to, I'll make sure the people upstairs know about it.'

Strangely, he feels little fear of Katherine. Maybe because she tries so hard not to be a woman, maybe because there isn't the sexual presence and the threat this seems to pose for him. He stares at her, sighs, then slumps a little further down into his chair.

'She's a good worker. Just because –'

'Look, I don't want any more excuses. Either deal with this complaint or I will.'

After throwing a memo onto his desk, she storms out. Chris picks up the piece of paper, crushes it into a tiny ball and throws it into the bin. As he does so, a smile returns to his face: in a few hours, he will be alone with Donna.

He meets her in the pub around the corner from the local government offices, just after six. He has been sitting in the virtually empty pub for twenty minutes by the time Donna walks in, and is already on his second bottle of German beer. Despite the alcohol, he is still terribly nervous and, when Donna sees him, smiles brightly and walks over to his table, he fights a very powerful urge to rush from the pub.

She is still dressed in the very sexy attire that had tormented his eyes earlier, and the other patrons, all men, stare at her with a sad longing that Chris tries to ignore.

'You started without me,' she says, her eyes filled with teasing curiosity.

'Sorry . . . I . . .'

She laughs. 'Don't apologise. I'm joking. Want another one?'

He nods weakly. She buys the round, two more bottled German beers, and returns to the table, sliding onto the leather-backed seat beside him, her beautiful, musk perfume washing over him and sending his desperately pumping heart into his mouth and very effectively gagging him. But even though he is struck dumb, his eyes say all that needs to be said: they caress her splendid body with a loving hunger and his erection burns into his trousers like a rod of molten iron.

They spend the next two hours talking and drinking. At first Donna talks and Chris listens, still amazed that he is actually sitting in this pub, with this glorious woman, this woman he has so desperately and secretly desired for over a year.

She talks about the office, her life, her history. At thirty-five, the single mother of a seventeen-year-old daughter, the father a long-forgotten teenage fling who she had no intention of involving in her child's upbringing. She talks of her daughter with an intense pride and Chris listens with genuine interest, his eyes fighting to meet hers rather than eat up the fine curves of her white nylon-sheathed legs and her very firm bosom. Then she tries to get him to open up about his life. But, even with the beer, Chris is reluctant to talk about himself. He

16

alludes to dead parents, to being an only child, to his university years and his accidental imprisonment in local government administration. He is far more forthcoming on his dislike of work, but only hints at his feelings for Donna. Yet she quickly seizes these hints and confesses to having secretly liked him for a very long time. To his astonishment, she confesses that she was always convinced he had a girlfriend, that such an attractive man must be involved with somebody. She tells him she finds his shyness 'sweet', that she has always had a very soft spot for 'sensitive, clever types'.

It is nearly ten when, after maybe six bottles of strong German beer, she asks him to come home with her.

'Lesley's out at a friend's,' she says, her eyes filled with a slightly drunken promise. 'The house is empty. Come back with me, spend the night. I know you want to.'

He can only nod, suddenly dizzy with an intense, alcohol-fuelled desire. She leads him from the pub, out into the warm evening. She hails a taxi. Then they are in the back of the car and her hands are pulling his beneath her skirt and she is pressing her hot, wet mouth against his. The shock is immediate and total. Suddenly, for the first time in his life, he is locked in a sexual embrace with a woman, his hands caressing her nylon-sheathed thighs, bathing in the moist heat of her flesh, journeying towards her greatest secret. They kiss, fondle, cuddle. He is lost in her and in this dream made reality. He is almost deliriously happy.

By the time they get to her house, she is almost ripping the clothes from his body, laughing, panting, her eyes glazed over with a powerful drunken sex-need. He tries to push her back so he can reciprocate the act of undressing, pulling at her sweater, lifting her short skirt up over her thighs and hips to reveal juice-soaked panties and very damp tights.

It is as he stares in mad hunger at the large damp patch around her sex and she unzips his trousers and

17

begins to pull them down his legs that that word comes back, that flashing red light word: tights. But it is too late: she has pulled the trousers down over his thighs and revealed his own panty clad, ultra-stiff sex and hose-encased, baby smooth legs. A strange moment of absolute numbness follows, a moment in which he is frozen solid inside a terrible humiliation. Her eyes are widening, confused, amused . . . amazed.

'What's . . . what's going on here, Chris?' she asks, her lovely blue eyes wide, her sexy mouth curved into a surprised half-smile.

Then the ice is broken and the horror is flooding in. He hauls up his trousers, tears welling in his eyes, and tries to push past her, saying nothing, his body rigid with a terrified embarrassment. She pulls at his shirt, but he shrugs her off. She shouts his name, but he is soon out of the corridor, out of the door and out onto the street, her voice loud yet muffled behind him. But he doesn't listen – he knows she is screaming outraged obscenities at him. All he wants to do is run. And he does run, down the long, sodium electric streets of a summer's evening into an oblivion of despair, all the time wondering in stunned horror how he could possibly have forgotten about the tights and panties and knowing, even as he replays the question, that the simple answer is *sex*, the drug of desire combined with too much booze. You fool, you absolute bloody fool.

He staggers into his flat just after midnight, tears pouring from his face. He rips all his clothes off, tearing the tights into shreds and cursing his sick cravings, realising that his dark, twisted desires have lost him the transformation of his life, the first true experience of the most intimate human communication.

He sits in the shower for over an hour, soaking himself in steaming water, trying to wash away the terrible, tormenting memory of Donna's startled face and her smile only seconds away from a declaration of disgust.

Eventually, at around two in the morning, the tears still flowing down his red cheeks, he collapses naked onto his bed and falls into a fitful sleep filled with a hundred nightmare recreations of his ultimate humiliation.

Two

He wakes just after 6.00 a.m., hung-over and engulfed by the appalling memory of his dreadful exposure. A sickening wave of embarrassment washes over him as he recalls, yet again, the look of amazement on Donna's beautiful face and his own near-hysterical reaction to this bizarre revelation.

He stares up at the ceiling in a semi-trance for nearly thirty minutes, tormenting his mind with the incident and contemplating the awful day ahead. At first he seriously considers not going into work, but knows that, in the long run, this will only make matters worse. So, eventually, he pulls himself off the bed and staggers into the shower. But this morning there is no elaborate washing and shaving and, after the shower, no delicate and ritualised dressing in delicate feminine undies. There isn't even a breakfast: at just after 7.00 a.m., he walks like a ghost out of his flat and into a very unsure future. And by 7.45 a.m., he is sitting in his office, over an hour early, staring blankly at his door, awaiting his doom with a pounding heart and wild, fearful eyes.

The knock at the door comes just after 9.00 a.m. He tries to mumble a nervous 'Come in,' but his desert-dry mouth can deliver only a pathetic gasp of despair. Then the door opens and, as he had expected and feared all along, Helen, Anne and Donna enter the office. They line up in a grim cinemascope row before his desk and he feels his face burn a bright, deep and very humiliated shade of crimson. His eyes bore into his paper-strewn desktop and tears begin to well up in his eyes. This is the moment of ultimate despair, and there is no escape.

'We've come to talk to you about last night,' Helen says, her voice surprisingly calm, even gentle, without a hint of the contempt or disgust he expects.

He nods painfully, still not looking up, tears now beginning to trickle from his eyes and down his burning cheeks.

'About what happened at my house,' Donna adds, her voice also quiet, even concerned.

'I know,' he mumbles. 'I'm sorry, I . . . I can't help myself.'

Then the tears are pouring from his eyes and his voice has collapsed into loud, pained sobs. He tries to turn away from the women, to hide in the corner, to shrink down to the size of a pinhead and disappear. But then there are hands on his shoulders, gently pulling the chair around, bringing him slowly back to face his fate. But then his face is being pulled into the soft, large cushion of Helen's shapely bosom. Suddenly his face is submerged in the warm, lilac scent of her and from miles away he can hear her voice, her maternal reassuring voice, telling him that there is nothing to worry about, that all they want to do is help him. Then Donna's voice and Donna's beautiful smell. She too is close and comforting, almost begging him to forgive her!

'I didn't mean to laugh, Chris. It was just such a shock. Exactly what I wasn't expecting. I tried to get you to stay. I wanted you to stay so bad . . .'

He pulls his head out of Helen's chest and she steps back. He wipes the tears from his eyes. This is all wrong, yet, of course, it is also all right. Through a teary blur he beholds the three women, all smiling, all clearly here to talk and sympathise rather than mock.

'You mean, you don't mind?' he asks, a question directed at Donna, but which all three answer with a resounding chorus of 'No!', 'Of course not' and 'Why should we mind?'.

And he is amazed, stunned, and then terribly, almost sickeningly elated. A huge tidal wave of relief crashes over him, a hard, powerful drug that fills him with a remarkable sense of happiness.

'I thought you'd be disgusted, that I'd have to leave. I . . . God, I'm so ashamed, so pathetic.'

'There's no need for all the self-pity,' Helen says, a tone of slight irritation in her voice. 'If this is something you want to do, then that's fine with us. But we really do want to know about it, about all of it. Then we'll see what we can do to help you.'

Still stunned by this totally unexpected turn of events, he asks them to sit down and tries to compose himself. Then, over the next hour, he tells them everything, a flood of relieved, desperate confession, a narrative so long suppressed that it virtually explodes from deep within him, a very secret and personal history. He confesses his lifelong desire to cross-dress, his deep sexual need to adopt a feminine persona. He tells them about Christina, about his secret identity and her strange virtual life. He talks about the clothes he is especially attracted to. Then he confesses his attraction to all of them, and his especially deep feelings for Donna. And finally, he reveals the deep core of masochism that lies at the heart of his transvestism, of his desire to be dominated and controlled by beautiful women, to be enslaved and forced to act as the sissiest of she-male maidservants.

And as he confesses, there isn't the slightest sign of mockery or contempt amongst the women. Indeed, if he sees anything in their lovely, sexy eyes it is fascination and, amazingly, beneath this fascination, a form of arousal. And in Donna's lovely eyes he sees something even deeper, something that might even be love.

At the end of his confessions there is a very brief silence, then Helen rises from her chair and stands over him like an ideal dominatrix, her brown eyes burning into his, a gentle smile filling his tormented heart with a sense of something approaching salvation.

'Well, I think the best way forward is for us to meet Christina,' she says. 'And as quickly as possible.'

At first he stares at her in disbelief. 'Meet Christina?' he mumbles. 'I don't understand.'

'Come to my house this evening and show us Christina. Bring your favourite outfit, all the make-up you need. Reveal your inner self to us.'

'To all of you?'

'Of course. We all want to meet her, and we all want to help. We can give you tips, show you how to improve her.'

Helen's words fill him with a sense of elation, yet also with terrible trepidation. Suddenly the brutal fear, the utterly unforgiving shyness has returned to possess his body and soul.

'I don't think I could.'

'I'd really like to meet Christina,' Donna suddenly says.

He turns to face her, his heart pounding, his mind racing with fear and desire. Today she is dressed in a tight pink sweater, a long black shirt, black hose and a pair of very high-heeled mules. As usual she looks fantastic; as usual the very sight of her gives him an instant erection. Her gorgeous blue eyes are filled with sympathy and arousal.

'It's time to live,' Helen adds. 'If you want to spend the rest of your life locked up in that flat, repressed, overwhelmed by fear, then don't come. If you want to experience the truth of yourself, to realise your potential and make all your fantasies come true, then come to my house at 6.00 p.m. tonight.'

He looks into her dark, fiery eyes, into two pools of shining black gold, and he nods.

'Yes. OK. I'll be there.'

'Good,' Helen says. 'We'll see you there. And don't be late.'

With this, she turns to leave and her beautiful companions follow her, Donna's eyes briefly meeting his one more time, her smile a smile of endless promise.

After they have left he sits perfectly still for a very long time, his heart gradually slowing, a sense of almost surreal calm gradually washing over him. The fear, the terrible, bleak fear that has possessed his life like a crazed demon, fades and then, for the first time in many years, it disappears. A slight smile crosses his thin, feminine face. He can hardly believe this is happening.

He manages to remain in this tranquil state for only a few hours. After lunch he finds himself pondering why Helen and her lovely friends have offered him this wonderful opportunity, why they have been so sympathetic to what is a particularly bizarre sexual tendency. Then the fear quietly returns, and with it a sudden, vicious paranoia. Perhaps, he finds himself thinking, there is a darker motive behind Helen's invitation. Perhaps the full revelation of Christina at the house is merely a means to ensure a more complete and inescapable humiliation. But then he remembers their words, their voices, their eyes. There is no evidence, no real proof of such a sinister motivation.

He leaves work early, unable to concentrate on anything except the night ahead. By the time he gets home, a cool terror sweat is covering his body and his hands are shaking with an intense trepidation.

He spends over thirty minutes in the shower, carefully re-shaving, soaping and scenting his girlish body. Dressed only in a very short Chinese silk dressing-gown, he selects a deliberately provocative and very sexy outfit from his secret wardrobe. First of all, a black satin panelled cross-dresser's corselette, a beautifully intricate device designed to provide an essential underlying feminine figure, complete with special padding at the hips and crotch, a very well-padded bra section and a very tight waist section. After this, he selects a pair of black silk panties frilled with delicate red French lace and a pair of very sheer black nylon tights. Next comes a shimmering black silk blouse, with beautiful puffed sleeves and black pearl buttons and a sexy black leather mini-skirt. Then, a pair of four-inch, stiletto-heeled court shoes made from gleaming black patent leather. This is followed by a beautiful blonde wig styled in the sultry fashion of the great fifties film stars, the favourite of his ten carefully maintained wigs. Finally, he selects his favourite jewellery and fills a pink make-up bag with the items essential for the creation of Christina. All this is then carefully packed into a large sports bag.

On the bus to Helen's house, the address taken earlier from his personnel files, the fear grips him yet again and he seriously considers turning back. But Helen's words of encouragement give him the strength to overcome the fear, the pathological shyness, her words and the memory of Donna's beautiful eyes.

It is a few minutes after 6.00 p.m. by the time Chris nervously walks into the very exclusive cul-de-sac where Helen lives. He can hardly believe his eyes when he reaches the driveway to her home and quickly rechecks the number on the crumpled sheet of paper in his pocket. But sure enough, he has the right house, a huge, Edwardian five-bedroomed monster, left to Helen by a rich and very guilty husband as a suitable divorce settlement – that and a very handsome monthly allowance.

In the driveway are Helen's beautiful Audi sports car, Anne's brand-new Peugeot 206 and Donna's slightly battered Ford estate. Seeing the cars only adds to the sense of panic and fear that tries to push him back down the road and onto the first bus into town. But he manages to force himself forwards to the door, where, with a hot, shaking hand, he uses a large brass knocker to announce his arrival.

Barely has the knocker struck wood than the door swings open and he finds himself facing Helen. Helen, looking totally stunning in a very tight, short black dress, black hose and stiletto-heeled mules, her hair flowing freely over her shoulders, her blood-red lips curved into a warm smile of welcome, her dark brown eyes filled with an amused anticipation.

'I'm glad you decided to come, Chris. You won't regret it. Come in.'

He can only nod weakly and follow her into the long, beautifully decorated corridor of this exotic, plush house. As he walks behind her, his eyes pinned to her long, elegant legs and their slow, graceful movement, he is also already violently erect, his heart pounding in his head, a tense, sticky fear sweat staining his forehead.

Helen leads him into the living room, a huge, perfectly square space filled with beautiful, expensive furniture, large, lace-curtained windows overlooking the spacious driveway and a stunning, ornate fireplace. Donna, still dressed in her lovely pink sweater and long pencil skirt, is sitting on a tan leather sofa drinking a glass of wine. Anne, now dressed in a pair of very tight black leather trousers, an equally tight white nylon sweater and a pair of very high-heeled stilettos, is standing with her back to the fireplace, also with a glass of wine, her lovely red hair a halo of sinful intent, her emerald eyes fixing Chris with a particularly intimidating gaze.

Donna asks him to sit down beside her. He does so nervously, placing the sports bag at his feet. Her powerful musk perfume washes over him and his erection stretches even more angrily against his trousers as she places a long, elegant hand on his knee.

'There's no need to be frightened, Chris.'

Helen, pouring herself a glass of wine, nods and moves closer to him. 'Try and relax, Chris. All we want to do is help you.'

Surprisingly, Chris finds himself vaguely irritated by her tone. 'Why?' he says. 'Why do you want to help me?'

'Because we're interested in you,' Anne suddenly interjects. 'Because it gives us pleasure.'

Helen nods, her eyes meeting Anne's, her smile widening. 'It's that simple, Chris. We enjoy exploring new avenues.'

She then comes over and sits next to him. Suddenly he is sandwiched between the two women who have fuelled so many of his sexual fantasies. Again, a sense of fear and unreality is quickly crushed by the brutal power of his desire.

'We won't offer you a drink,' Helen continues. 'I don't think it would be appropriate. In fact, it would probably be best if I showed you the room where you can change and we get straight on with meeting Christina.'

And so Chris follows Helen from the room, the smell of Donna still tormenting him. Helen leads him up a wide staircase to a first-floor landing, then down a corridor lined with doors. The room is at the end of the corridor, a large, sparsely decorated bedroom with a double bed, a built-in wardrobe and a dressing table.

'The spare room,' Helen says. 'A bit Spartan, but it'll do for now. The bathroom is just opposite, so if you need to shower, etc, feel free. We'll see you downstairs a little later.'

With this, she leaves him alone in the room. He remains standing, not moving, gazing nervously around the room for five very painful minutes. Now the fear is at its height: this is the moment of truth, his last real opportunity to escape the revelation of Christina. He places the sports bag down on the bed and turns to face

27

the dressing table. He sits on the small leather-backed stool by the table and stares at his reflection in the oval mirror. Then he remembers Helen's earlier words: it's time to live, to truly experience life. And that, he knows, means truly to experience himself, or rather, perhaps, herself.

He returns to the bed and opens the sports bag. He stares at its sexy contents and then begins to undress. Soon he is naked and looking down at his stiff, desperate sex. This is the very essence of every desire, his life quite literally bared. As he takes the corselette from the bag, his sex rubs against its soft, silken surface and a moan of helpless pleasure escapes his lips. It is only now, when the power of pure physical pleasure has transcended all fear, that the transformation from Chris into Christina truly begins.

With the corselette drawn over his lean, surprisingly muscular body, he feels the first exquisite transformative effects of the dressing. With its carefully and very realistically padded bra section, he experiences the glorious pulling sensation of a full, feminine bosom. His erection is already hidden in the soft padding of the crotch region of the corselette, but as he adjusts the bra he feels the fierce, rock-hard meat burn into the woollen padding and demand some form of release and again cannot avoid a moan of the most intense pleasure.

After the corselette comes his very favourite moment in this erotic ritual: the slow, teasing entrapment of his long, silky-smooth legs in the sheerest black nylon tights. Each movement now is careful, elegant and feminine and, as he guides the tights up his legs, a little more of Christina is revealed. As the soft, gentle and intensely pleasurable material slides over his legs, it is as if Christina is washing over Chris, as if a doubtful, tormented personality is being replaced by a calm, sensual and totally relaxed personality as if a skin is being shed.

Once the tights are firmly in place, he rises from the bed, gently smoothing the sublime nylon material over his thighs and knees. He takes a few dainty, feminine steps, his whole body movement now changed, and smiles helplessly. Christina is now firmly in control! Then he takes the super-soft, ultra-sexy black silk panties from the sports bag and elegantly steps into them, pulling them up his hosed legs and around his tightly restrained waist with a sigh of pleasure.

The dressing is then suspended while he applies his make-up. Sitting at the dressing table staring at his reflection like an artist considering his model, he applies a light tan foundation cream, taken from the pink make-up bag, to his freshly shaven, smooth face. As he massages out the already weak male angles in his cheek-bones, he finds himself marvelling, as he always does, at the ease of this profound change: just a few drops of foundation and already his indistinct masculinity has been destroyed.

Satisfied with the smooth base created by the foundation cream, he quickly applies highlighter to his eye-brows and then attaches a pair of very long, vampish false lashes to his eyelids. After a touch of pale blue eye-shadow, he applies peach-coloured rouge to both of his cheeks. Already he is staring at the early form of Christina, a pretty she-boy with short hair whose lovely sky-blue eyes twinkle with a helplessly feminine desire. And as he carefully applies a strawberry-coloured lipstick to his full, inescapably girlish mouth, as he teasingly runs the soft tip of the stick over his equally soft lips, Christina becomes stronger, clearer, more sharply in focus.

With the make-up complete, he rises from the stool and elegantly minces back to the bed, his tightly pantied and hosed buttocks swaying with a quite deliberate and provocative femininity. From the sports bag, he takes the glorious blonde wig and the items of jewellery. He then returns to the dressing table. Placing the jewellery on the table, he takes a deep, infinitely pleasurable breath and carefully pulls the thick blonde wig over his own close-cropped hair.

He has created Christina many times before, but as he positions the spectacular wig over his head, he knows there has never been a transformation like this. In a few minutes he will reveal his feminine persona to three beautiful women; for the first time, Christina will truly step out of the closet. A sweet, sexy smile crosses his lovely face as he contemplates both this exciting fact and the stunning image that is staring back at him from the mirror. He beholds a beautiful blue-eyed blonde with a full, sensual mouth and a long, slender swan's neck. As usual, he is both elated and disturbed by the success of the transformation. As usual, he regrets the blinding shyness and fear that has prevented him from stepping out into the world, from meeting other TVs socially, even just arranging for a photo to send to the gorgeous Annette.

Satisfied with the position of the wig, he carefully attaches two emerald clip-on earrings to his ears and wraps a band of silver-grey pearls around his neck. Then he once again rises from the dressing table stool and returns to the bed. From the sports bag he carefully extracts the beautiful black silk blouse and the matching leather mini-skirt. After laying them out carefully on the bed, he pulls the stiletto-heeled court shoes from the bag and places them on the floor. His erection burns into the soft but very firm fabric of the corselette, but thanks to the clever use of padding it remains completely invisible. As he takes up the blouse, a moan of helpless pleasure slips from his glistening, painted lips.

The caress of the silk against his bare arms is like a thousand teasing kisses, a brutally erotic caress that leaves no alternative but an intense, almost painful physical pleasure and a further deepening of the sense of sissy femininity that is gradually possessing his body and soul. And once it is buttoned up to the top of its high-collared neck, he steps into the tight black leather skirt and pulls it into position around his slender waist, a very arousing, but also relatively simple process.

Then there is the final startling element of the transformation, the final item of feminine attire that signals the true realisation of Christina. He takes the four-inch stiletto-heeled court shoes in his hands and sits down on the bed. He delicately crosses his sheer black nylon-encased legs and slips the first gleaming, black patent leather shoe over his right foot. He then repeats this process with his left foot and, with a tiny moan of apprehension, stands up. Suddenly elevated by four inches, a familiar sense of sensual dizziness washes over his intricately feminised body. He takes a tentative step forwards and it is almost as if he has walked through an invisible barrier into the dimension where Christina lives. Then he is suddenly taking the tiny mincing steps that the elegant, sexy shoes seem to demand, steps that create a helpless wiggle of his hips and an erotic swaying of his backside which is teasingly enhanced by the tight black leather skirt. As he moves so effeminately around the room, he revels in the electric tingle of nylon against nylon as his thighs rub together and the gentle caress of the sheer silk blouse against his upper body. Then there is the wonderful sense of counter-balance induced by the expertly padded brassiere section of the corselette. As this substantial chest sways, it seems to do so in a complex syncopation with his bottom and hips, a syncopation whose fundamental rhythm is set by the quick step demanded by the stiletto heels. And the result of this intricate interaction is the most erotic and provocative of sissy walks, a walk he has perfected with the obsessive enthusiasm that lies at the heart of Christina.

He minces from the room in a state of ecstatic terror, his heart pounding fearfully yet joyously. As he carefully descends the stairs of this large, plush house, his sense of helpless femininity is almost overwhelming, as is his sense of terrible yet erotic trepidation about his exposure before Helen, Donna and Anne. As he reaches the ground floor and approaches the doorway into the living room, he wonders if this is in fact some elaborate deception designed to expose him as a pervert and ensure his absolute humiliation. He imagines entering the room and being submerged in the blinding white light of camera flash-bulbs and the deafening roar of mocking laughter. Yet this fear is nothing compared with the excitement he feels, the excitement and intense sexual arousal inspired by his imminent exposure.

Then, in this state of high anxiety, so carefully and wonderfully feminised, his heart leaping desperately into his mouth, he enters the living room.

Donna is standing by the fireplace. Anne is sitting reading a magazine. Helen is gazing with an expression of boredom out of the large front windows. And it is Donna who sees him first, Donna who nearly drops her half-full glass of wine in amazement, Donna, whose look of surprise suddenly turns into a wide, generous smile.

'Bloody hell,' she almost cries out, 'you're beautiful.'

Helen spins around and, although there is no exclamation of surprise, it is clear she is taken aback by the scale of Chris's transformation. Anne rises from her seat, an impressed smile slowly spreading across her gorgeous face, a smile spiced with conspiracy and, ultimately, cruelty.

Helen and Donna immediately walk over to him, while Anne remains by the seat, her eyes appraising, cool, considering a mysterious future.

'I'm very impressed, Chris – you look quite stunning,' Helen says, her lovely dark brown eyes feasting on this striking she-male manifestation.

He smiles weakly and nods, his voice trapped in a vice of sudden nervous fear, despite his considerable inner elation.

'You must have been doing this for a long time,' Donna adds, her own eyes filled not only with surprise but with a very real arousal. 'It must have taken a lot of practice to look this good.'

The two women examine him very carefully, asking questions about his figure, his make-up, his clothes – questions he answers slowly, shakily, still unable to believe this is really happening to him.

'You've got fantastic legs,' Donna says. 'The tights really show them off well.'

He virtually swoons at this lovely compliment. Then, to his amazement, Donna rests a hand on his right thigh and begins to caress his hosed skin, a teasing and very suggestive smile on her gorgeous face, her blue eyes burning into his. He fights to maintain his balance, his erection now a rod of molten iron burning into the heart of his very being.

'We can help you,' Helen says. 'With your make-up, your deportment, your dress. You've obviously come a very long way but, if you want, we can take you further.'

He looks at her, knowing now that there is no secret plot against him, that these beautiful women are genuine in their desire to develop his feminisation.

'I'd love that,' he says. 'It would be all my dreams come true.'

Donna removes her wayward hand and steps back to get a clearer view of the beautiful she-male. His own eyes drink her up, her splendid, petite figure, her perfect poise, her lovely clothes, her promising, eternal smile. How much I want you, he thinks. And how much I love you.

'That's what we do,' Donna jokes, 'make dreams come true.'

33

Three

Virtually as soon as Chris accepts the offer of help to develop Christina further, Helen leads him to the large leather sofa and asks him to sit between Donna and herself, thus directly facing Anne. Almost instinctively, Chris finds himself elegantly crossing his long, black nylon-sheathed legs and wallowing in the vaguely jealous glare this inspires in the gorgeous redhead.

'Before we proceed,' Helen says, 'we need to know you are absolutely serious. If we are to allow Christina to reach her true potential, we will require you to submit to our authority completely. This is not just a matter of feminisation, it is also a question of enslavement. You've told us of your desire to be feminised and dominated, to live your life as a sissified servant of beautiful women. Well, if we develop Christina, it will be as our personal maidservant. Not only will we train you in the arts of dress, make-up and deportment, but also in the domestic arts essential for a slave girl and, of course, certain very fundamental sexual skills with which you will pleasure us. This will require your absolute and unquestioning surrender to our every word. Are you really prepared to go this far?'

Chris listens to Helen with increasing astonishment and arousal. This is indeed a dream come true, the wildest, sexiest dream he has ever had!

'Yes,' he replies, with an uncharacteristic confidence. 'I want to go all the way. It's all I've ever truly wanted. I want to be your slave; I want it more than anything else.'

'Even if it means giving up everything you have – your job, your flat, all your possessions?'

Again, a confident nod. 'Yes, absolutely.'

A slight smile crosses Helen's lovely face. 'Then we'll start immediately. You will spend each workday evening and each weekend of the next fortnight undergoing induction training at this house. At the end of this period you will be required to take two weeks' leave, so that you can begin detailed training. This will be carried out on a twenty-four-hour basis here and at the homes of Donna and Anne. During the coming two weeks, you will be permitted to continue to attend work, but there will be the strictest expectation that you will remain fully feminised at all times beneath your male work clothing. During the two weeks of detailed instruction, you will be permanently feminised.'

Chris listens to Helen in amazement. It is now quite clear that she has been planning this since his earlier tearful confession, that for some strange reason of her own she and her beautiful associates are bent on realising all of his deepest dreams and transforming him into a sissy maidservant.

'For the rest of this evening,' Helen continues, 'you will serve us. Now you may indicate your acceptance of your enslavement by kneeling down and kissing our feet.'

This first command is delivered with an erotic authority, and he instantly obeys, rising from the sofa with a series of careful, delicate movements, gently smoothing out his short, leather mini-skirt and then slowly, almost teasingly, lowering himself to his hosed knees before Helen, making sure as he does so that his skirt slowly rises up his backside and his hosed and pantied behind is fully exposed to Anne.

Helen kicks off her high-heeled court shoes and stretches out two shapely feet sealed in sheer grey nylon, her cherry-red toenails clearly visible through the sensual film of hose. Now on his knees, he leans forwards and places a long, passionate kiss on each foot, loving the feel of the warm nylon and hot flesh against his lips, plunging himself into aromas of feminine sweat and scented soap mixed with the residue perfume of the leather shoes, then moaning with the most masochistic pleasure as he turns his attention to Donna's outstretched and now shoeless feet. Sensually imprisoned in the sheerest black nylon, her pink toenails erotically apparent, her feet are petite masterpieces which he worships with long kisses, kisses which turn Donna's initial girlish giggle into a slow-burning moan of pleasure. How desperately he wants to spend the rest of his life in this position of absolute servitude, prostrate before the true goddess of his strange, utterly unyielding desire. I am yours, he says to himself. Absolutely and forever. Yet even as he thinks this, a foot has slipped between his hosed buttocks and is pushing against his crotch. Anne, it seems, is getting bored with waiting. And so he turns from Donna's exquisite feet and positions himself subserviently before Anne. Tall, slender, regal Anne, her red hair a burning beacon of her fiery, unforgiving nature, her emerald-green eyes staring into his with a truly frightening intensity.

Like the others, she has kicked off her shoes and stretched out two elegant, delicately hosed feet. This hose is of a very fine pink nylon and heavily scented. As he places his painted lips against the surface of the sheer fabric, it is almost as if he has received a tiny but powerful electric shock, a harbinger of the cruel adventures that he will have with this beautiful, quite wicked woman.

In a state of supreme arousal, Chris is then ordered to stand. He does so with a series of almost balletic movements, his natural feminine grace once again clearly impressing the women.

'Now you must pledge to serve us, Chris,' Helen announces. 'Agree to follow every instruction and obey every commend without question.'

'I pledge to serve you in any way you wish without question,' he says, his voice hoarse with desire, but showing no signs of fear or doubt.

'From now on,' Helen continues, 'you will address each of us as Mistress. During these first stages of your training, you will be known as Chrissie. When we feel you have demonstrated the necessary attributes of a true she-male maidservant you will be known as Christina. Do you understand?'

'Yes, mistress.'

'Good. You will also be required to acknowledge each instruction with a curtsey. Do you understand?'

He demonstrates his understanding by performing a very dainty curtsey that produces a look of sheer delight from Donna and a smile of quiet satisfaction from Helen.

His maid duties begin immediately. Helen tells him to go to the kitchen and open, then serve a bottle of wine currently located in the fridge. Once again, he curtseys his understanding. Then he wiggle-minces to the kitchen, deliberately exaggerating each ultra-feminine movement for the amusement of his new mistresses. He quickly retrieves the bottle, opens it and returns. Then, curtseying sweetly before each mistress as he does so, he refills the glasses, hesitating before Donna as their eyes momentarily lock in a gaze of powerful mutual attraction.

'From today you will be forbidden to drink any alcohol or any other form of stimulant, including tea or coffee,' Helen says, watching the exchange with Donna. 'Tomorrow I will give you a special diet plan, which you will stick to rigidly.'

Turning from Donna, he curtseys his understanding, thrilled by the way Helen is seizing control of his life. Then he turns to refill Anne's glass. As he does so, the gorgeous redhead, her eyes drinking up his delicate, feminised form, suddenly pulls the glass away. Chris reacts quickly, but not before Anne's trousers are splashed with wine.

Anne leaps up and begins brushing angrily at the stain. Poor Chris apologises, despite knowing that the spillage was not his fault.

'You stupid girl!' Anne snaps. 'You've ruined a perfectly good pair of trousers. How on earth do you expect to become a proper maidservant when you can't even pour a glass of wine?'

Then, to his amazement, she grabs the bottle from his hands, places it on the coffee table by her chair and takes a very firm hold of his thin, slender wrists. She then forces his arms behind his back and pushes him over the leather arm of the chair, causing his skirt to rise up his long, nylon-enveloped thighs, thus exposing his pert pantied and hosed backside to the view of all three women.

He has had so many fantasies of being spanked, of being taken across a beautiful woman's knee in such an intricately feminised state and soundly thrashed, but as Anne begins to deliver a series of very hard slaps to his bottom, reality proves itself rather more painful than fantasy. Within a few seconds, the spanking brings tears to his eyes and soon his poor backside is wriggling furiously under the barrage of blows. By the time she has finished, his backside feels as if it is on fire and tears are pouring from his lovely blue eyes. He is then pulled to his feet and turned to face Helen. Through tear-stained eyes he notices that Donna is staring at him in an even more aroused state.

'From now on, any perceived failing on your part will be instantly punished,' Helen says, clearly excited by the spectacle of Chris's suffering. 'A spanking will be the most common form of punishment, but there are many more ways to deal with your naughtiness, Chrissie, and I am sure you will get to experience quite a lot of them.'

Yet even as she details his future sufferings, Chris's eyes are drying and the pain in his hosed backside is turning into a strangely pleasurable heat, a heat that travels from his buttocks, between his legs and then into his still very stiff sex. Then, as the heat reaches its deeply arousing peek, the pain is forgotten, and he is gripped by a new, intense pleasure.

For the rest of the evening, he serves the women with a deep, sissy enthusiasm, helping Helen and Donna prepare a meal, then serving it to his three lovely mistresses via a ballet of careful, ultra-feminine movements. Throughout this highly exciting adventure, he receives constant advice from the women on movement and general deportment and at least one hard slap to his backside from Anne for failing to obey her instructions. The general tone of the women quickly changes from one of fascination and sympathy to command and dominance. Now he is simply the sissy maid and, the more curt and hash their instructions become, the more excited he feels.

After the meal, he is left to struggle with the washing up and then made to clean the kitchen very thoroughly. By 10.30 p.m., he is exhausted, having been denied any food or drink since he arrived. Following a teasing inspection by Helen, he is grudgingly congratulated on his domestic skills and told he can go.

'There's no need to change,' she adds. 'Donna wishes to take you home in her car. Your clothes are in your bag in the corridor. You can leave your make-up here. I will talk to you again at work in the morning, and you will be expected to report here tomorrow evening at 6.30 p.m. promptly.'

Chris delicately curtseys his understanding and follows the lovely, regal Helen out into the living room
where Donna is waiting for him, a soft, sexy
smile igniting her beautiful face, her eyes filled with
a powerful desire.

Chris notices that Anne appears to have left. He
performs a final farewell curtsey for Helen and then
follows Donna from the room.

Donna leads her pretty sissy charge down the long
corridor, his eyes pinned helplessly to the long, tight
skirt and the wonderfully accentuating effect it has on
her shapely, swaying bottom. Then, suddenly, they are
both out in the cool night air. Chris can hardly believe
it: he is outside fully dressed as Christina! A sense of
nervous elation washes over him as his high heels strike
the concrete surface of the driveway. This is surely the
most exciting moment of his life!

Anne's car has gone and this makes access to Donna's
somewhat battered Ford much easier. She opens the front
passenger door for him and gently helps him to slip
modestly into the leather seat. As he carefully adjusts his
short leather skirt, Donna climbs into the driver's seat
beside him. Without a word, she then places a hand onto
his hosed thigh and then slips it beneath his skirt. He gasps
with pleasure as her hand seeks out his well-hidden sex.

'Where is it?' she laughs, moving closer to him.

'There's a lot of padding in my underwear,' he gasps,
his erection struggling angrily into the warm prison of
the panty corselette.

Then she is kissing him, her hot, soft mouth pressing
against his, her tongue deep in his mouth. They
embrace, his hands seek out her plump, perfectly shaped
breasts through the tight sweater. She moans into his
mouth. Then she is pulling away.

'Not yet – not here.'

She composes herself and starts the car. Soon they are
on the road, heading back to his flat.

'It was like kissing a real woman, Chris,' she eventually says. 'And it turned me on terribly. I'm soaking wet.'

He is so aroused he cannot reply. His heart is fit to burst out of his padded bra, and suddenly breathing is very difficult. All he can taste is her, all he can smell is the powerful scent of her splendid, perfumed body, all he can see is the vision of sensual feminine beauty he has secretly worshipped for such a very long time.

He crosses his long, nylon-sheathed legs and feels the intense fetishistic pleasure of this expert feminisation mix with his furious passion for Donna. Her eyes momentarily stray from the road and he feels an incredible sense of deeply feminine pride as she whispers her admiration in a sex-charged, husky voice.

'I'm so jealous of those legs. You should be banned from wearing trousers and kept in tights permanently.'

Her teasing words produce a gasp of helpless, mad pleasure.

'Would you like that?' she asks, knowing full well what his answer will be, her pale blue eyes filled with a playful and deeply erotic amusement.

'Yes, mistress,' he gasps. 'Especially if you put me in hem.'

She laughs, enjoying this sexy game. 'Oh, I'm going to make sure you wear them all the time, Chrissie. Except when I need your body, of course.'

By the time they pull up outside Chris's apartment building, Donna is driving with one hand and caressing his hosed knees with the other, while Chris is gently massaging Donna's splendid breasts through the tight sweater. The car has hardly stopped before they are in each other's arms once again.

'I want to stay the night,' she says, breaking the tight, desperate embrace, a red-hot flame of need lighting her perfect face.

'Of course, mistress,' he replies, amazed, elated. 'But your daughter?'

41

'She's spending the night with a friend again. Let's go up to your flat and fuck.'

She leads him mincing desperately behind her into the building, then into the lift. In the lift they kiss and cuddle and he is so distracted by hard lust that he is no longer aware of being so profoundly out of the closet, not even here, in this most exposed of places.

They stagger from the lift, their high heels clicking violently against the tiled floor of the third floor hallway. They reach his door. He struggles to open the door with the key that is hidden in a small pocket of the sexy, black leather skirt. Then they are in his house, in the living room.

'Strip me first,' she says. 'Slowly, gently. Strip me naked.'

And, of course, he must obey his beautiful, all-powerful mistress. First, he kneels and removes her black patent leather court shoes, revelling in the erotic precision of their design and the endlessly erotic feel of the gleaming, warm leather. He kisses the heels of each shoe, before placing them by her petite, hosed feet. He then elegantly rises back onto his own high heels. Their eyes meet and lock tightly together as he reaches around behind her skirt and slowly edges the zipper down from her   waist   to the middle of her splendid bottom. He grips the waist of the skirt and pulls it down, sighing with an almost unbearable pleasure as her own perfectly shaped, black nylon-sheathed legs are revealed to his wild, sex-crazed eyes.

'You're so beautiful, mistress,' he gasps. 'I want you so badly.'

As the skirt passes over her thighs he notices that her tights are soaked in sex-juice and he leans forwards and slowly licks droplets of come from her crotch. She moans loudly and then violently grabs his wigged head, forcing his face deep between her legs. The skirt falls to the floor and his hands grip her buttocks tightly. He breathes in her sex, he swallows it up with a gasp of infinite pleasure. The pungent smell of her infects every tormented inch of his being.

Then, his make-up staining the sheer fabric, his boiling, flushed face drenched in her come, he delicately slips the tights down her legs and off her feet; then, with a teasing care, he slips the black silk panties over her thighs, revelling in her powerful sex-scent and beholding a perfect upside-down triangle of glistening, jet-black pubic hair.

The panties removed, he stands upright and slowly helps Donna to wiggle out of the tight sweater. A moan of shocked delight escapes his strawberry-red lips as a sexy, lace-edged pink brassiere is revealed, a bra which holds firmly in place a pair of large, heaving, pale rose breasts, their hard, long nipples clearly visible through the soft silk fabric. After discarding the sweater, he gently strokes each plump breast through its delightful silken prison and teases each rock-solid nipple. Donna responds with a gasp of girlish pleasure. He then slowly unclips the bra to expose these splendid orbs in all their sensual, natural glory. And almost immediately he is smothering her breasts in kisses, leaving a mass of lipstick tattoos and inspiring more desperate moans of pleasure. But even as she writhes under his hungry caresses, she is attempting to pull the tight leather skirt over his padded hips and down his long, nylon-encased legs.

'Now it's your turn,' she whispers.

He stands back and allows her to pull the skirt down over his legs. He daintily steps out of it and then watches with a fierce, burning desire as she slowly unbuttons the black silk blouse and gently eases it over his shoulders. Then, with the blouse discarded, she is staring at the fiendish intricacies of the lovely cross-dresser's corselette.

'This is really clever,' she whispers. 'An artificial body frame. No wonder you look so curvaceous.'

She tells him to take off his high-heeled shoes and then gently guides the black panties and the sheer black tights down his silky-smooth legs, eventually leaving him in only the wig and the corselette. He shows her how to unbutton the corselette and, as she pulls it from his body, he feels the most acute and delightful sense of absolute submission wash over his body. Eventually, Donna helps him to step out of the corselette and thus reveal his true, distinctly male physical self, the most prominent feature of which is his large and very erect penis. Donna's lovely blue eyes widen with an intense arousal and her gorgeous smile widens.

'My, my,' she teases, 'you are a very big girl.'

Then she slowly wraps a hand around the rigid, engorged sex-shaft and brings a squeal of surprise and pleasure from Chris's helplessly girlish mouth. As she begins to slowly caress his sex, her eyes wander hungrily about his body.

'You keep yourself in good condition, Chris. And not a hair to be seen anywhere. I'm really impressed, especially by this.'

Then she leads him from the living room and into the bathroom, her hand still firmly in possession of his sex.

'We should shower first. Get rid of all that make-up and stuff. We can wash each other.'

She releases him and he slowly, shakily runs the shower. Then he helps her step beneath the powerful jet of warm water. Soon they are both engulfed in a thick cloud of steam and Donna is carefully soaping every inch of Chris's lean, surprisingly muscular body. Moaning with a pleasure he had not thought possible, his body swaying erotically beneath Donna's careful, teasing caresses, he takes up a second bar of scented soap and begins to apply it over this gorgeous woman's perfect frame, paying particular attention to her sublime breasts. She giggles and gasps and concentrates her own efforts on his straining, angry sex. Then her soapy hands are between his legs and gently pushing his thighs apart. Then, to his extreme surprise, her hands are slipping between his buttocks.

'Turn around,' she whispers, pulling her hands free. 'Turn around and spread your legs.'

He obeys and waits fearfully as her finger returns to the darkness between his buttocks. Then, amazingly, a long, soapy index finger is gently working its way into his anus. He cries out and instinctively hops forwards. She wraps her free arm around his waist and holds him firmly in place, pushing her finger deeper into his most intimate region. He moans with a strange, undeniable pleasure.

'You like it, don't you?'

'Yes, mistress,' he gasps. 'Very much.'

She laughs and continues to tease his anus, causing his penis to stretch even further up his stomach.

'That's good. Helen wants to make sure you're fully trained in the pleasures of the arse.'

Her strange words signal the removal of the finger and a return to the mutual caresses that soon have them both gasping with a desperate, crazed pleasure.

Eventually, she leads him from the shower and they gently, teasingly dry each other before she orders him to take her to his bedroom. His heart pounding, his knees shaking, his entire body wrapped in a field of nervous electric energy, he leads her into the bedroom. Then, suddenly, they are on the bed and in each other's arms. He is covering her in kisses, she is stroking his sex and licking his chest. They lock in a long, hard kiss, her hands grasping his short hair tightly, even angrily. She climbs on top of him, slowly lowering her soaking sex onto his stiff, enflamed penis. This is the moment he has been waiting for all his life: the first genuine sexual encounter with a woman. Her smile widens into a grimace of animal pleasure as his cock slips deep into her cunt. And within seconds she is riding him, pumping both of them to a violent orgasm, a mutual fit of screaming and bucking that leaves Donna spread over his body like a boiling-hot blanket of soft, female flesh and him seeing stars through tear-filled eyes. Then his arms are around her, tightly hugging her, and he is begging her never to leave, swearing complete, absolute and eternal obedience.

'I love you, mistress,' he cries.

Hours pass, the night ignited by the red-hot spark of a truly profound desire. They make love continually. She insists he pleasure her orally, pushing his head between her long, sweat-soaked legs. He plunges his tongue deep into her oceanic sex and, with the guidance of her increasing screams of pleasure, finds her clit. He brings her to at least three loud, fierce multiple orgasms and his body is soon soaked in his sweat, her sweat and a pungent film of her sex-juices. Then, as a reward, she slips her lovely lips around the head of his angry, desperate, rock-hard cock and quickly sucks him to his own very violent orgasm, drinking every drop of his thick, rich come with a rapt smile of extreme pleasure.

When sleep comes, it is a beautiful abyss of blackness. Exhausted, overwhelmed, sated, they lie naked, spent, wrapped in each other's arms. Tonight he has been initiated into the joys of sexual being via a truly volcanic encounter with a most beautiful and imaginative woman, a woman who, along with the gorgeous, regal Helen and the emerald-eyed goddess Anne, has begun to map the long, ultra-kinky pathway to his future of joyous she-male enslavement.

PART TWO
The Making of a Maid

Four

He wakes from a deep, dreamless sleep, a slow emergence. Instinctively, he turns to embrace Donna, to reassure himself that the previous night hadn't been some wonderful hallucination. But she isn't in the bed: only a slight, warm dent remains. Suddenly, he is wide awake, panic gripping his heart. Suddenly, he is terrified he has been dreaming. He pulls himself from the bed and rushes naked into the living room. There is no sign of her anywhere! Then he sees the note on the dining table, a sheet of yellow writing paper. He picks it up and reads her neat, careful handwriting, her gentle, loving, teasing words.

Chrissie,

I had a fantastic night. You're the first virgin I've ever slept with and now I know what I've been missing! But I doubt very much I'll be sleeping with any more – you're more than enough to keep this girl happy! Make sure you wear your sexiest undies today, because I'll be coming to see you in the office later.

All my love

Mistress Donna

An almost overwhelming sense of relief washes over him as he reads the note, and it is only now he realises it is daylight. He has no idea what the time is. He checks the kitchen clock: 7.40 a.m.! He rushes into the shower and spends the next half an hour washing, scenting and carefully shaving every inch of his body, the wonderful memories of the night before ensuring an immediate and very intense erection.

Once dried and perfumed, he returns to the bedroom and follows Donna's instructions, taking a pair of beautiful white silk panties and drawing them up his smooth legs and over his rampant sex with a gasp of almost agonising pleasure. He follows the panties with a pair of very sheer, seamed black nylon tights, pulling them up his legs with a series of helpless moans. This is all he wants: the incredible thrill of feminisation combined with absolute servitude, a heavenly subjugation, a silken slavery.

He deliberately avoids slipping socks over the tights and is very tempted to wear one of his more shirt-like white silk blouses, but instead he opts for his usual office attire and is soon rushing from the flat, his heart beating out a rapid rhythm of addictive and deeply masochistic desire, his cock straining with a savage energy against its silk and nylon prison.

And by the time he gets into his office, he is almost half an hour late. He dashes through the main office, hardly noticing his three mistresses. In his office, his mind possessed by a supreme, all-pervasive hunger and a wild anticipation of his forthcoming servitude, he collapses into the seat behind his desk and fights to regain his breath. Yet hardly has he sat down than the door opens and Helen strolls in. His first, now redundant reaction is a bizarre irritation at her failure to knock, but then he is out of his seat and standing obediently before her, his eyes staring modestly at her black patent leather court shoes.

'I expect you to curtsey when your mistress enters the room,' she whispers, her deep voice filled with a relaxed but absolute authority.

He performs a sweet, very feminine curtsey and apologises.

She walks past him and lowers herself into his seat.

'You were late this morning, Chrissie,' she says.

He turns to face her. 'I'm sorry, mistress. It won't happen again.'

'No, it won't. And to make sure, tonight I'll give you a very sound spanking. I want you here at 8.30 a.m. sharp each morning. As soon as you arrive, you'll be expected to make coffee for Anne, Donna and myself. I will also expect you to give me a foot massage.'

As she delivers her instructions, she kicks off the lovely high-heeled shoes and raises her black-hosed feet upwards. He performs another delicate curtsey and kneels before her.

This morning she is wearing a very tight black sweater, a knee-length red skirt and black tights, her gorgeous brown hair tied in a very tight bun. Her beautifully plump figure is perfectly displayed by this simple costume, particularly her very large, yet still very shapely breasts. His eyes stare down at her nylon-encased feet. His erection stretches against his trousers and beads of sex sweat fall into his eyes as he leans forwards and takes a lovely, hosed foot in his hot, shaking hands. The feel of her warm, soft flesh through sheer black nylon is heavenly and he cannot resist a moan of pleasure as he begins very gently to massage the sole of her foot.

'Press a little harder, Chrissie – the pressure loosens up the muscles and helps me relax.'

He obeys, wary at first, but noticing her positive response he soon finds a confident yet careful motion.

'Do you like my feet, Chrissie?' she asks, a jagged edge of obvious arousal cutting through her husky voice.

'They're lovely, mistress. The beautiful feet of a very beautiful woman.'

She smiles at this complement. 'Donna tells me you're no longer a virgin.'

He blushes and cannot resist a smile of his own. 'No, mistress.'

'She also tells me that you're a particularly eager and gifted lover.'

His blushes deepen and he bows his head in embarrassment.

'She says you have a particularly skilled tongue.'

Her words are now filled with sexual intent and Chris increases the pressure on her gorgeous feet.

'I'll expect to be shown these talents, Chrissie.'

Amazed, he looks up at her. Their eyes meet: there is no doubt she means what she is saying.

'Of course, mistress. Whatever you require.'

Her only response is another enigmatic smile.

Following the strange, exciting massage and the teasing conversation that accompanies it, Helen orders Chris to his feet and hands him a sheet of paper covered in very small, neat handwriting.

'This will be your diet for the next two weeks. You will eat the same food each day and nothing else. A slice of brown toast and a glass of pure orange juice for breakfast, an apple at eleven, a simple salad and a banana for lunch, a peach at three. Your evening meal will be provided at my house. There will be no more coffee, tea or alcohol. Besides the orange juice, you will be allowed to drink only mineral water.'

He listens and reads in a state of stunned disappointment. How an earth will he survive on this? But he quickly curtseys his understanding and watches her leave in a state of absolute amazement, his eyes never leaving her long, elegant legs, his sex pressing angrily into his stomach, the promise of the evening already driving him mad with anticipation.

For the next hour, he sits behind his desk, staring into a drugged abyss of sexual hunger. Work is now utterly beyond him. All he can think of is the look of sinful promise in Helen's eyes, the feel of her beautiful feet through the teasingly sheer nylon and, overlapping with these powerful images, his incredible experiences with the gorgeous Donna. And it is as he remembers the previous night, as his hands rub helplessly against his imprisoned sex, that the door opens once again. Shocked, he quickly withdraws his hands and rises to his feet. Standing before him like the apparition of the goddess of all his desires is Donna. Dressed in a black sweater, a very short check skirt, black tights and high heels, her lovely blonde hair bound in a bun, her face lit up by a beautiful, life-enhancing smile, she is his perfect vision, his dream made startling reality. He curtseys sweetly and her smile broadens.

'Very good, Chrissie: you must never forget to curtsey before your mistress.'

She strolls up to him, takes his head in her cool, elegant hands and gives him a very long, wet and hard kiss. His knees buckle, her powerful musk perfume fills his nostrils. He almost collapses against her before she gently pushes him away.

'Take down your trousers – let's see what you've put on for me.'

Embarrassed, yet also terribly excited, he unzips his trousers and lets them fall around his knees, revealing the very sheer, black seamed tights, the panties and the extremely angry erection straining beneath them. She laughs and runs a long, red-nailed finger down the length of his hosed, panty-imprisoned and very erect cock. He moans loudly and she clamps her free hand over his girlish mouth, pressing her shapely, substantial breasts into his chest as she leans forward.

'Dear me, you are in a state,' she whispers, teasing his sex a little more, pressing harder against the imprisoned shaft, 'but you look wonderful. Such a shame you have to wear trousers. But not for much longer. In a few hours we'll have you all wrapped up in feminine frillies, with a nice short skirt to show off these sexy legs.'

He moans louder into her hand gag and pushes his crotch into her skirt. She tuts and slips her teasing hand between his hosed legs.

'What a noisy little sissy you are, Chrissie. You really do need to be gagged. I think my panties should do the trick. Yes, I'll have to make sure this naughty, sluttish mouth is well filled with my panties tonight.'

His eyes widen with a terrible, helpless arousal.

'Put your hands behind your back,' she orders.

He obeys and she begins to caress the dark, warm gap between his buttocks. He squeezes his buttocks together around her hand. She gasps playfully, pulls her hand free and then redoubles her teasing efforts on his burning, aching sex.

'Just imagine the taste of me, the taste of my come and my piss, the taste of my arse. All filling that dainty, sexy mouth.'

Then he explodes. She presses her hand tightly into his mouth. A terrible muffled scream fills the room and his thick white semen floods into the skimpy, delicate panties. He falls into her embrace and she then guides his spent, shaking body back to the chair.

As he collapses into the chair, a profound, bottomless happiness washes over him.

'I love you so much,' he gasps.

She smiles and steps back from her drained lover.

'Good. And to prove it, you'll keep those pretty spunk-filled panties on for the rest of the day. I'll see you tonight at Helen's – we've got a very special treat planned.'

Before he can say another word, she leaves the room, his eyes fixed upon her startling body in stunned adoration.

He spends the rest of the day in a state of some physical discomfort, but never once considers changing. His commitment to his new mistresses is absolute and he will obey their commands completely and without question.

By the time he arrives at Helen's house that evening, the stain has almost dried, and as he knocks on the large, imposing front door his heart is once more pounding with a heavenly anticipation.

He is made to wait some time before Helen opens the door. She is now dressed in a beautiful, semi-transparent, cream-coloured silk blouse and a knee-length black skirt, her legs sealed in the almost uniform black hose. She is also wearing very high-heeled, black patent leather court shoes. Her very large bosom is tightly restrained by a white, lace-edged bra that is clearly visible through the shimmering silk. Her lips have been painted a deep, glistening cherry-red and at the centre of each of her lovely dark brown eyes is a fierce, threatening flame of wicked passion.

'Come in, Chrissie,' she says, her voice harder, cooler, the voice of a true dominatrix.

Chris instinctively curtseys and follows her into the house, up the long, dark stairs and back into the spare room, his eyes never once leaving the plump but shapely outline of her ample bottom and the dead straight seams of her hose.

'Now,' she says, turning to face him, 'I want you to undress and get into the shower. You'll find everything you need to wash, shave and perfume your body. When you've finished, return to this room. You have twenty minutes.'

Following another sweet curtsey, he begins to undress before her, his own eyes cast down on her sexy shoes, his attitude one of complete subservience.

By the time he gets down to the stained hose, his massive, desperate erection is embarrassingly obvious. Yet he makes no attempt to hide it, feeling a strange, highly charged pride in his state of furious arousal. And as he pulls the tights and panties down his silky legs, his sex almost leaps out like some starved, chained snake.

A smile crosses Helen's face as she studies his sex, a teasing, calculating smile that only serves to make him even more excited.

Then he is naked, his hands behind his back, his eyes still pinned to her shoes.

'Donna told me you were rather well endowed for a sissy,' Helen says. 'I can see she wasn't joking. Now off to the shower with you.'

He curtseys again and minces out into the corridor. It is only then that he realises he has no idea where the bathroom is! As he turns, he feels Helen's distinctive presence almost directly behind him.

'The first on the right,' she whispers, her hands gently caressing his naked buttocks.

Gasping with aroused shock, he curtseys again, the smell of Helen's lovely rose perfume filling his nostrils, and minces down the corridor.

Washing, shaving, drying and then scenting his body in twenty minutes is no mean feat, and by the time he returns to the bedroom, he is at least three minutes late. He also finds himself facing the gorgeous backs of Helen and Donna, both of whom are now leaning over the modest single bed.

It is Donna who turns to face him, her stunning blue eyes widening in amused excitement at the sight of her slave/lover.

'Well, don't you look a pretty picture?' she says, walking up to him, her eyes carefully examining every inch of his baby smooth, naked body.

Donna is now wearing a very tight pink woollen sweater, a very short white mini-skirt, white tights and pink stiletto-heeled shoes. Her beautiful blonde hair spills freely over her shapely shoulders and her pink coloured lips have soon extended into an even more teasing smile. She looks absolutely fantastic and he moans helplessly as she stops only a few inches in front of his quivering, naked form.

Then, to his astonishment, she grabs his sex. He squeals in shock, his eyes virtually popping out of his head, as Donna proceeds to lead him forwards by his sex. He totters behind her, both appalled and wildly aroused by this ultra-kinky guidance, and, as he is pulled to a halt before the bed, a spasm of pure, masochistic pleasure vibrates through his girlish body.

As he fights to recover from the shock of Donna's bizarre intervention, he notices what the two startling women are pondering on the bed. Laid out before them is a beautiful black satin dress edged at its sleeves, very high neck and very short skirt with inches of fine white French lace. By the dress is a cream silk pinafore, also exquisitely edged with French lace, and what appears to be a black version of the cross-dresser's corselette. Next to the corselette are a pair of black nylon tights, a pair of black silk panties and a dainty maid's cap.

'Your uniform, Chrissie,' Helen announces.

Chris stares at this sexy array in absolute astonishment. This is his most powerful, most consistent fantasy about to be made reality and he nearly swoons before its terrible sexual power.

It is only as he staggers before his uniform that he notices Donna has produced a very sheer black nylon stocking and is running it teasingly through her hands, a wicked smile on her beautiful face.

'But before we get you all dolled up, I think we need to make sure your naughty cock is well and truly under control. Put your hands behind your back.'

He obeys and watches in horror and helpless excitement as Donna slowly bunches up the stocking, her teasing, sexy eyes never leaving his, then very slowly and very carefully slips it over the engorged purple head of his sex. The feel of this cool, soft fabric against the boiling, ultra-sensitive surface of his sex is incredible and there is nothing he can do to prevent the loud, angry moan that explodes from his mouth as Donna stretches the stocking down over his sex and positions it tightly around the base of his swollen testicles.

'Be quiet, you silly girl,' Helen snaps, her eyes burning into him, her tone that of an angry schoolmistress, a tone that only inspires even greater arousal in poor Chris. 'If you don't stop that silly squealing you'll be gagged for the rest of the evening.'

Her threats serve only to excite him even more, as she knows they must.

'Oh, I think he'd like to be gagged, Helen,' Donna whispers, now gently caressing his sex through the stocking. 'And I've got the perfect gag. I've been working on it all day, making sure it tastes just right.'

Both women laugh as Chris's squeals turn into a low moan of animal pleasure.

And as if this wasn't enough torment, Donna then produces a thick pink silk ribbon and uses it to tie the terrible, teasing stocking in place around his testicles in a fat sissy bow.

'As you can see, Chrissie,' Helen explains. 'The stocking is black. It will show the slightest sign of a naughty male emission immediately. If, at any time, there is evidence of such a release, you will be soundly spanked. You will wear the stocking permanently until your training begins in earnest, when a more suitable form of restraint will be introduced.'

Helen's hard, dominating words sound like the sexiest poetry to Chris, her deep, husky voice a tool of slow-burning sexual torture that would make a recitation of the telephone directory sound like the most exciting erotica.

By the time Helen takes the corselette from the bed, poor Chris is almost on the verge of passing out from the effects of the intense pleasure coursing through his body. It is only the sight of this beautiful variation on the corselette that revives him.

'I spent the afternoon in the city visiting some fetish fashion stores,' she says, holding the corselette before him. 'They really do have an incredible range of stuff.'

He smiles weakly and nods.

'The great thing about this is that it acts like a proper corset. So you get the body shape, plus figure training.'

Chris examines the corselette, noticing that, unlike his version, it is fitted at the upper waist with two red satin panels beneath which is a row of stays.

'Not genuine whalebone,' she says, a hint of disappointment in her sexy voice. 'They're made from a form of extra-strong plastic lined with rubber and then sewn into the satin panels.'

At the back of this part of the corselette are two rows of metal eyes through which run a complex mass of criss-crossed silk laces. Above this is the chest section: two large bra cups filled with what looks like extremely realistic padding.

'A forty-inch chest, Chrissie,' Helen continues, watching his eyes fix onto the bulging cups. 'Not padding, but special rubber bags filled with silicon. They look and feel very realistic.'

Donna then helps Chris to step into the black lace-frilled legs of the stunning corselette and Helen then draws it carefully up his body. He feels the tight elastane fabric of the corselette grip and squeeze his stomach and is almost immediately overwhelmed by the most exquisite sense of restriction. This is increased as Helen pulls the corselette up over his chest and slips the surprisingly strong silk shoulder-straps up over his arms and then over his slender, girlish shoulders. Then two sensations seize him at once. First, the amazing effect of the perfectly shaped artificial breasts which fill the beautifully designed, lace-edged bra cups. Suddenly he feels himself pulled forwards by their very real weight and has to stand virtually to attention to counteract this strangely pleasurable effect. Second, there is the tightness around the waist, a tightness made almost immediately more severe as Helen takes up the silk laces and begins to use them to pull in the satin panelled sides and press the tough plastic stays into his sides and push the air from his lungs. He gasps in pained amazement as she pulls the corset to a tightness that is more than uncomfortable and then sustains this level of restriction by tying the silk laces in a series of very tight and fat bows. This tightening provides a strange, rather enthralling counterbalance to the pulling effect of the breasts and he now finds himself forced to stand almost bolt upright.

He cannot help but marvel at the effect of the corselette and finds himself running his shaking hands over the smooth, soft material and moaning with pleasure at the sense of intense femininity the garment produces. This sense is significantly enhanced when he notices that the corselette, like his own, less exotic version, has a specially padded crotch section which completely obscures his rock-hard, tightly stockinged sex and more padding at the hips to produce a genuinely feminine figure.

'You look fantastic already,' Donna purrs, taking the tights from the bed and handing them to him.'But these will really add that special sissy touch. They're the finest we could find, and they're seamed. They'll do wonders for those gorgeous legs.'

His heart hammering against his delicately feminised chest, Chris is then helped to sit down on the bed by Helen. As he does so, the tight panels of the corset bite deep into his sides and he gasps in pain.

'The corset will be rather uncomfortable for a while,' she says, her splendid eyes filled with a cruel amusement, her own substantial breasts rising and falling rapidly with an obvious excitement through the fine fabric of the expensive silk blouse. 'But diet and regular exercise should reduce your waist to a less restricted size quite quickly.'

As he very carefully pulls the tights up his legs, he is very much aware of the eyes of the two dominant beauties burning into his every gesture. Yet, rather than being intimidated, he finds their fascination highly exciting and produces a series of elegant, balletic and very feminine movements for their entertainment, demonstrating his natural skill at slipping sexily into the hose. He gently rises from the bed to slip the tights over his upper thighs and secure them around his tightly restricted waist, a smile of intense pleasure lighting up his pretty face. The tights feel incredibly light, soft and sexy and, as he carefully straightens the pencil thin black seams, he notices that Donna seems to be lost in a sex-trance.

'You're really good at this,' she mumbles. 'How an earth did you ever manage to pass as a boy?'

'He should have been completely feminised ages ago,' Helen adds. 'It's absurd that he should be anything other than a she-male slave.'

Her sexy words only add to his almost unbearable sense of arousal. Yet this, he knows, is only the beginning. And as if to demonstrate the fact, Donna then takes up the black silk lace-edged panties and holds them before him.

'Put these on, Chrissie, then we'll begin making you up.'

He takes the lovely undergarment from Donna, his eyes glued to hers. This is sex Nirvana, he thinks, pulling the panties up his hosed legs; this is absolute perfection.

He is then led by Donna to the dressing table, each step in his finely hosed feet a strange, new and delightful experience of feminine movement, the corselette's various restrictions and weights forcing him to take smaller, much more feminine steps, his bottom already beginning to wiggle with a helplessly sissy enthusiasm.

He is made to sit before the large, oval dressing table mirror. Laid out on the table before him are a vast array of bottles, tubes and canisters, a much more complete collection than he could ever have hoped to bring together. He stares at this incredible cornucopia through wide, stunned eyes. Donna leans forwards and takes up a tube of foundation cream. They stare at each other in the mirror. Her full breasts press against his bare shoulder as she leans forwards. His cock feels as if it is about to burst out of its delicate stocking prison at any moment.

'I'm soaking,' she whispers.

'I want you so much,' he replies.

She eases a long line of light tan cream from the tube and then begins to massage it into his face. He watches in a state of almost paralytic sexual ecstasy as she begins to transform him into Christina, her long, elegant hands spreading the cool cream across his cheeks and chin, over his forehead, under his eyes, around his neck, removing any sign of the abrupt angles of masculinity and carefully replacing them with the gentle curves of femininity. Soon, a complete, flawless mask has been created. This is followed by a further layer of a much lighter cream, which manages to produce the illusion of a perfect, unblemished skin tone. Then she sets to work on his eyes. First, a jet-black highlighter pencil is drawn across each eyebrow, creating two identical, perfectly curving lines of teasing femininity. After this, she carefully fixes a set of extremely long and helplessly fluttering false lashes to his natural eyelashes and adds a hint of scented mascara to each. Then pale blue eye-shadow is delicately applied with a tiny, soft brush to each eyelid.

After the eyes come the lips. Donna gently runs a thick, cherry-red lipstick across his full, always feminine lips, transforming them into a gorgeous sissy bow of pure subservience. This is followed by a clear lip-gloss that makes his lips shine like two red pools of bottomless desire.

After the lips, pink rouge is carefully applied to each cheek, and then Donna stands back to admire her work.

Chris stares in disbelief at the power of even this incomplete transformation. Where he had tried so hard for a classic feminine authenticity in Christina's make-up, Donna has quite brilliantly created the impression of a natural feminine beauty. It is almost as if it is not make-up that has been applied, but a new face!

'It's amazing,' he mumbles. 'You've made me seem so . . . real.'

'I've just brought out your natural femininity a bit more, Chrissie. You *are* real. You're a girl at heart. It's so obvious.'

As he stares at her through the mirror, Helen steps forwards to fill the reflection with her stunning, ample presence, a triumphant smile on her beautiful face.

'This is brilliant, Donna. Well done. Put the wig on and we have the perfect she-male.'

As Helen's teasing, husky tones fill his sissy ears, Chris watches as Donna takes what looks like a large pink hat box from beneath the dressing table, removes the oval lid and carefully takes from inside it a stunning black wig, a thick mass of carefully styled brunette locks, surprisingly long, that seem to meet at a perfectly oval plateau with a square front. Almost immediately, he recognises this classic style.

'Bettie Page,' he whimpers.

Donna smiles, obviously impressed. 'Yes. Helen chose it. I've never heard of her.'

Helen steps forwards and takes the wig from Donna.

'Yes, Bettie. I've always been a great fan, and I'm pretty sure Chrissie has, too.'

Chris can only nod in astonishment as Helen then carefully places the wig over his own close-cropped hair, adding a further wonderful touch to this startling transformation. And as the wig is pulled gently into place, the power of the resemblance between the image that these two women have created and the legendary fetish model is immediately apparent: they have very successfully performed a quite deliberate act of beautiful pastiche.

'Wonderful,' Helen whispers, her eyes meeting his through the mirror.

He can only agree with her simple analysis and sigh with a deep, erotic pleasure. Before him is a truly beautiful, sensual woman, a gorgeous sex-bomb created in the image of a true goddess.

Yet even now the transformation is incomplete. Overseen by Helen, Donna proceeds to add to this changeling masterpiece a pair of clip-on diamond stud earrings and a set of long, blood-red false nails, peripheral touches to a vision of ultra-feminine glamour. Finally, his neck and arms are covered in a very powerful and obviously expensive perfume.

Satisfied that this stage of their work is complete, the two women help Chris back onto his feet and guide him across the room and back to the bed. Once again he is overwhelmed by feelings of intense feminine submission produced by the small steps and helpless wiggle created by the corselette, and he cannot avoid a small moan of intense pleasure.

At the bed, Donna takes up the stunning black satin dress and holds it against his body. He squirms with helpless pleasure.

'Oh, dear, you really are turned on, aren't you?' she teases, her eyes filled with an almost sadistic pleasure at the sight of her lover's erotic suffering.

'Yes, mistress,' he mumbles, his cock straining with an increasing fury in its delicate nylon prison.

'Remember,' Helen says, a smile spreading across her gorgeous face, 'the slightest sign of naughtiness down below and your bottom will be stinging for days.'

Her words are, of course, designed not to prevent further excitement but to *inspire* it and poor Chris can only produce a tiny, tormented curtsey of understanding and fight an increasing urge to come, an urge which is only increased as Donna carefully unfastens the black pearl buttons running down the back of the stunning satin dress and then holds it open for him to step into.

She pulls the soft, scented dress up his delicately feminised body with a sigh of pleasure. The dress is truly beautiful: cut from the finest black satin and carefully decorated with a pattern of elegant crafted black silk roses. It is very short, and billowing out from beneath the tiny skirt is a cloud of gorgeous, very fine white lace petticoating which, when positioned over his waist, has the effect of pushing the skirt up at almost a right ankle to his hosed legs and exposing his heavily frilled, black silk panties to full view. The dress is pulled over his expertly padded chest and Helen helps him slide his silky smooth arms into the long sleeves, each of which is elegantly puffed out at the upper arms and shoulder areas and trimmed at the wrist section with more beautiful white lace. As the dress is guided up to his neck, he feels it tighten around his body, a perfect fit which accentuates his considerable bosom. The neck of the dress is very high and also frilled with white lace, and the row of pearl buttons runs from the top of the rear of the neck right down to the base of his back. It takes Donna nearly five minutes to secure each button, increasing the tight, figure-hugging fit of the dress quite considerably as she does so.

'Rather ingenious, really,' Helen says, her eyes glued to Donna's patient efforts. 'You're literally imprisoned: the pattern of the buttoning means it's virtually impossible to remove the dress without help.'

Chris revels in her teasing words and feels a sense of genuine, absolute enslavement. Yes, he is very tightly imprisoned in feminine frillies and he is loving every moment of it.

Once the dress is secured, Donna takes up the large, cream silk, white lace-frilled pinafore and carefully places it over the lovely dress, slipping a thin silk strap over Chris's beautifully wigged head and then tying the two very thick ribbons affixed to the waist section in a very fat and dainty bow at the base of his back. Helen then carefully pins the delightful white lace maid's cap to the gleaming centre of the spectacular Bettie Page wig.

'He looks incredible,' Donna whispers to Helen, as the women stand back to admire their handiwork.

'Yes,' Helen says, her eyes drinking up this sexy she-male confection. 'He does. But this is only the beginning. Can you get the shoes?'

Donna then slowly bends down before the bed, making sure as she does so that her short pink skirt rises up her long, white nylon-sheathed legs and that poor, tormented Chris gets a spectacular view of her hosed, pantied and very shapely backside. From beneath the bed she takes another pink box, which she places on the bed. She removes the rectangular lid to reveal a truly stunning pair of black patent leather, stiletto-heeled court shoes. As she pulls them from the box, Chris immediately notices that the heels on the shoes are at least six inches – far higher than anything he has ever worn. Fear and desire are mixed into a potent sex brew that seems to be boiling over inside his sex as Donna holds the shoes before him with a teasing smile.

'Six-inch heels; rather higher than anything you've tried before, Chrissie,' Helen says. 'As our maidservant, you will be required to wear the highest heels at all times, so it's important you get used to them as quickly as possible.'

Donna places the beautiful, gleaming shoes at his hosed feet and, without a word of instruction, he carefully steps into them. He gasps in amazement as he is immediately made half a foot taller. The heels themselves are razor-sharp stilettos that make balancing a very precarious and constant effort. Chris quickly finds himself swaying fearfully and instinctively reaches out for Donna's helping hand. The heels are made even more dangerous by the strange set of restrictions and weights imparted by the corselette.

'The key is to find the checks and balances,' Helen says. 'There is a point, a very fine point, where your new shape and the heels meet in perfect unison – a sissy centre of gravity. All you have to do is find that point. And the only way you can do that is to walk in the shoes.'

Still holding Donna's hand, he tries to take a step. Almost immediately, he loses his balance and topples forwards, but Donna manages to pull him back from the abyss. He smiles fearfully and takes another step, this one successful. Then another. And then he feels it, the strange union of the downwards pressure applied by the false breasts, the rigid counterbalancing posture demanded by the tight corset and the erotic balancing act enforced by the heels. By taking very small steps, by wiggling his hips and backside, by holding his hands carefully at his sides, it is indeed possible to find a small portion of time and space where it is possible to walk, or, rather mince, in the shoes. Yet this is more than a walk – this is a pretty, visual demonstration of his absolute sissification. Suddenly, he is tottering forwards in the sweetest, daintiest manner imaginable, his frilled bottom swaying with a helpless provocation, his large, false breasts bouncing beneath their layers of tight, sensual restriction. And within a few minutes he is almost confident in his tiny, sissy steps, and he is revelling in the intense sense of helpless femininity each high-heeled movement inspires.

'Very good,' Helen says, her eyes betraying surprise. 'I thought it would take you much longer to get used to the shoes. You really do have a natural affinity for feminisation.'

He slowly turns and minces back to Helen. He stops before her and then attempts a short, quick curtsey. This, however, is far too ambitious, and as his delicately hosed knees bend he loses his balance completely and falls heavily onto his backside, leaving his legs splayed before him and his sexy undies on full, hilarious display.

Laughing loudly, Donna and Helen help him back onto his feet.

'We'll have to work on the curtsey, I think,' Donna says, her smile both warm and cruel.

And so for fifteen minutes, Donna tutors her she-male love slave in the art of curtseying in very high heels, playfully slapping the back of his sheer black nylon-sheathed thighs as he fails to follow her instructions. Helen leaves the room after a few minutes of this sissy circus, returning a little later to discover Chris curtsey-ing deeply and confidently, a proud, aroused smile on his face.

'Well, I think it's time we set our little sissy to work,' Helen says. 'But I think we should show her what a little cutie she's turned out to be, first.'

The two women guide Chris from the room, down the corridor and into another much larger bedroom. With each tiny mince, he becomes more confident in his movements. It is as if he has been injected with a drug that is gradually turning him into the sissiest, daintiest she-male ever created, and that with each tiny step its effects are becoming more intense, more irreversible.

The large bedroom belongs to Helen. It is a beautiful, simply decorated room whose main feature is a huge oval bed covered in white silk sheets. An ornate white dressing table has been placed by a far wall, next to a large walk-in closet. The only other item of furniture is a very tall, full-size mirror that is currently standing on a white rug in the dead centre of the room. The two women lead Chris up to the mirror and for the first time he is able to see the vision of sissy subservience they have created.

A gasp of genuine amazement escapes his carefully painted lips. He is facing a tall, very beautiful woman with long, perfectly shaped legs, her substantial bosom straining against a very sexy French maid's uniform which barely reaches the top of her hosed thighs and whose sexy black silk panties are visible through a mist of fine white lace petticoating. Her full, sensual lips curve into a smile of astonishment, her long eyelashes flutter with girlish excitement. Two white silk ribbons run from the edges of her sweet maid's cap and travel down a gleaming, thick waterfall of long, black hair that spills onto her soft shoulders. A perfect and classic image of submissive femininity. Yes, Chris is amazed.

'I can't believe it. This is so realistic,' he says.

'All we've done is reveal what's been there all along,' Helen whispers. 'And remember: this is only the beginning. If you let us, we can turn you into a perfect she-male.'

'I want that,' he replies, turning to face her. 'I want that so much. I never want to be a man again. I want to be like this forever.'

Helen laughs. 'You were never a man, Chrissie. But if you behave yourself and do what we tell you, you'll never have to pretend to be a man again.'

Five

Following the incredible revelation, Donna and Helen lead their wiggle-mincing slave from the bedroom to the stairs. Descending the stairs is a new, precarious test for Chris and each ultra-high-heeled step, assisted by his two mistresses, brings a girlish gasp of fear.

'Nice and slowly, Chrissie,' Donna encourages. 'You'll soon get the idea.'

By the time they reach the bottom of the stairs, Chris is sweating and his heart is pounding. A wave of relief washes over him as he is subsequently led to the living room.

Anne is waiting in the living room. Dressed in a very tight white nylon sweater, figure-hugging black leather slacks and high-heeled ankle boots, she is a vision of elegant dominance. Her thick, glistening red hair bound in a tight bun, her lips painted a light peach, she beholds him with beautiful green eyes that seem to burn into the core of his sissy soul. There is a painful and strange silence as Chris is brought before Anne. He performs a deep, sexy curtsey and then stands rigidly to attention.

'Incredible,' Anne whispers. 'He's stunning. I mean . . . Well, I don't know what I mean.'

Helen laughs. 'Yes, it's really rather difficult to believe.'

Anne continues to stare at the she-male in amazement.

'There is wine in the fridge, Chrissie,' Helen says. 'You'll find the glasses and tray in the usual place.'

Chris curtsies once more and minces off to the kitchen, very much aware of Anne's emerald eyes drinking up his long hosed legs and the dead straight seams that mark out their simple perfection.

He takes the chilled wine from the fridge and fills the three glasses resting on a silver tray by the sink. He is now deeply aware of every movement and attempts to ensure that each is as feminine and graceful as possible. It is almost as if he has been possessed, that since his presentation to Anne, his true feminine essence is finally seizing complete control of his body, and that the sensations produced by this possession produce a shockingly intense, all-pervasive pleasure. As he minces back into the living room, the tray held before him, he knows he has never been happier.

The three women are now all seated and Chris totters up to Helen, performs an impressively balletic curtsey and leans forwards to allow his beautiful, fiery-eyed mistress to take a glass of wine from the tray. He then repeats this servile act before Donna and Anne, then stands to attention, hosed legs tightly together, with the tray at his side, awaiting her instructions.

'We want to break you in slowly, Chrissie,' Helen says, her eyes traversing the she-male's delightful form with hungry, conspiratorial eyes. 'These evening sessions before the beginning of your more intensive training will act as a series of introductory sessions designed to give you a general idea of your duties and the trajectory of your transformation. This evening we will concentrate on general deportment and behaviour.'

Despite being rather confused by Helen's slightly academic tone, Chris curtseys his understanding.

'You will never speak unless directly instructed to by a mistress,' Helen continues. 'When asked to speak, you will refer to each of us as "mistress". You will not use our names – you are now subservient to all women and will refer to them all as "mistress". You will not speak when issued with an instruction – a simple curtsey will suffice as a general signal of understanding. You will not look directly at a mistress without permission. Your eyes should always be cast down modestly at a mistress's feet, unless instructed otherwise. When a mistress enters the room, you will stop whatever you are doing, curtsey and await instruction. If you receive no instruction after thirty seconds you will continue with your duties. Do you understand me so far?'

Chris curtseys and Helen smiles.

'Good. We have the highest hopes for you, Chrissie. If you perform well, I promise we will change your life in ways you never dreamed possible.'

His eyes pinned to Helen's beautiful court shoes, Chrissie curtseys his appreciation of her kindness.

'If you fail to perform,' Helen continues, 'you will be punished. We will not hesitate to administer appropriate punishments if you let us down.'

As he curtseys yet again, Chris wonders what the appropriate punishments might be, and knows that he will not only accept the punishments but most probably enjoy them. A deep vein of masochism has always run through his cross-dressing and now Helen and her beautiful colleagues are obviously determined to mine it as part of their plans for his distinctly sissy future.

'Later on in the week we will start to train you in your basic domestic duties. You will be expected to clean this house and, when required, the homes of Mistress Donna and Mistress Anne. We will also expect you to wash and iron all our clothing. We have no interest in teaching you to cook, but you will be taught some basic domestic skills associated with the kitchen so that you may assist us in the preparation of food. You will also be expected to help us shop. This does mean that you will be required to go out as Chrissie but, from what we've seen so far, this shouldn't be a problem.'

Chris listens in amazement and with considerable excitement. All he wishes is to serve these beautiful women in any way they see fit, and it is clear that they intend to make a great deal of use of their new she-male slave!

It is at this point that Anne orders Chris to return to the kitchen and fetch the bottle of wine. The lovely she-male obeys with a delightfully sissy curtsey, making a point of ensuring that his sexy panties are on full display for his beautiful red-headed mistress, and then wiggle-minces back to the kitchen. He returns with the chilled bottle of lime-green Chardonnay and leans forwards before Anne to fill her glass. It is at this point that, once again, Anne suddenly pulls the glass away. Chris tries his hardest to avoid spilling the wine, but a small drop still manages to splash onto Anne's leather trousers.

'You foolish little slut!' Anne suddenly explodes and slaps Chris's hosed thighs twice with considerable power.

Chris releases a high-pitched yelp of surprise and outrage. It seems that the lovely, cruel-eyed Anne is determined to get the sexy sissy into trouble as often as possible!

Helen immediately rises to her feet and examines the minute spillage.

'This is really unacceptable, Chrissie. Your clumsiness demonstrates quite clearly that you lack even a rudimentary understanding of the absolute necessity for complete and constant physical control. And this isn't the first time: there is still the question of your poor performance in the office this morning. You will be spanked and then I think a little bondage therapy will be required.'

Her sharp, hard words echo through the she-male's head like ringing bells of supreme injustice. Yet, despite

73

the obvious trick played by Anne, Chris says nothing: he merely curtseys before Helen, his beautiful, fire-eyed mistress, and awaits his no doubt strange and painful fate.

The wait itself is short, for no sooner has Helen passed sentence than Anne jumps up from her seat and rushes over to a large leather bag sitting by the fireplace. From inside she takes a number of lengths of what appear to be black rubber-coated cording and a thick roll of silver masking tape. As she returns, Helen orders Chris to face the front windows so that his back directly faces his mistresses. He obeys, and Helen then removes the sexy silk pinafore. She then slowly unbuttons the lovely satin maid's dress. As the dress falls to the floor to reveal the wondrous delights of this particularly gorgeous she-male's undergarments, Helen forces Chris's arms behind his back. She then grasps both of his slim, feminine wrists and crosses them, allowing Anne to step forward and bind them very tightly together with a length of the rubber cording. As Anne ties his wrists together, Donna stands in front of Chris and, in a slow, ultra-teasing motion, begins to wiggle her short pink skirt up her beautiful, white nylon-sheathed legs.

'I promised you a very fragrant gag, Chrissie, and I've been working on it all day. Now it's time to try it out.'

He can only watch with a deeply aroused fascination as Donna proceeds to hitch her skirt up over her waist to reveal her hosed panties, again clearly soaked in her apparently perpetual flow of come. Chris's sex strains angrily against its delicate yet absolute stocking imprisonment, his sissy eyes popping out of his pretty little head. His wrists straining with a fundamental masochistic pleasure, he witnesses the stunning blonde kick off her high heels and then wiggle out of the tights, a dance of teasing promise that leaves the helpless she-male moaning with a vast, desperate need. Once the tights have been discarded, she takes the white nylon panties by their elastic waist band and then slowly pulls them down her long, elegant legs, her startling blue eyes never leaving her fascinated slave's, her smile a beacon of endless sensual promise. Pulling the panties from her ankles, she then steps up before Chris and pushes the gusset section firmly against his nostrils. The smell of Donna hits him like a fist, the smell of her body, of its most intimate functions and its deepest arousals. Her pungent sex, the perfume of her animal life, all of it is suddenly deep within Chris, filling every pore and every tormented, sexed thought.

'Open wide, Chrissie,' she teases.

And he does, and then the panties are rammed deep into his mouth. He moans with a desperate, twisted desire as the panties are virtually forced down his throat. Coughs and splutters are met with cruel, mocking laughter. He strains against the tight bonds securing his wrists and watches with wide, terrified and intensely aroused eyes as Helen takes up the roll of masking tape and tears from it a long, thick strip.

'Lips together, Chrissie.'

He obeys Helen's teasingly matter of fact words and then his gorgeous mistress applies the tape to his soft, ripe, girlish lips, spreading it firmly over them with the palm of her hand and thus tightly gagging her excited, swooning she-male charge.

Chris squeals with a powerful, masochistic need into the panty gag, the many intimate tastes of Donna tormenting his sealed, filled mouth. Helen then applies a second length of the rubber cording to Chris's elbows, forcing them painfully together into a highly uncomfortable position with a tight, utterly unforgiving knot. The she-male is overwhelmed by an utterly delicious sense of complete and inescapable helplessness as Helen then guides her sexy charge to a wooden dining chair that Anne has placed in the centre of the room. Donna and

Helen then carefully bend the unfortunate she-male over the chair, ensuring that his tightly pantied bottom is presented for a no doubt sound and merciless punishment. Once satisfied that he is adequately positioned, Helen then binds his hosed ankles with another length of the wicked rubber cording. Chris whimpers helplessly into the gag as he is tied tightly in place, his lovely eyes wide with fear and the most wonderful sense of absolute submission. His dreams of becoming a gorgeous she-male damsel in distress are now about to be realised and the incredible fact of this realisation is almost too much to bear.

'Given your repeated clumsiness, Anne will use a hairbrush this time,' Helen announces. 'Twelve hard strokes. Next time they will be on your bare behind.'

Hardly have these terrible words escaped Helen's splendid lips when a sudden sheet of black fire envelopes Chris's tightly tethered she-male form. A brutal, sharp, stinging pain spreads across his buttocks like the shock wave from a meteor impact on the soft earth of a virgin moon.

The poor, helpless she-male screams into the pungent panty gag, but the only sound that escapes the thick, unyielding tape is a pathetic, high-pitched squeal of agony, a squeal that is repeated eleven times as Anne administers the spanking with a cruel enthusiasm, her green eyes alight with the sadistic pleasure of inflicting pain on a helpless and very beautiful victim.

By the end of the spanking, Chris is sobbing desperately into his gag. His buttocks are on fire and thick, pained tears are pouring from his lovely, wide, sissy eyes. As he is pulled back to his feet by Helen and Donna, he can hear Anne's laughter filling the room. He is then positioned so that he is staring directly at the three gorgeous women through a film of tears.

'Yes, Chrissie, it hurts,' Helen teases. 'But I get the distinct impression you like it to hurt. However, I think you need some time on your own to think about what

has happened and how you can improve your performance. So we're going to wrap you up nice and tightly
and put you in the broom closet for an hour.'

Bemused by these words, Chris can only watch
helplessly as another length of rubber cording is applied
to his knees. Then, to his horror, he is made to hop out
of the living room in the high, high heels, down the
corridor and up to a small door beneath the stairs. Here
a new and even more bizarre moment of humiliation
occurs. Helen pulls open the door and then, from a
pocket in her skirt, she produces another pair of panties,
black, rather large, and made from a very smooth and
no doubt very expensive silk.

'I've had these on all day at work, Chrissie, and I
must admit I'm rather jealous of Donna's little torment,
so . . .'

She then proceeds to pull the panties over her slave's
delicately wigged head and position them carefully over
his face, ensuring that the gusset section is pulled tightly
over his nostrils and the two leg sections are positioned
over his eyes, thus creating a most unusual bondage
mask. To the sublime tastes of Donna are thus added
the powerful and very personal odours of the gorgeous
Helen. Each desperate, sexed breath that Chris takes is
a breath of Helen's sexual scents and his own sex
struggles angrily in its delicate stocking prison as the
masochistic pleasure this new humiliation brings floods
through his delicately feminised body. But this is not the
end of his restraint, for no sooner are the panties
stretched tightly over his girlish face than Anne has
produced another black nylon stocking. She then proceeds to wrap it over Chris's tape- and panty-sealed
mouth, adding a second gag and in the process forcing
the gusset section of Helen's odorous panties even
tighter against his flaring nostrils.

'Right,' Helen says, 'I think she's ready for her new
home.'

Smiling cruelly, Anne opens the door, leans inside and flicks on a light switch. A very small, confined space is revealed. Chris looks inside with a renewed sense of fearful apprehension. On the floor is what appears to be a rubber mattress. Other than this, the cupboard is completely empty.

Anne and Donna then help a whimpering Chris totter into the cupboard, forcing his head down beneath the low beam of the doorway as they do so. They then help the lovely she-male damsel in distress to kneel on the rubber mattress and carefully lower him onto his stomach. Once he is fully stretched out, face down, his legs sticking out of the doorway, Anne ties another length of the black rubber cording to his already bound ankles and then pulls the cording up towards his tethered wrists, thus forcing the gorgeous she-male into a tight, painful hog-tie that is secured in place when Anne ties the free end of the cording to the length so effectively binding his wrists together. It is only now that poor Chris's trussed form is completely contained by the tiny cupboard: bound, double gagged, his senses tormented by the sweet perfume of his mistresses, locked in a tight, inescapable hog-tie, unable to move an inch. He is strapped ultra-tightly in a grim, claustrophobic prison, a prison which is suddenly made doubly terrifying by a simple flick of the light switch and his subsequent descent into an awful, total darkness.

'I think an hour should help you understand the importance of absolute body control, Chrissie.'

Helen's cruel, cold words fill him with a very genuine fear, which is made more intense as the door is closed and locked. The wooden panelling of the door immediately presses against his tethered, heeled feet and pushes him into an even more uncomfortable position. He tries to move, even an inch, but the ultra-tight bonds and the tiny space he has been forced into make any movement utterly impossible. All he can do is listen to the hoarse, desperate sound of his laboured breathing and feel the terrible burning deep in his tormented buttocks begin to melt into a gentle sex-heat and spread teasingly between his legs and into his tortured, rock-solid sex. All he can do is feel ever more excited by his strange she-male predicament, feel increasing waves of powerful masochistic desire occupy and possess his sissified body and infect his mind with an absolute addiction for feminisation and complete submission to these three beautiful women who have so quickly and effectively taken over his life.

As the delicate tastes of Donna and the pungent perfumes of Helen fill his mouth and nose, as he plunges through this boundless darkness into a realm of total sex sensation, he knows this is all he has ever truly desired, that due to some bizarre, heavenly intervention by the forces of fate, he has been given the opportunity to become his own fantasy, an opportunity he is now accepting without a moment of hesitation, despite this terrifying ordeal of deprivation, this heart-stopping premature burial in hose, panties and the very highest of heels.

Then there is Donna, the glorious, transcendent Donna. Now his first lover and foremost mistress. The woman he has so secretly desired for so long, who has accepted his true nature with an obvious erotic attraction. Not only does Donna want Chris, she most clearly wants Christina even more!

For the next hour, he is lost in this realm of desire and destiny, contemplating his future, committing himself utterly to the fate that his three wonderful mistresses have planned for him. And by the time they return, by the time the door is unlocked and the light explodes into his momentarily blinded eyes, he knows there will be no return to his old male self, no slow, painful road twisting regretfully into the past. Now, there is only the truth of the ultra-feminine moment.

He is untied and helped back to his feet. The layers of bondage are removed. Gradually, slowly, even painfully, he is allowed to regain his balance. He curtseys his gratitude and it is clear to all his mistresses that he has loved every moment of his sissy imprisonment. Soon he is back before the dressing table mirror, Donna lovingly touching up his near-perfect make-up. Then, after a quiet, secret kiss between the two lovers, a kiss that leaves poor Chris swooning in his mile-high heels and drinking deep of the look of unconditional need in Donna's soft, sparkling blue eyes, he is redressed in his sexy maid's attire and returned to his new life of servitude, spending the rest of the evening mincing happily before Helen, Anne and Donna, obeying each command with a sissy smile, ensuring that each task is carried out with a beautifully exaggerated feminine delicacy.

Of course, the end comes too soon. At just before midnight, Chris is returned to the spare room and carefully turned back into Chris, his eyes so easily betraying his disappointment as he is transformed back into a mere male.

'Don't look so upset, Chrissie,' Helen says, as Donna helps her she-male lover to remove his layers of make-up. 'I've bought these for you ... to help you through the days ahead, and to help reinforce your new feminine persona.'

She then steps back to reveal a new set of clothing laid out on the bed. At first sight the clothing seems to be the various separate elements of another male business suit. But then Helen takes up the jacket and holds it before him.

'I believe the expression is "hide in plain sight". The jacket and the trousers are cut from a very fine and expensive black silk. From a distance they look just like a simple male suit, but they are actually the most feminine of garments disguised as male clothing. The trousers are made from the same material, but there is no zipper and they have a deliberately tight, bottom-enhancing back panel. You will wear these with this blouse.'

She places the jacket on the bed and then takes up a semi-transparent white silk shirt with gleaming silver-grey buttons.

'The blouse can be worn with a tie. You will also wear these shoes.'

Anne then steps forwards, holding another pink rectangular box. Inside is a pair of black patent leather, slip-on shoes, with rather high, square heels and a silver buckle. On the face of it, male shoes, but cut from very feminine materials: the theme of this entire and very appropriate disguise, a disguise that fills Chris with a new, powerful arousal.

Then Donna walks up to the bed and produces one more item of sexy attire: a very beautiful, white silk, lace-trimmed teddy.

'Wear this beneath the suit, with a pair of your very best tights. I chose it for you especially, Chrissie.'

Chris smiles at her helplessly, lovingly, obsessively. He is enslaved, possessed, completely and inescapably enthralled. Now, every second of every day he will be feminised! The permanence of his transformation strikes him like a fist in a velvet glove. Shocked, excited, amazed, he watches as the suit is carefully packed into a black leather hold-all and then placed on the bed before him. Then, his make-up removed, he is undressed by Donna, slowly stripped down to his fierce, rigid and tightly stockinged erection and the wig. Then Donna makes her slave lean forwards so that she can carefully remove the wig, a smile of darkest desire caressing her lovely face. As Chris leans forwards, Donna pulls the wig free of his head and then lets her free hand idly brush against the tormented, imprisoned sex. Poor Chris can only gasp with a fundamentally tortured need and press his sex against the offending hand.

'Not tonight, Chrissie. As Helen said – it's time for you to learn restraint.'

For a split second a look of anger fills the she-male's lovely eyes, his terrible frustration all too evident.

'Now, now, Chrissie. You promised to obey me, didn't you?'

Then the anger has gone. Chris curtseys his acknowledgement of this inescapable fact, a small tear trickling from his right eye.

'Good. Now get dressed and meet me downstairs. I'll give you a lift home.'

The three women leave the room. On the bed, by the hold-all, he finds his original work clothes, plus a pair of white nylon panties. The uniform of Chris, the dress that makes him a weak, useless man. Still tightly stockinged, and now very disappointed, he dresses quickly and then walks from the room, his movements still unavoidably feminine: even in his original work shoes, he cannot help but take small, sissy steps and wiggle his pantied backside provocatively.

He presents himself to his three gorgeous mistresses just before half past midnight. Helen makes it clear that he will be expected to return to work in the morning in his new clothes and that he will continue to act as their maidservant each evening for the next fortnight. She also makes it very clear that she will expect to see Chrissie in his office first thing the next morning for a foot massage. The thought brings a moan of pleasure to the sissy's lips and he performs a particularly deep curtsey to register his understanding and intention to comply without question.

A few minutes later, he is in Donna's car, his mind spinning, amazed at what the evening has brought, more committed than ever to following the path that Helen, Donna and Anne are laying out before him.

Donna says nothing as she drives across town. Despite this, he cannot keep his sex-maddened eyes off her long, nylon-sheathed legs and fights the terrible urge to lean forwards and slip a hand beneath her skirt.

By the time the car pulls up outside his apartment building, he is almost gasping with sexual need.

'I can't come in tonight, Chrissie,' Donna says, turning to face him with a rather sad smile. 'But I want you to be very good for me. I know you want me and that you're really very horny at the moment, but it's not up to you to decide when you can have sexual release any more. I decide. I'm your lover and your mistress, and you must obey me. And I need you to prove your obedience and your love. So I want you to go upstairs and slip into your sexiest lingerie and go to bed. And I want you to keep that stocking on. I want you to dream of me, Chrissie, to dream of all the fun we're going to have together. But you must not, on any account, play with yourself. You must not even touch your cock. Just go up, get changed and go to bed. Do you understand?'

'Yes, mistress,' he replies, his eyes so sad, tears beginning to trickle down his crimson cheeks.

Then, to his surprise, Donna leans forwards and quickly unzips his trousers. He gasps as she pulls his stockinged sex from behind the panties and then pulls the sheer sexy material as tight as she can against his scrotum, bringing a loud moan of pleasure from his sissy lips.

'Nice and tight. The way I expect it to be all the time. Now put it away and off you go.'

Without a kiss or even the slightest embrace, his sex burning into his stomach like a rod of fire, he zips himself up and climbs reluctantly from the car. No sooner has he closed the car door than Donna starts the engine and leaves him standing on the pavement outside the apartment building.

By the time he enters the flat, his mind is totally overwhelmed by desire and tormenting memories of the incredible evening he has just spent with his mistresses.

As he undresses, the urge to masturbate is almost unbearable, yet at the same time totally unacceptable. Eventually, he stands before his full-length bedroom mirror staring at his smooth, feminine form and at the large, stiff sex sealed so tightly and so frustratingly in the sheer black nylon stocking and all the masochistic need in his sissy heart is brought to bear to convince him that the only genuine way forwards is to obey his mistresses. So he seeks the sexiest item of nightwear in his extensive collection. And by the time he has slipped into a lovely pink silk baby-doll nightdress with matching pink panties and curled up beneath sheets that are still marked by the beautiful and now terribly tormenting scent of Donna, he knows there will be little real sleep, and that he will spend the few hours before dawn tossing and turning in a hot, sweating pit of frustrated need, his mind filled with thoughts of his gorgeous mistresses, his dainty sissification at their hands and the further, no doubt ultra-kinky adventures that await the sweet, long-legged, soft-lipped she-male they have christened Chrissie.

Six

The next two weeks pass in a dense fog of perverse desire, frustrated need and the steady, inevitable development of Chris into Chrissie, a sissy she-male maid whose only aim is to serve her mistresses in any way they see fit.

The morning after his amazing bondage adventure, he bathes and perfumes his body with a new fascination, remembering the way in which the incredible maid's uniform had transformed his body and, without a doubt, his soul. To shower, he must remove the stocking, an act of sheer torture that brings tears of appalling frustration to his tired, sex-tortured eyes. Then, once dried, he must replace it, moaning angrily and desperately as he slips the sheer, soft fabric over his rampant crimson sex and ties it tightly in place with the silk ribbon. And after the pain of the stocking, he must face the teasing pleasures of the strange silk suit. His freshly restockinged sex complains bitterly as he first slips into the sexy white silk teddy and then glides his most expensive pair of black silk tights up his freshly shaven and scented legs. The violent, unending erection stretches angrily against the nylon stocking and also against the tight, soft silk material of the teddy. He stares at himself in the mirror and feels a strange, narcissistic attraction to the deeply ambivalent image that confronts him. Memories of maid Chrissie, the beautiful she-male Bettie Page lookalike, come flooding back and he moans helplessly with a powerful, all pervasive pleasure, a deeply masochistic pleasure, a pleasure which has made him its absolute slave.

The suit itself is as light as silken air and a disturbingly perfect fit. It caresses his body and when he moves it is as if he is covered by a sheet of the sexiest, softest and flimsiest of materials imaginable. And, as he carefully secures the knot in his black silk tie, there can be no doubt in his mind that, despite its design and function, this is the most feminine of garments. As he slips his hosed feet into the patent leather shoes, as his eyes study the way the trousers encase and accentuate his long, feminine legs and particularly how they fit so tightly and provocatively around his shapely backside, he knows the suit is in fact designed to expose very subtly rather than hide his femininity. As he moves in the suit, as he walks from the bedroom to the living room, he feels the power of the sissy she-male in a way that he has never felt before, a power that he can no longer control, a power that has taken complete possession of his body and now forces him to take small, mincing steps and make dainty, delicate gestures, to behave in a completely new yet at the same time deep-rooted manner.

To walk out onto the street, suddenly to be among other people, in the hard, harsh, no longer deniable real world is a truly terrifying and at the same time totally electrifying experience. At first, he is convinced that everybody is staring at him, that every pair of eyes is filled with loathing and disgust and directed angrily at this strange girl-boy. Yet after only a few minutes it becomes apparent that no one is actually staring at him; indeed, the ease with which he disappears into the agitated commuter mob is almost embarrassing.

By the time he gets into work that morning he is almost comfortable with his new, distinctly feminine appearance. He makes sure he arrives before his mistresses, so that he can prepare their morning coffee without a difficult interruption. He moves around the office kitchen with a feminine grace, preparing coffee and biscuits and ensuring that a hot cup and two biscuits are placed at the desk of each mistress only a few minutes before they arrive. Then he enters his office, slips off the beautiful black silk jacket and becomes immediately aware of a terrible, unavoidable effect of the suit trousers. The silk blouse is tucked neatly into the trousers and as he looks down at his waist area, he sees that the trousers are so tight around his crotch and buttocks that his erection is quite blatantly apparent, stretched tight against his waist like a large, thick metal pole. As there is no zipper attached to the trousers, he cannot make an effective adjustment. So, utterly humiliated, he rushes behind his desk and quickly sits down behind it. Yet no sooner has he made himself rather fearfully comfortable than the door to his office opens and the gorgeous, imperious Helen strolls into the room, forcing him to rise from the desk and present himself before her, curtseying deeply, his face crimson red, his utter degradation complete.

'You look lovely, Chrissie,' Helen whispers, a quite wicked smile lighting up her beautiful, dark-featured face.

Chrissie curtseys his appreciation, his eyes pinned to her high-heeled feet.

'But you're rather obviously excited by it all, and I'm sure the other ladies in the office will find that particularly amusing.'

He moans despairingly as she fights a sadistic laugh and knows immediately that the trousers have been purchased with these humiliating consequences well in mind, thus that part of his training during the next two weeks will be, whatever Helen may have said to him previously, a very public humiliation. Yet even as this terrible knowledge sinks deep into his sissified heart, his excitement increases. And this too is an essential part of his training: to enjoy each new, deliberately humiliating test and to enjoy it in exact proportion to the size of the embarrassment he must endure: the more he is humiliated, the more excited he becomes.

And so, after giving the stunning Helen another gentle and very erotic foot massage that brings a series of helpless moans of pleasure to her perfect, blood-red lips, he faces this new day of sissy servitude with a tortuous mixture of terror and intense sexual excitement, his paranoia about exposure now doubled by its apparent justification.

Although there is no direct comment, he is painfully aware throughout the office of the sniggers and the strange, vaguely contemptuous looks, and his sense of male self, always weak, always prone to easy damage, slowly but surely crumbles to a speck of memory. And he remains in this state of discomfort, doubt and worry for most of the day, right up until the glorious moment when he is led back into Helen's spare room and slowly transformed back into the gorgeous sex bomb she-male that is the maid Chrissie.

And it is during that very night, as he minces in the ultra-high heels, wiggling his hosed and delicately pantied bottom with such enthusiasm before his mistresses, that he learns even more about the expectations of these beautiful, demanding women. After he has served dinner and spent an hour tottering back and forth between the dining table and the kitchen, the women retire to the living room and Chris is made to stand to sissy attention before them.

'I think it's time for you to learn a little bit more about our needs, Chrissie,' Helen says, a conspiratorial smile lighting up her sublime face. 'As I've mentioned before, part of our plans for you include ensuring that you are able to give women physical pleasure, a very special kind of pleasure that Donna has told us you are already rather good at providing.'

He listens, but there is really no real need for explanation. He curtseys his understanding and obeys without hesitation as Helen insists that Chris kneel before her and place his hands, wrists crossed, behind his back, wrists that are then quickly and expertly bound together with a length of the rubber cording by Anne. He then watches as Helen raises up her long, black skirt to reveal her shapely, black-stockinged legs and her fully exposed and very wet sex, her panties clearly having been removed earlier.

'I hope you don't need telling what to do next, Chrissie,' Helen purrs, as Chris shuffles forwards on his hosed knees and positions his head between his mistress's legs, his heart pounding like a mad jack-hammer in his head, his own nylon-restrained sex fighting its sensual prison with a blind and utterly useless fury.

The smell of Helen's sex, the elemental scent of cunt, smashes into Chris's pretty face long before his anxious, darting tongue tentatively licks at the droplets of sex-juice dripping from her pubes. Then Helen's hands are grasping his head and pushing his face deep into this black forest of dark, eternal desire. And it is only a matter of a few seconds before Chris's instinctively expert tongue has slipped through her bush and deep into the tunnel of love, quickly seeking out her boiling, slippery clit with a slave's helpless desire to please.

Helen comes almost immediately, her thighs suddenly closing around Chrissie's feminised head and squeezing him painfully as she lets out a loud moan of almost painful pleasure that fades slowly into a bass growl of contentment. Her legs part and Chris is allowed to pull his come-soaked face free of the dark, pungent prison. But, inevitably, this is only the beginning; for no sooner has he freed himself from Helen's sweaty clutches than Anne has swivelled around his tethered, petticoated frame and presented the poor she-male with her own dark, uniquely perfumed sex forest. And after the strange pleasure of bringing the lovely, cruel-eyed Anne to a thunderous, screaming orgasm, he is placed between Donna's lovely marble thighs and left to service his most beloved mistress.

Left exhausted by this terrible, demanding pleasuring, he is then once again panty-gagged (this time with Anne's most intimate garment) and placed in the tightest of hog-ties. Yet rather than imprisonment in the cupboard, he is now left to squirm helplessly on the floor before his mistresses as they recover from his expert ministrations, a recovery that involves the rapid consumption of two bottles of wine and a great deal of laughter and swearing, most of it at their new slave's expense.

If there is a point at which time turns into a whirlpool, an endless, disorienting succession of intensely erotic adventures collapsing into each other with no real sense of the past, present or future, it is this one, this moment of absolute bondage, this come-splattered coda to an evening of perverse but beloved submission. Days pass and even more bizarre, erotic adventures mark their coming and going, but the fortnight leading up to his induction proper into the realm of slavery is truly a dreamtime, a landscape without beginning or end across which he totters in the highest of heels and the tightest of bondage, a landscape made even more intense and alien by the fact that his own sexual release now seems to have been completely banned. Although Donna remains friendly and even loving towards him, it is clear he will not be allowed to get anywhere near her in a sexual sense until his full induction has begun. And so the sexualisation of every moment of every day is assured, as is his increasing masochism and femininity.

Yet reality is not that easily cast aside, and for Chris, the world of work is its meanest, most brutal manifestation, and on the Wednesday before his 'special leave' begins, he again finds himself confronted by the severe, angry form of Katherine, his line manager.

'I'm afraid there is nothing else I can do to help you now, Chris,' she says, her voice riddled with the hypocrisy of false sympathy, her shark eyes betraying the pleasure she takes in this ridiculous, pathetic expression of power. 'Nothing has improved since our last talk and I can't allow the situation to deteriorate. So I'm issuing you with a formal warning. I'll also be taking the matter up directly with the Personnel Office. When you return from this leave you insist on taking, I intend to undertake a complete review of the office and its management, with the aim of removing those members of staff who are failing to meet the set performance standards.'

It would be an exaggeration to say that he actually listens to this grim monologue of spectacular self-importance. But what he does do is watch Katherine's eyes; for at no point during this verbal spanking does she in fact look at him: her eyes are directed through the open door of his office, out towards Helen, who is sitting at her desk, typing. He also notices that Helen infrequently looks up from her computer screen and holds Katherine's gaze in a very frank and obviously sexual manner. The rumours of Katherine's lesbianism have always struck Chris as typical office gossip, but recently, on more than one occasion, he has noticed the strange, furtive looks she exchanges with the lovely Helen and the rumour has seemed to approach fact.

Then, during a pause in this tongue-lashing, Chris, perhaps to his surprise, confronts her.

'Are you happy, Katherine?'

At first she responds with a distracted grunt, but when he repeats the question, she turns to face him.

'What? What on earth does that mean, am I happy?'

91

'You don't seem very happy. You seem rather frustrated.'

Her initial response is a slightly incredulous gasp. 'I wouldn't be too concerned about me, Chris: I'd be concerned about *you*, about how happy you'll be feeling when you're unemployed.'

With this last, harsh remark she turns and leaves the room, her distinctly masculine stride as stiff and angry as the tired, bleak and very desperate gaze she fixes upon the lovely, regal Helen.

As she leaves him, he feels no anger, not even a sense of irritation. Instead, there is only the inescapable truth of his ongoing transformation and the simple fact that he is now absolutely certain he cannot go on working in this soul-destroying, pointless job, and thus that his future most assuredly lies at the high-heeled feet of his glorious, beautiful mistresses.

Two days later, he reports to Helen's house in the full knowledge that he is about to spend the next two weeks continually feminised and enslaved, spending every waking second serving his mistresses and undergoing a detailed induction into a new level of sissy servitude. As he enters Helen's house, it is almost immediately apparent that things have changed. Helen is dressed in a tight black sweater and a very long black skirt that reaches down to her black-hosed ankles. A choker of silver pearls is wrapped around her surprisingly slender neck and she is wearing a pair of very high, black patent leather mules. As usual, he avoids her soul-burning, majestic gaze and meekly follows her up the steep flight of stairs to the spare room that has become the locale of each highly erotic and increasingly detailed feminisation.

And it is in the spare room that he confronts the strange, terrifying truth of this new level of his sissification. For where before this had been a simple, somewhat sparse spare bedroom, he now finds himself in the centre of a very large and utterly bizarre baby's nursery! Where there had been a small, functional single bed, there is now a large, adult-sized and metal-barred cot. One complete wall of the room is now lined with rows of wooden shelves upon which rest a vast and bizarre collection of materials, including ultra-large nappies, baby bottles, dummies, rolls of masking tape and the ominous black rubber cording, a number of lengths of very odd-looking rubber tubing, fat rubber ball gags of all colours, paddles of various sizes and, to his final shock and utter astonishment, a series of ribbed dildos, all of varying length. And if this wasn't strange enough, positioned by the cot is a large baby's high-chair and directly opposite the cot what appears to be a huge playpen filled with dolls and a disturbing variety of other baby playthings.

As he stares in horror at this new, ultra-kinky chamber, Helen steps in front of him and orders him to strip naked immediately. Despite the strangeness of his surroundings, he obeys her without a moment's hesitation, noticing as he does so that the walls of the room have now been painted a very striking hot pink and that a new, thick white carpet has also been fitted. How such a transformation could have taken place in just twenty-four hours is something of a mystery, but Chris has become very much aware that Helen can, when inspired, work miracles.

'You're probably wondering about the new room design, Chrissie,' Helen says, a slight, cruel smile on her lovely face.

Now stripped down to his tights and panties, he curtseys and nods his head warily.

'We've decided that, in order to ensure the necessary level of mental conditioning required for your new role, and to eliminate the last, fundamental traces of your masculinity, it will be necessary to reduce you to the status of a baby girl. You will therefore spend the first seven days of the induction period completely babified. The only time when you will be freed from this condition will be the dance and deportment training you will receive from Donna.'

Despite his surprise and shock at this new, devilish twist, he can only curtsey his assent and wiggle sexily out of the tights and panties, his still tightly stockinged sex popping up angrily as the panties are pulled down over his silken thighs.

'If you perform as a baby girl with sufficient skill, you will be allowed to progress to the level of full maid training at the end of next week. You should note that part of this next level of training will include ensuring that you can pass as a woman in public.'

Amazed, appalled, yet also helplessly aroused by this extreme development of his feminisation, Chris soon stands naked before Helen, his nylon-sheathed sex pointing up at his flat stomach like a terrible harbinger of doom for his already considerably weakened sense of masculinity, yet his eyes betraying a deep and inescapable excitement.

Helen's smile widens. She then steps forwards and slips her hands over his rigid cock. He gasps with surprise and frustration and cannot avoid staring up longingly into her beautiful dark brown eyes.

'Yes, it's been a long time since you came, Chrissie, and it's clear that you're suffering. But I'm afraid suffering is very much a key component in your training. Actually, I'm surprised you've managed to control yourself so well during the last two weeks. All you need to remember is that this, your angry little cock, is no longer your property – it belongs to us, to your mistresses, as does the rest of you, body and mind. If you manage to get through the next seven days, then there will be a reward, a reward that I'm sure will make all this suffering worthwhile.'

The stunning dominatrix then begins gently to tease the stocking off Chrissie's boiling, rock-hard sex, producing more whimpers of frustrated despair. And as she discards the damp, warm stocking, a smile of true sadistic glee crosses her lovely face. It is clear that she is deeply aroused by Chris's humiliation and frustration, and by her complete power over him.

'Now go to the bathroom. Wash, shave and perfume yourself as usual, then return to me. Take no more than twenty minutes.'

In the shower, his mind races with thoughts of the week ahead, of his impending babification and of the other mysterious plans this beautiful, determined woman has for him. The desire to masturbate is almost unbearable, and he finds himself racing through his preparations to escape temptation and is soon once again standing before Helen, his cock, like the rest of him, at very firm attention, his heart pounding with a helpless, sissy anticipation.

Helen appraises his body with a cool, detached eye, plotting the map of his babification, pondering the true, devastating extent of a new level of terribly exciting humiliation. And the first item of feminine attire she produces is a very sheer, white nylon stocking. Before his wide, madly aroused eyes, she then proceeds to cover the stocking in a mist of powerful rose-scented perfume, her own gorgeous, soul-melting brown eyes quickly capturing his gaze, her smile now a beautiful warning of torments to come.

'Eyes down, please, Chrissie.'

He curtseys and diverts his gaze to her splendid black patent leather mules, her sexy toes, painted a blood red, clearly visible through a fetishistic film of black nylon.

Then she steps closer, her hands still within his range of vision, and he can only watch in excited and horrified anticipation as she rolls the scented stocking into a ball and then begins to gently slide it over his burning, aching, sex-maddened cock.

His agonised squeals of tormented pleasure inspire a grunt of utter contempt from his beautiful, unyielding mistress. Soon tears of frustration are trickling down the poor sissy's crimson cheeks and he is fighting to prevent his girlish buttocks from wiggling in an almost sluttish dance of sexual agony.

'The stocking was Donna's idea,' Helen whispers. 'She really is a very imaginative woman. You're very lucky to have her as a mistress.'

Once the stocking is pulled firmly into position, Helen then takes up a long length of pink silk ribbon and uses it to tie the gentle nylon prison tightly in place, securing the ribbon with a large, babyish bow at the base of his very full, almost bulging testicles.

Yet even this terrible torment is not the end of his sexual sufferings; for no sooner has Helen secured the stocking than she has returned to the dressing table and taken from it the strangest object he has yet seen. At first sight, it appears to be a weird metal sculpture – two small metal hoops joined by a curved silver bar. As she returns to him, he quickly returns his gaze to her feet.

'You may look up now, Chrissie,' she says, standing only inches from his tormented body.

As he raises his eyes, she holds the strange device before him and then clicks open one of the two hoops. She then repeats this process with the second hoop, her smile widening as his confusion increases.

'As I have made clear, Chrissie, the key to your training is restraint. You are already learning this, but with the induction we must step onto a new plateau of denial, a new stage in the arena of overcoming and self-control. And I'm afraid this will involve a certain amount of suffering, but suffering is part of the core of true submission. Without it, you can never truly understand what it is to surrender completely to a mistress.'

As she speaks, she draws the device towards his rigid, sheathed sex and it doesn't take too many seconds before Chris realises that it is designed to fit over his already tortured cock!

And as Helen slips the open hoops over his stockinged sex, her words, spoken in a voice of pure velvet, strike deep into his sissy heart.

'Yes: a rather wicked cock-restrainer, designed to prevent full erection and thus to make ejaculation impossible. The more excited you get, the more painful the resistance of the restrainer, as I'm afraid you're about to discover.'

It is then that she clicks the two hoops shut around his tightly stockinged sex. The metal instantly bites deep into the engorged flesh of his cock and he releases a helpless cry of genuine pain.

'I suggest if you want the pain to go away, you think of work.'

Her teasing, black comic words only add to his discomfort. To make matters worse, the restrainer pushes the soft nylon of the stocking deep into his stiff sex, and in some strange way manages to make the erotic caress of the delicate nylon material even more exciting!

As tears of genuine pain well up in his wide, baby girl eyes, Helen then orders the poor sissy to bend over and spread his legs wide. Horrified and agonised, he leans forwards, letting the tips of his fingers brush against the thick white carpet and then slowly spreads his legs wide apart, his painfully restrained sex pressing into his stomach, the feel of cold, utterly unforgiving metal an awful announcement of this new level of control.

Unable to see Helen, he can only listen fearfully to her movements and await the next bizarre turn of the screw. And this soon becomes terribly apparent as her hands suddenly rest on his buttocks, but it is not her skin resting against his skin – her hands are sheathed in a soft, cool fabric: she is wearing what feel like rubber gloves!

'It isn't just your cock that will need special attention, Chrissie. There is also your arse. Donna has already told me that you find anal stimulation very exciting, and this is very important for your development as a sissy she-male. We want you to learn that this particular orifice is a source of a very real and intense sexual pleasure. Indeed, we want you to come to regard your anus as the primary source of sexual pleasure. So as we control and restrain your cock, we will train and excite your arse.'

He listens in absolute amazement, initially horrified by the idea that he is to be denied sexual release from his cock and trained instead to find his pleasure through what amounts to anal sex! Yet even as these terrified thoughts are flooding his mind, Helen is slipping a well-greased, rubber-sheathed index finger deep into his back passage and the true extent of the pleasure offered by this stimulation is becoming blindingly apparent. Indeed, the helplessly loud, sissy moan of arousal that escapes his pretty mouth as Helen pushes her finger as deep as it will go is all the confirmation she needs that Chrissie is indeed the ideal subject for the plans she has drawn up for the creation of the perfect she-male maidservant.

Once satisfied that his anus is sufficiently lubricated, Helen slowly removes her finger, producing another moan of helpless sissy pleasure. He then waits in a state of even more excited and fearful anticipation as Helen moves about the room behind him. Eventually he becomes aware that she is standing behind him once again. Then there is the strangest, most disturbing sensation: something hard, cool and rather sticky is being pressed into his back passage!

'Just relax, Chrissie. It's only a small anal plug. Over time we'll increase the size of the plugs, and very soon you'll be able to accommodate the most substantial of intruders.'

He gasps, he moans, he squeals as the anal plug, a phallus-shaped piece of hard pink rubber, is slipped slowly and carefully deep into his anus. This is the most intimate and profound invasion of his remaining masculinity, a terrible, yet incredibly exciting ravishment that opens a new door of physical sensation and reveals the true nature of the pathway to sissidom that lies beyond.

Once the plug has been pushed firmly and inescapably home, Chris is made to stand. As he does so, as his thighs come together and his legs straighten, the plug is pushed even deeper into his back passage and another helpless, hopeless moan trickles from his girlish lips. Even worse, the strange pleasure provided by this bizarre intrusion also sends particularly powerful signals of arousal to his inflamed and tightly imprisoned cock, creating yet more discomfort! This will be the awful dialectic of his feminisation: pleasure followed inevitably by pain.

He is truly appalled by the startling power of the pleasure induced by the plug. Although he had experimented with Donna, nothing has prepared him for the weird delights of the anal plug!

'I can see you're enjoying yourself, Chrissie. And that, as you now no doubt realise, is a punishment in itself. The plug and the rings will remain in place permanently for the next seven days. They will only be removed to allow your natural functions.'

He listens, or rather tries to listen, as the battle between pain and pleasure rages across the landscape of his feminised form. And he watches with tears of frustration and confusion filling his lovely eyes as Helen walks over to a newly fitted extra-large wardrobe and slides open its long, white doors to reveal a spectacular array of babified femininity, a row of adult-sized little girl dresses in a suitable selection of sissy colours: hot pink, bright yellow, snow white, pale blue. Each dress is made from gleaming satin, each is covered in frills and thick frou-frou petticoating. Indeed, it quickly becomes apparent that, besides the wide variety of colours, each dress is in fact identical!

'I had them made especially, Chrissie. One for each day of the week. An essential part of any true sissy's wardrobe.'

Poor Chris moans as Helen selects a hot pink dress and brings it over to the bed. As she carefully places the dress on the bed, her cruel smile increases and their eyes inadvertently meet.

'That's the second time you've failed to avert your gaze, Chrissie. If you do it again, I will spank you with a hairbrush on your bare bottom. Now I suggest you get a good look at this lovely little item, while I prepare your other baby attire.'

The threat of a spanking is merely another terrible tease, another evil tickle of his outraged, tortured sex. And as Helen returns to the wardrobe, he can only stare at this lovely, intricate dress and feel a yet even more painful sexual arousal. As previously noted, the dress is cut from a very expensive, hot pink satin. It has a very high, white pearl-buttoned neck, which is topped off with a row of very thick white French lace. The bodice and very short skirt are covered in what appear to be a pattern of roses and the skirt itself, as well as being frilled with the same ornate lace as the neck area, is laden with inches of spectacular frou-frou petticoating. The long, puffed arms of the dress lead down to pearl-buttoned, lace-trimmed sleeves and another row of pearl buttons traverse its back, from the base of the short skirt right up to the bottom of the neck section.

And as he stares in utter bewilderment, Helen returns carrying a large pile of even more embarrassing dainties. She dumps them on the bed and then begins carefully to sort out the various items before his wide, horribly excited eyes. A thick towel nappy, white nylon, self-supporting stockings, a very large pair of white plastic panties, a pair of delicate pink silk booties with pink silk ribbon laces, a white leather mini-corset, and a pair of pink silk fingerless mittens.

'I think this is everything,' Helen says, almost speaking to herself. 'I ordered most of it from the internet. You can find anything on it.'

She then takes up the thick nappy and tells Chris to spread his legs. As he looks on, his face crimson with shame, a sense of devastating humiliation dissolving what remains of his sense of masculinity, she slips the nappy between his legs, draws it up over his soft, feminine buttocks and pulls the two ends of the thick towelling fabric together around his slender waist. Then, from her skirt pocket, she takes a very large, silver safety pin and secures the two ends tightly together, her cruel smile widening by the minute. The nappy is followed by the stockings. She hands the first pretty, ultra-sheer white stocking to Chris and tells him to put it on. As he sits down on the bed, the plug presses even deeper into his arse just as the cock ring presses harder into the unfortunate flesh of his engorged cock. It is difficult to tell whether the resultant moan is one of pain or of pleasure, and Chris is fast coming to realise that there is now probably very little difference between the two.

The stocking feels wonderful against the silky smooth, scented skin of his leg and as he guides it up over his knee and along his thigh he feels a familiar and very intense thrill. Unfortunately, this thrill also ensures that his poor, brutalised penis is locked in an even tighter, more painful grip by the terrible, unyielding restrainer and once again he finds himself releasing a series of highly ambiguous moans as he secures the self-supporting stocking around the top of his thigh, a process which he then repeats with the second stocking, with the same, rather predictable results.

After the stockings come the white lace-frilled plastic panties. Seemingly huge, thick and embarrassingly noisy, he pulls them up his legs with a sense of complete damnation. Now he knows there is no turning back from this bizarre turn of events, this headfirst dive into the whirlpool of babification. And once the panties have been wiggled into place, Helen takes up the compact, stream-lined white leather mini-corset and wraps it around his already slight stomach, her hot, excited breathing caress-ing his chest and shoulders like a delicate virgin's kiss as she carefully works the corset into place, then takes up the white rubber laces and begins to pull very hard.

At first, Chris feels only a slight discomfort, already used to the restrictive effect of the corselette, but it quickly becomes apparent that Helen intends to move beyond the previous levels of figure training and soon the pressure being applied to his waist is considerable, if not downright painful.

'Restraint, Chrissie. Remember what I have told you: restraint is everything.'

Her words are of little comfort as the air is pushed from his lungs and fat, sissy tears begin to well up in his pretty eyes. But then the pressure has levelled out and Helen is tying the laces tightly into place. He is appalled by the pressure on his waist and feels sure he will soon pass out. Helen, however, is disturbingly indifferent.

'It may feel unbearable, Chrissie, but you'll soon get used to it. I think you'll be surprised by just how much restriction your waist will take, especially after the diet takes effect. Believe it or not, I think there's at least another inch we can take off you.'

His eyes widen in horror at this last sentence, yet, to his amazement, he finds himself nodding with a resigna-tion that is more evidence of his absolute enslavement and devotion to this stunning, fiery-eyed woman.

After the corset comes the dress, the amazing, intri-cate, soul-consuming dress. He watches in pained fascination as she slowly unbuttons this spectacular pink creation and then holds it teasingly before him. As he steps into the dress and she begins to draw it up his body, a sense of utterly divine surrender washes over him. The true, deep, nerve-tingling pleasure of absolute submission to this stunning woman has never been more apparent than at this exact moment. He swoons in her powerful, sensual grasp as she pulls the dress over his feminine shoulders and neck and then begins carefully, slowly, erotically to secure each of the gleaming white pearl buttons, sealing him tightly and totally into a realm of absolute baby girl servitude. His tormented cock struggles against nylon, metal and towelling, buried deep in a sweet prison of endless sissification, as Helen's long, deceptively gentle hands secure the buttons around the very high neck of the dress and the lace frillies tickle his pretty, dimpled chin.

'You look gorgeous,' she whispers, her soft, damp lips brushing against his ear. 'Tell me how much you want this.'

'More than anything, mistress,' he gasps, as her hands wander beneath the dress and into the sea of frou-frou petticoating fixed to the wide, short skirt. 'I want to be your slave forever. I want nothing else.'

'I'm sure we can arrange that,' she replies, her beautiful, deep voice resonating with sexual arousal. 'But how much do you want to be restrained, to be nappied, to be tightly bound and gagged, to be utterly, endlessly humiliated?'

As her sex-honey-coated voice teases him, her hands slip down his plastic-pantied bottom and between his legs. He moans, he wiggles in her warm, teasing embrace, he feels the pain of the restrainer and the pleasure of her wicked caress.

'I want it so very much, mistress. I want to be kept this way forever.'

She takes his hands and guides them to her full, heavy breasts. Helplessly, urgently, he begins to caress these tightly restrained orbs. Then, once again, their eyes meet. Yet he fails to avert their powerful, hungry, animal gaze. Instead, he falls into it, into this look of nova-bright sex, this cosmic heart of a savage, eternal passion.

'I told you what would happen, Chrissie. You'll be spanked. Soundly. Bound, gagged, in this delicious baby state, and then spanked.'

'Yes, mistress.'

But there is no spanking there and then. Instead, suddenly, shockingly, she pushes her she-male slave away and takes the pair of pink silk booties from the bed, telling him to sit down as she does so. Dazed by this sudden change of mood, he finds himself obeying and then watching with adoring eyes as Helen proceeds to kneel down by her slave and then slip the dainty, elegant and incredibly sissy booties over his stockinged feet. She secures each bootie with a thick pink silk ribbon lace tied in a fat, babyish bow, then rises to face him.

'Before we go any further, I think a spot of suitably sissy make-up is required.'

She then takes him by the hand and leads him over to the dressing table. Walking in the booties is surprisingly difficult. Indeed, it soon becomes apparent that, because they have no real soles, the booties slip relentlessly against the soft, thick carpet and normal walking of any kind is impossible. Instead, he finds himself shuffling absurdly behind his mistress, fighting desperately to keep his balance, yet with his eyes still pinned hungrily to Helen's beautiful, black-hosed ankles and very high, black patent leather mules. And, as well as the problem of balance, there is the inescapable torment of the plug and the restrainer. As he shuffle-minces forwards, the movements of his stockinged thighs and nappied, pantied buttocks exert a powerful pressure on the plug and seem to push it deeper into his anus, thus increasing the waves of teasing pleasure that pour between his legs and up into his tightly restrained sex, and thus increasing the discomfort so relentlessly provided by the fiendish metal re-strainer.

Once at the dressing table, he finds himself facing the strangest manifestation of Chrissie yet, a very attractive, very feminine but still obviously male slave imprisoned in an intricate and very sexy baby girl's dress!

'Yes,' Helen whispers, recognising Chris's concern, 'you do look rather odd. But it won't take me long to fix that.'

And so he watches as this gorgeous, plump beauty sets to work on his face, applying a heavy tan foundation followed by a much lighter, almost cream-coloured facial paint, a mixture which produces a startling pale marble effect and leaves his face looking vaguely like that of a nineteenth-century china doll. This impression is then heightened by the application of two large circles of hot pink rouge to his very feminine cheeks followed by exactly matching lip colouring. A pale blue eye-shadow is then applied, to match his lovely, girlish eyes. Despite his previous experience, this transformation is still quite shocking, and suddenly he is facing a beautiful doll-like sissy, a babified masterpiece which is then stunningly topped off by a truly marvellous blonde wig, a mass of carefully sculpted baby curls which Helen, her eyes filled with a now familiar erotic fire, holds before his reflection with a broad smile.

'I had it made specially, Chrissie,' she purrs. 'The perfect topping for this lovely sissy cake.'

Chris gasps with pleasure and surprise as she then proceeds gently to guide the wig over his head and pull it firmly into place. This final act of transformation is perhaps the most profound for, within seconds of the wig being positioned, Chris finds himself confronting a beautiful, wide-eyed, helplessly pouting baby sissy doll, a fantasy creation straight out of his most intense dreams of enforced feminisation and servitude. He moans with she-male pleasure as the full extent of this new work of sissy art comes alive before his amazed, sex-maddened eyes. Yet his are not the only eyes filled with the dark heat of desire. For Helen is staring at her creation with an intensely erotic surprise.

'My, my,' she mumbles. 'My, oh, my.'

And as he stares at this gorgeous manifestation, he knows he can never ever truly be a male again, that this is the final stage of the destruction of what little remains of his sense of masculinity. Yet there is no sense of loss here: as he revels in this dainty, befrilled creature, he celebrates a beautifully irreversible changing and a true changeling. At last he is free to cast off the shackles of a masculinity that has always felt forced, artificial, inauthentic.

As he surrenders so willingly to this glorious babification, Helen slips away to the wardrobe, returning a few moments later with a very large pink cardboard box. She places the box on the table before him and then quickly returns to the bed to retrieve the lovely, delicate mittens. Chris watches in a state of ecstatic anticipation as Helen places the mittens beside the pink box and then opens a drawer in the dressing table, taking from within it a small, black wooden box, little larger than a soap dish. She places this box next to the mittens. She then picks up one of the mittens.

'Hold your left hand out, Chrissie.'

Trembling with deeply masochistic excitement, Chris obeys, his sex struggling painfully in its metal prison, his sweetly hosed thighs pressing together to force the plug deeper into his anus and ensure that even more powerful shock waves of pleasure crash into his beautiful, sissified body.

Helen slips the petal-soft fingerless mitten over his outheld hand, and it is only now that the quivering she-male notices that the mitten is fitted with a row of exquisite pearl buttons down one side of its pink silk and satin surface, and that the glove is designed to slip under the frilled sleeves of the dress. On closer examination, it also becomes apparent that there are a number of tiny holes in each sleeve of the dress and that the mitten can in fact be tightly secured to the dress sleeve via the pearl buttons. And as the mitten is secured over his hand, he becomes aware that the sexy, babyish glove is lined with surprisingly thick rubber, which effectively immobilises his fingers. As Helen secures the second glove, an even more profound and complete sense of utter helplessness washes over him and he almost cries out with a wild sissy pleasure.

After double-checking that the mittens are tightly positioned, Helen takes up the small wooden box and slides open its lid to reveal, to his surprise, a very large baby's rubber pacifier resting on an equally large pink plastic base, attached to the ends of which are two long pink silk ribbons! And if this wasn't strange enough, the huge teat of the dummy is shaped exactly like a penis!

'You will be kept dummy-gagged permanently during the first week, except when you are fed or we need your mouth for our own pleasure. Now open wide.'

He obeys and Helen teasingly slips the large rubber phallus deep into his mouth. The teat almost fills his mouth to bursting point, flattening his tongue against the floor of his mouth and making even the most pathetic of squeals impossible. The plastic base fits over his painted lips perfectly and once the ribbons have been tightly tied in place in a fat sissy ribbon at the back of his becurled head, it creates a perfect seal and adds to the devastatingly effective power of the gag.

His eyes wide with fear and angry arousal, the sense of feminine weakness and helplessness now at its shattering peak, poor Chris can only watch in silence as beautiful, ample, flame-eyed Helen, a smile of triumph spreading across her gorgeous face, then opens the large pink box and takes from inside it a truly spectacular and very beautiful adult-sized baby bonnet, an epic wonder of sissification designed to add the final cosmetic touch to this spectacularly erotic transformation.

'It really is quite beautiful, Chrissie. You're a very, very lucky sissy.'

Poor Chris finds himself nodding helplessly in agreement at the sight of the stunning bonnet, a mass of very fine pink silk trimmed with a very intricately patterned white lace, a long, thick pink silk ribbon running from each frilled, curved end and a very large silk rose fixed to the front right hand side. As Helen pulls it over his wigged head he manages to force the slightest moan of almost transcendent pleasure from his so efficiently stopped mouth and, as the thick ribbons are tied in place beneath his sissy chin in a very fat, sexy bow, the gorgeous, tormented she-male is truly lost in a state of pure ecstasy.

Satisfied that the bonnet is adequately secured, Helen then helps Chris to his feet and leads him over to the full-length mirror built into the front of the new wardrobe. As his complete reflection is revealed, Chris gasps silently into his tight, phallic dummy gag. The vision of sissified loveliness before him is almost too ideal, too perfect, an image from his most extreme dreams of absolute domination and submission brought to grand, spectacular life. A beautiful, baby doll she-male, her long, shapely legs wrapped in the finest, sheerest white nylon, her feminine frame encased in the darling baby dress, her lovely, china doll face surrounded by the intricate, helplessly sweet bonnet, her eyes wide with excitement and sissy anticipation.

'You look perfect, Chrissie, even better than I could ever have imagined,' Helen says, her own continuing excitement all too apparent in her gorgeous golden-brown eyes.

Still stunned by his sissified visage, Chris is then led over to the playpen. Helen releases the clever child-proof lock and helps Chris inside, insisting he stand with his arms behind his back, facing away from her. There is then a brief pause, during which Chris's sense of feminine helplessness intensifies to such a terrible, passionate level that he finds himself wiggling uncontrollably.

'Dear me, you are getting all heated up,' Helen says, taking his wrists, crossing them and then binding them tightly together with what feels like another piece of the rubberised cording. She then repeats this process with his elbows, forcing them together and binding them painfully tight, and a moan of discomfort fights to escape Chris's well-stopped mouth. Then, to his surprise, she forces him to kneel down in the centre of the large metal-barred pen, but now so that he is facing Helen and the door to the room. She has three more lengths of the cording in her hands and a very wicked, almost horny smile on her face. She kneels down by his bootied ankles and uses two lengths of the cording to bind tightly together his ankles and knees.

Chris is thus totally immobilised in the centre of the pen, a trussed sissy completely at the mercy of his beautiful, utterly determined mistress. Yet his bondage is not complete, for no sooner has she finished binding his ankles than the third and final length of cording is used to bind his tethered ankles to his tightly bound wrists, thus forcing him into a kneeling hog-tie which effectively denies him the opportunity of any form of movement. Not only this but, as the final length of cording is secured, the weight of his sissified body is forced onto his thighs and backside, which in turn forces the anal plug even deeper into his back passage. And if this isn't enough, the helpless sitting position forces the very tight corset to dig even deeper into his sides. Thus, the poor she-male beauty is locked into a

109

very uncomfortable and also very exciting bondage, a state which can only serve to heighten his deeply masochistic pleasure and make him crave even greater humiliations.

Having trussed her sissy slave so securely and wickedly, Helen rises to her sexy, high-heeled feet and steps out of the playpen.

'I think you need a little while to come to terms with what's happening to you, Chrissie,' she says, her lovely, deep voice cut through with sexual arousal. 'So I'm going to leave you here for about an hour or so, then come back with Donna and Anne. I'm sure they'll be thrilled by what a sexy little sissy you've turned out to be.'

He stares desperately at her lovely back as she glides from the room. As an added touch, Helen turns as she reaches the door and releases a truly erotic smile of endless promise. The helpless sissy squeals uselessly into his fat gag as her hand wanders teasingly towards the light switch. But his protests are, of course, futile. Helen flicks the switch and then leaves the room, locking the door and plunging poor Chris into an absolute, yet highly erotic darkness.

In the complete darkness of the room, Chris struggles in his baby bondage for over an hour, trying desperately to avoid becoming too aroused by this ecstatic imprisonment and thus relieve the terrible, sadistic pressure on his stiff, tormented sex. Yet the position he has been tied into has been designed to inflict the maximum excitement and therefore the maximum discomfort and, without the distraction of sight, he is forced to concentrate completely on this awful, yet perversely exciting struggle for virtually the whole period of his so-called 'contemplation'. Tormented by the restrainer, fiercely aroused by the plug, his body teased by the gentle fabrics caressing his shaven, scented body, the only contemplation he is capable of is the contemplation of his tethered body and its bizarre ordeal at the hands of the divine Helen.

By the time the sound of a key turning in the door lock rings in his sissy ears like bells of liberation, he is covered in sex-sweat, moaning relentlessly and straining angrily but quite uselessly against his various, inescapable bonds.

The door opens. Light from the hallway floods into the room to reveal a very shapely, dark figure. Then a much brighter light floods the room and he is temporarily blinded. And by the time his eyes begin to focus, he discovers the wonderful form of Donna standing over him, her eyes wide with amazement, a very broad and cruel smile igniting her beautiful face.

Despite the strict demand that he avoid her eyes, he finds himself looking up at Donna with a mixture of sex-hunger and utter humiliation. He feels his china-doll face burn with embarrassment, but knows the thick, pale face-paint will easily hide the wave of crimson spreading across his sissy cheeks.

'Who's a pretty little baby, then?' Donna suddenly purrs, her voice filled with the exaggerated tones of classic baby talk.

Chris squeals into his dummy gag and shakes his head angrily. Donna bursts out laughing and then, to his utter horror, she holds up a very large plastic baby's bottle filled with a thick white liquid and topped with a huge rubber teat.

She unlocks the playpen and steps inside. She is dressed in a very tight black nylon sweater, a very short black leather skirt, black hose, and high-heeled, black patent leather court shoes. Her hair is loose, flooding over her shoulders like a golden waterfall, and her lovely blue eyes shine with cruel amusement and a barely disguised sexual excitement.

As she kneels down before him, her skirt rides up her thighs to reveal flower-patterned stocking-tops and red satin suspenders, a revelation that brings even more squeals from Chris.

Her smile widening even further, her powerful sandal-wood perfume teasing his baby girl nostrils, she then torments him further with an incomprehensible litany of baby talk, tickling his dimpled, bowed chin with her free hand and waving the bottle before him threateningly with the other.

Yet even as she so knowingly humiliates him, how terribly, how fundamentally he wants her. As his cock strains harder against its painful metal tyrant, his desire for this beautiful woman pours like a stream of molten lava over his sissified body.

His eyes fall on her splendid, tightly restrained breasts as she leans forwards to untie the bow holding the bonnet in place, her skirt crawling further up her legs as she does so to provide a wicked glimpse of red silk panties.

She carefully removes the bonnet and places it at her side, then frees the bow holding the dummy gag in place. As she pulls the dummy from his painted mouth, he tries to declare the force of his continuing desire and the reality of his love, but no sooner is his mouth free than the fat teat of the plastic bottle has been forced between his lips.

'Drink up.' She laughs. 'I want you to take all of it, Chrissie, every last drop.'

Almost involuntarily he finds himself sucking on the teat and beginning to drink what tastes like warm, sugared milk laced with cinnamon. And as he does so, her free hand slips beneath Chris's wide, short skirt and disappears into the mass of frou-frou petticoating. As her hands seek out the thick plastic panties he splutters into the teat and tries to spit it from his mouth. Donna's response is to push the bottle even more firmly against his lips and press her free hand deep into the panties, thus bringing even more uncomfortable pressure to bear on his restrained, nappied sex.

112

'Hope you like the restrainer and the plug,' she says, her soft voice filled with a paradoxical love. 'I know it hurts, but I want you to prove yourself, Chrissie. I want you to suffer for me. There'll be no release for at least another week. You'll be in agony most of the time – unable to come. And all the time surrounded by sexy, kinky women determined to ensure you're permanently turned on. And there'll be nothing you can do about it, because you'll be all babified and tied up. But I know you, I know you'll really love every second of it. The more we dominate and humiliate you, the more you want to serve, to do anything we tell you. Isn't that true?'

He can only nod furiously between gasps as he sucks up the last of the milk, now violently aroused and in some considerable pain.

Satisfied that he has consumed all the milk, she pulls the teat from his lips and takes up the dummy gag.

'I love you,' he whispers, as she prepares to fix the gag back into his mouth.

She hesitates and then kisses him, a long, warm, passionate kiss, which he returns with a helpless desperation. Then she pulls her mouth away and quickly repositions the dummy gag, his submission absolute, his adoration total, as she ties it tightly in place. She then coyly pulls her skirt down over her black stockinged thighs, smiles gently at him and gets to her feet. His wide eyes never leave her fantastic body and he moans angrily as she turns her back on him, then steps out of the playpen. As she reaches the door, she turns, her smile slighter sadder now.

'I'm missing you terribly, Chrissie. But if you really behave yourself, if you show us what a good little baby you can be – well, there'll be a really special treat for you at the end of the week.'

Then she leaves and tears of frustration, of hopeless, crushed longing well up in his pretty eyes. Yet even as the first tear is trickling down his porcelain cheeks, the tall, regal, cruel Anne enters the room. Dressed in a very short black and white check skirt, a semi-transparent white silk blouse, very sheer black hose and relatively low-heeled court shoes, she strides over to him, laughing loudly, her piercing green eyes filled with a mocking contempt.

'Oh, yes,' she says, 'this is so you, Chrissie. The perfect sissy baby she-male. Some men would pay thousands for this. You should thank your lucky stars.'

She steps into the pen and, like Donna, kneels down beside him. Yet there is no sexual tension in this encounter. Chris has learned to fear Anne and as she produces a second large baby's bottle filled the same, thick creamy milk, a sense of true dread and fear washes over him.

'We should keep you like this permanently,' she snaps, untying the dummy gag, pulling it roughly from his mouth, then stuffing the teat of the bottle into his far from willing mouth. 'Drink it all, babikins, otherwise I'll personally thrash that soft sissy arse of yours until it bleeds.'

Poor Chris can only obey instantly, filling his mouth once again with the sweet, cinnamon-flavoured milk.

'You really are a pretty little thing,' Anne continues, as he tries to drink the milk without staring at her large breasts and the clearly visible lace-edged bra that imprisons them. 'And seeing you so sweetly attired and secured has definitely given me some very interesting ideas.'

She hesitates, her mind turning over, her eyes momentarily glazed as she considers a wicked scheme.

'How would you like to be a baby model, Chrissie?' she then asks. 'There are loads of internet sites where men who like dressing up as babies post pictures of themselves and their sad friends. Most of them look utterly ridiculous. But you – Well, you're on a completely different level. I think there'd be a lot of fellow perverts who'd pay good money to look at pictures of pretty Chrissie all babified and tethered. Yes, your own website, full of photos of sweet Chrissie in baby bondage. Better still, full of photos of Chrissie tied up in *all* her lovely clothes. Sounds good, doesn't it?'

Sucking desperately, now feeling quite sick, Chris can only nod wearily, Anne's plan filling him with utter horror.

By the time he has managed to empty the bottle and the dummy gag has been tightly resecured, Anne has set out her initial thoughts on a kinky personal website dedicated to the gorgeous she-male Christina, a website with a decidedly sadomasochistic edge featuring page after page of pictures of Christina intricately feminised, tightly bound and inescapably gagged; Christina as Baby Chrissie, Christina as maidservant, Christina as office girl in bondage, Christina as nurse in bondage, Christina at the feet of her shark-eyed mistresses. And as Anne enthusiastically details her plans, Chris's horror fades, to be replaced by a strange, disturbed excitement, as if to be exposed in this manner, to be revealed as a transvestite sadomasochist via the vast electronic arena of the internet, is to be delivered into a new realm of perverse delights.

By the time Anne slinks out of the room, his mind is reeling from the prospects of becoming an internet bondage model, and he is still in a state of some mental distress when Helen returns, kneels down at his side and produces a third bottle of warm, thick milk. Of course there is absolutely no question of him refusing the bottle and the unfortunate she-male is soon sucking reluctantly on the fat teat, his eyes pinned helplessly to her ample bosom.

'I hope you've been enjoying yourself, Chrissie,' she teases. 'But not too much: I wouldn't want you to damage that poor little penis. But I must say, you do take to the bottle very naturally. Anne no doubt told you she wanted you to be kept in nappies permanently. I'm afraid I couldn't agree to that. But I'm sure they'll always be there as a very necessary disciplinary tool, although I don't really see Anne as the maternal type. I think Donna will make you a much better mummy.'

It takes him some time to drain the third bottle and, by the time he has reached the last few drops, Anne and Donna have returned.

'Right,' Helen announces, removing the teat. 'It's way past your bed time, so let's get you tucked in.'

The dummy gag is quickly replaced and then the cording securing the hog-tie is released. Assisted by Donna, Helen then helps the dazed, giddy and somewhat nauseous she-male to his feet. His hosed legs are by now as stiff as wooden planks and only a few wayward shuffles up and down the room can bring them back to life. And once he is able to walk freely, he is led over to the large, barred cot. As Helen unlocks a side panel and pulls it down, Anne carefully repositions the lovely bonnet on his wigged head and ties it in place with another fat bow. Poor Chris is then helped into the cot by Donna and made to lay flat out on his back on a pink rubber mattress that is the only item of actual bedding in the cot. It is only as he lies down that he notices the leather shackles fixed into the frame of the cot, a set at the level of his waist and a set where his bootied feet are now resting. And as Helen teasingly straightens his pretty, sexy baby clothes, Anne and Donna secure her mittened hands and bootied feet in the heavy shackles, thus ensuring that the she-male is held firmly on his back for the rest of the night.

Satisfied that he is tied tightly in place, Helen then pulls up and locks the side panel. Because of the bonnet, Chris can only see directly above him and he soon finds himself staring up as if from the bottom of a well at the beaming faces of his lovely three mistresses.

'What a lovely sight,' Anne teases. 'It'd be a crime not to share her with the world.'

Helen and Donna laugh and Chris finds it very difficult not to release a moan of deeply masochistic pleasure.

The three women then take turns in placing long, wet kisses on Chris's marble forehead and wishing him a suitably excited night. Then they disappear from view and within seconds he is plunged into darkness again, the sound of the bedroom door closing and locking a simple announcement of the coming night of immobile, helpless baby bondage that awaits him.

As he ponders the utterly bizarre events of the last few hours, his sense of sexual excitement seems to increase rather than diminish and he is soon deeply frustrated and, thanks to the restrainer, far too uncomfortable to sleep. The urge to masturbate, an urge always unthinkingly surrendered to in his own bed, is now almost unbearable, and soon new tears of agonised frustration and pain are filling his eyes. Yet even as he strains against the shackles and imagines Donna's soft, elegant hands caressing his sissified body, a new urge is making itself known: the urge to urinate, an urge which quickly moves from a vaguely uncomfortable need to a painful demand, an urge he soon finds himself battling with desperately in the pitch blackness, an urge that brings fresh tears to his sissy eyes and to which, eventually, he surrenders. The humiliation of flooding his thick nappy with what feels like a gallon of warm urine is indescribable. Surely, this is the last nail in the coffin containing what is left of his masculinity. But even as tears of despair and embarrassment pour down his cheeks, the sense of relief and the physical relaxation the urination brings, together with the exhaustion induced by the struggle, lull him towards a deep, dreamless sleep, a sleep that leads like the dead straight seam of a sheer, black silk stocking towards a distinctly feminine future.

Seven

The next morning he is woken by Helen and released from the cot, only to be immediately stripped down to his now very heavy nappy. Once his gorgeous mistress discovers that he has wet himself, she drags him over to the bed, hauls off the offending nappy and carefully dries him with a towel, all the while scolding him angrily for this lack of restraint. And no sooner is the poor sissy dried than Helen administers twelve very hard slaps to his bare bottom, producing a symphony of tightly dummy-gagged squeals and a two deep crimson buttocks. Sobbing in pain, yet knowing that the final effect will be pure pleasure, he is then led to the bathroom. To his relief, the terrible cock-ring is removed, as is the stocking beneath, and, watched carefully by Helen, he is allowed to thoroughly wash and shave his body. Once dried, powdered and perfumed, he is led back to the bedroom and then turned back into baby Chrissie, complete with a fresh black stocking restrainer, a painfully resecured cock-ring and a very fat, scented nappy.

Within the hour, he is back in the playpen, bound in the kneeling hog-tie and now secured in a beautiful yellow version of the darling baby dress, complete with matching mittens, booties, stockings and bonnet, moaning into his dummy gag, straining against the cords binding his arms and legs, a beautiful, and intricately

118

made-up sissy awaiting his next bizarre and no doubt very erotic adventure.

His breakfast consists of another large bottle of creamy milk and two baby's rusks fed to him as he sits bound in the pen by a smiling Helen. To his deep embarrassment, she is now talking to him in the soft, gentle voice of a mother talking to her baby daughter. Yet even as his porcelain painted face burns with unseen humiliation, he cannot help but be excited by this sudden change of personality, particularly as Helen has also dressed in a very tight white nylon sweater which quite deliberately accentuates her large, matronly bosom, a knee-length blue skirt, white tights and low-heeled blue leather court shoes, all of which make her look like a very beautiful and marvellously buxom wet-nurse.

Yet this is only the beginning. After the feeding, he is tightly regagged and left alone for another tormenting, frustrating hour. When Helen does return, it is with Anne and Donna, both of whom spend the next thirty minutes or so teasing their babified charge remorselessly. Anne, dressed in a red silk trouser suit and perilously high heels, towers over him like a satanic messenger, her smile cool and cruel, her emerald eyes filled with cunning and contempt. Donna, however, almost immediately replaces Helen in the pen and begins to torment him with gently mocking baby talk. Dressed in a very short white dress, matching hose and a pair of white court shoes, she too resembles a nurse, and as she leans forwards to kiss his rouged cheeks his eyes are once again allowed to feast on her long, nylon-sheathed thighs and her superb, tightly restrained bosom.

And for the rest of the day, he is at the absolute mercy of these beautiful, dominant and very imaginative women. By mid-morning, they have brought him down into the living room and presented him with a pile of furry toy animals. His arms and legs now freed, but with the dummy gag, the mittens and the bonnet still firmly in place, he is made to play with the toys, his pathetic imitation of a baby girl crawling around the living room bringing peals of sarcastic laughter from the women. Yet even this tiring, savagely embarrassing torment is intensely exciting, and as the day progresses, and each new humiliation is introduced, he finds himself more and more aroused, lost deep inside a vast maze of masochistic desire that seems to have no exit point.

It becomes clear early on that Donna, despite being sexually unavailable, will play a very significant role in the week of babification. It is she who, after the initial humiliation of the furry animals, leads him to the kitchen and secures him inside a large, adult-sized high-chair. And it is she who removes the dummy gag and teasingly feeds him a meal of baby food, another bottle of milk and another rusk, all the while whispering sweet baby nothings in his ear and ensuring that his excited eyes are kept busy with the wondrous spectacle of her beautiful breasts.

'Did baby enjoying her din dins?' Donna asks, her hands now resting on Chris's yellow stockinged knees.

Poor Chris can only nod and moan as Donna suddenly moves her hands up his legs and beneath the thick frou-frou petticoating attached to the short skirt of the dress. Soon they are once again teasing the noisy fabric of the plastic panties and pressing deep into the nappy beneath.

'Baby must be getting very horny by now, what with all these sexy undies and the lovely stockings. I bet your poor willie is suffering quite badly.'

Eventually, she removes him from the chair and takes him back into the living room, where he spends another uncomfortable hour being forced to play with a collection of Barbie dolls and a surprisingly ornate doll's house.

By mid-afternoon, the women's enthusiasm for these teasing games has waned and Helen returns the beautifully babified sissy to the nursery for his 'afternoon nap'. However, as soon as they reach the room, Helen shuts and locks the door and leads him over to the bed rather than the cot. As he shuffles along behind her, his eyes pinned desperately to the backs of her shapely, delicately hosed legs, he wonders what new, wicked torment she has in store for him.

She sits down on the bed and then orders him to stand before her with his arms behind his back. He sweetly curtseys his understanding and obeys. She then tells him to lean forwards and, very carefully, she removes the bonnet and the dummy gag.

'I think you need to relax a little before I put you to bed, Chrissie. So I'm going to allow you to suckle me for a few minutes. Now I want you to lie on the bed and put your head in my lap.'

Disturbed by the slightly obscure reference to 'suckling', Chris curtseys and climbs up onto the bed, a difficult undertaking given the constantly restrictive presence of the mini-corset, the slippery nature of the dress, mittens and booties. But, determined to obey his mistress, he soon finds himself on his back and carefully lowering his head into her soft lap. Once appropriately settled, he finds himself staring up at Helen's spectacular bosom, two sensual mountains straining against the material of the very tight white nylon sweater. He moans pathetically and pushes his thighs tightly together, thus forcing the plug to press deeper into his arse.

Yet this initially, highly erotic positioning is nothing compared with what follows. For as Chris stares up at Helen's generous bosom, the beautiful, plump brunette suddenly edges the bottom of the sweater out of her skirt and begins to pull it up over her torso, revealing as she does so a large, very pretty white silk bra filled to bursting point with her incredible pale rose breasts, their very long and stiff nipples clearly visible through each smooth cup of the bra.

Chris squeals with a brutally frustrated pleasure as Helen places the sweater on the bed and then slips her arms behind her back and begins to unhook the bra. His poor eyes nearly pop out of his sissified head as she slips out of the slender cream shoulder-straps and allows the large cups to slip free of her breasts to reveal the two magnificent orbs in all their considerable glory. She then discards the bra and takes Chris's sissy head in her hands.

'There, there, babikins,' she purrs, her beautiful eyes now fixed on his. 'There's no need to worry: Mummy's here.'

As his head is guided towards her left breast, tears of pain and desire well up in his girlish eyes, the cock-ring now biting into his straining, furious sex. And as he slips his lips over her rock-hard nipples, as his mouth brushes against the soft, warm flesh of this holy fruit, his feet wiggling helplessly, he is filled with an almost holy sense of joy. He is a feminised priest worshipping his deity with absolute devotion.

He sucks hungrily on her teat. At one point he accidentally nibbles at her breast, but the loud moan she subsequently emits is one of pleasure rather than pain, and she quietly encourages Chris to continue. Soon, she is moaning continually and demanding he transfer his very effective oral ministrations to the other breast. After five more minutes, a powerful shudder runs through Helen's body and a cry of pleasure explodes from her wide, sensual mouth. Her orgasm is a terrible reminder of the pleasure he is denied, yet even as she comes violently he continues to suck desperately on her large, silken bosom.

Eventually, Helen gently detaches the sexy sissy slave from her breast and orders him to get up from the bed.

As he does so, she slips back into the bra. He faces her in a state of shock, his eyes cast modestly down at her shoes.

'You seem to have a lot of erotic talents, Chrissie. I will expect you to suckle me regularly.'

He eagerly curtseys and her smile widens.

'Now, as a special reward, I think you should be very tightly bound and gagged. Would you like that?'

Another deep sissy curtsey makes it very clear that he would and she orders him to shuffle over to the cot. As he does so, his heart beating with masochistic anticipation, Helen slips back into the sweater then glides over to the dressing table. From within one of its drawers, she takes a familiar roll of silver masking tape. From another drawer she takes a pile of black stockings.

'Kneel down,' she says, her eyes still quite glazed by the pleasure of Chris's expert suckling.

He curtseys and then carefully kneels down beside the cot. She walks up to him and drops the stockings and tape at his side, leaving his face inches from her blue skirt.

'I'm rather wet now, Chrissie, so I'll have to change my panties and tights,' she purrs, 'but it seems such a shame to put them in the wash when you're here to appreciate all their secret aromas.'

His eyes wide, his cock struggling angrily against the evil metal rings, he watches in an agony of frustrated desire and amazement as she then proceeds to unzip her skirt and let it fall to the floor before him. Her long, strong, yet still very shapely legs, so elegant and sensually sheathed in the sheer white nylon, are revealed to him in all their statuesque glory, as is a very large damp patch around her panties and the powerful, arousing aroma of her sex.

As she slowly teases her legs out of the tights, poor Chris moans with a new desperation. Yet even this is merely an overture; for as soon as the tights have joined the skirt, Chris finds himself facing head-on Helen's soaking, white silk panties, panties that the splendid dominatrix then proceeds to pull slowly down her smooth, muscular legs, revealing a thick sex-forest covered in the golden honey of her come. Chris moans wildly as she lets the panties fall to her knees and then presses his face into her sex.

'It's a pity there isn't more time for you to use that gifted sissy mouth of yours,' she whispers, rubbing her flooded pubic hair against his marble chin.

Then she steps back, leaving him gasping with almost deranged hunger. Now completely naked from the waist down, she steps out of the panties, picks them up and presses them into his face. The smell of her, the powerful, sweet perfume, is a brutal aphrodisiac that inspires another loud moan. She then insists he open his mouth as wide as possible, rolls up the panties and rams them home. He gasps as his mouth is completely filled with her most intimate garment and the scents and tastes of her flood once again deep into his consciousness. And no sooner have the panties been forced into place than she has taken up the roll of masking tape, tears off a long, thick strip and spread it firmly over his sissy lips, thus trapping the panties deep inside his mouth. Then, to his surprise, she carefully removes the gorgeous blonde wig and places it at her feet, taking up the tights as she does so and beginning to roll one of the legs into a wide open bowl. He watches in confused fascination as she then proceeds to reverse the bowl, place it on his head, and then begin to pull the widened leg down over his face. Soon, thanks to her considerable strength and skill, he is literally enveloped in hose! His face is pushed flat against the tight nylon and breathing becomes very difficult. A sense of panic overwhelms him as Helen then carefully positions the hose mask so that the soaked gusset section is directly over his nose and taped mouth and the free leg is dangling from the front of his face like a weird nylon trunk! Once she has done this, she takes the free leg and tightly wraps it around his eyes and uses another, longer strip of the masking tape to hold it in place, spreading the tape from ear to ear and thus also across his eyes. He is blindfolded, deafened and gagged. His only remaining unrestricted senses are touch and smell, yet even these are severely limited by the mittens and the pungent hose gusset stretched so tightly over his squashed nostrils.

Sealed in a sex-soaked sensory deprivation chamber of hose and feminine frillies, his breathing now hard but eventually even and regular, he is helped to his bootied feet. In an utter sex-perfumed darkness, all sounds muffled to the point of incomprehension, he is helped into the cot and made to lay face down on the rubber mattress. His arms are then forced behind his back and tied tightly together with two of the stockings at his mittened wrists and elbows. His hosed ankles and knees are likewise bound with more stockings. Then another stocking is tied to the stocking binding his ankles and used to pull his ankles upward towards his tethered wrists. Very soon he has been pulled into an extremely severe hog tie and his ankles and wrists have bound tightly together.

It is in this uncomfortable, pinioned, utterly helpless state that he is left. He feels Helen's hands stroke his hosed cheeks and moans helplessly and fearfully. But then there is nothing. He cannot move, speak, see, feel or hear. He is lost in a terrible, absolute numbness where all he can contemplate is the intense, powerful smell of his mistress and the memory of his mouth suckling her large, warm breasts. And in the centre of this bizarre ordeal is the most profound pleasure, the most delicious sense of all-pervasive helplessness. The plug tickles his widening anus, the cock-ring tortures his stiff sex; he cries with pleasure into the fat panty gag, and all he can hear is the sound of his sissy heart pounding with masochistic ecstasy.

He has no idea how long he is kept in this divine, fetishistic state of imprisonment. Maybe an hour, maybe two. He quickly loses track of time and space and finds himself falling into a bottomless pit of pure sensation and molten desire. How desperately he now wants, indeed *needs* to serve his three glorious mistresses; how desperately he wants to submit to all their inventive, wicked humiliations. He is nothing without this and the burning femininity that is now flowing over his psyche like a river of flames.

By the time he feels hands exploring his tethered body, he is numb in both mind and body and desiring only more of this absolute servitude. Gradually, his intricate bonds are freed and he returns to the mysterious reality of Helen's beautiful home. And eventually, the hose mask is carefully removed and he is allowed to see the flat, sweat-soaked surface of the cot's pink rubber mattress.

'Just relax, Chrissie; let me get you out of all these stockings. Helen's got a bit of a thing about tying you up.'

Donna's voice inspires a sense of deep relief and a renewed excitement. He moans thankfully into the tight panty- and tape-gag and lies ·still while she slowly struggles to free him from Helen's kinky handiwork.

Eventually, all the stockings have been removed. Donna turns him over and helps him sit up. As life returns to his body, she peels off the tape-gag and then eases the fat, pungent panty-gag from his tormented mouth. It is only as she does this that he notices she has removed the white dress and now stands before him in a white leather basque, white stockings and the high-heeled shoes. His eyes widen and she laughs.

'Helen warned me you might be a bit sweaty, so I slipped out of the dress – just in case.'

He finds her explanation slightly odd, but doesn't really care: the sight of this beautiful woman, this gorgeous muse who has entered his life and so lovingly taken his virginity, who has proven his masculinity in the very act of ensuring his sweet, silken slavery as a she-male maidservant, fills him with an intense, almost overwhelming joy and a fierce sexual arousal. Yet this arousal has its own unique consequences, and he is soon wincing as the restrainer bites mercilessly into his hardening, restrained sex.

'Don't get too carried away, Chrissie – you know what'll happen.'

But her words can have no real effect: his desire, his brutal masochistic need, has complete control over his every thought now, and it is a need these glorious women are manipulating with a terrifying ease.

She unlocks the barred side of the cot and helps Chris step down onto the carpeted floor. He is then led from the impromptu nursery into the bathroom and made to strip down to the cruel restrainer, her smile widening as each item of sissy attire is slowly removed, his poor, tormented eyes never leaving Donna's splendid, ultra-sexy form.

Once he is standing naked before his most beloved mistress, she steps forwards and looks deep into his eyes.

'I'm going to remove the restrainer, Chrissie. Then I'm going to remove the stocking. And then I'm going to bathe you. This will be the sternest test of your love for me. You have to prove that you really do love me. It will be simple yet also very hard to do this. All you have to do is avoid coming. Do you think you can manage that?'

He looks at her with desire-stricken eyes, then performs the weakest of curtseys. She smiles and then slips

127

her long, elegant hands over the cock-ring. He moans as she opens the two rings and pulls the device from his long-tormented sex.

An even bigger moan follows the slow, teasing removal of the stocking and the full revelation of his sex, so fully, brutally erect, and so very desperate. Then, to his horror, she runs a teasing finger along its enflamed shaft.

'Only a week, Chrissie, then I'll show you what real pleasure is.'

As he gasps his appalling frustration, she takes him by the hand and leads him into the shower. Then, before his utterly defeated, appalled, sex-starved eyes, she performs a slow, wicked striptease, and within a few dreadful minutes is in the shower with him, her glorious naked form rubbing up against his. She turns the shower tap and they are both immediately covered in a warm sheet of water. She then takes up a scented bar of soap, smiles sweetly and begins to drive him insane.

She covers his body in a thick layer of soap suds, paying particular attention to his cock and balls and quickly producing angry cries of intense frustration and even fear as all the while the threat of an uncontrollable, explosive orgasm hangs over his pretty, sissy head.

'Control, Chrissie; restraint. Remember what Helen said.'

Tears fill his eyes as she then proceeds to explore his back passage with a soapy finger, seeking out the plug and pushing it in a little deeper.

'You like the plug, don't you, Chrissie?'

He moans his assent and she laughs gently.

'Next week, I'll use a full-size dildo for a few nights to widen you a little further. Soon you'll be able to take a very big, tasty cock.'

He prays, he pleads with all the mysterious forces of the universe. She rubs her warm, soaking breasts against his chest and he imagines the end of the world, the largest fireball ever seen engulfing him in a blinding moment of startling orgasmic fury.

Then, to his relief and despair, she has stepped back from his body and is turning the shower off.

'You did very well, Chrissie. I'm impressed and touched – you tried really hard for me.'

His eyes glazed, his cock like a rod of white-hot steel, he moans pathetically and feels hot tears of brutal frustration begin to trickle down his scented cheeks.

Once they are out of the shower, Donna carefully dries her adoring slave and herself, at one point wrapping them both in the large white towel and returning Chris to the whirlpool of teasing and frustration Donna seems determined to make his mental home.

Once dried, he is covered from neck to toe in a rose-scented perfume and led back to the nursery. Here, to his surprise, a new outfit has been laid out on the bed – a cherry-red version of the baby girl dress, together with matching red plastic panties, seamed red stockings and an even more spectacular red silk and satin bonnet. Also on the bed is a large, fresh nappy, the white mini-corset and a beautiful white silk pinafore. As he is led up to the edge of the bed, he also notices that on the floor is a very dainty pair of red patent leather Mary Jane shoes.

'You'll be required to act as our baby maid this evening, Chrissie, so Helen has provided a suitable costume.'

Staring with utter fascination at this new and very elaborate costume, Chris performs a curtsey of understanding. Then, over the next hour, he is carefully recreated as Baby Chrissie. A fresh black nylon stocking is slipped teasingly over his cock and the terrible rings are snapped painfully back in place. As before, he is dressed in the humiliating baby underwear and then made up in the china doll style. After this, the dress and the lovely pinafore are carefully positioned over his sissy body and he moans with pleasure as the gorgeous Donna secures the pinafore in place at the base of his spine with a very large baby bow.

After the dress and the pinafore, the wig is refitted, as is the large, phallic dummy gag, which she pops between his lovely red lips with a teasing laugh and the loveliest of smiles. The gorgeous red bonnet is trimmed with even more lace than its predecessor and decorated with a pattern of silk roses. Then, satisfied that her charge is suitably transformed, she helps him to step into the square-heeled Mary Janes and buckles them tightly in place.

'You look absolutely stunning, Chrissie.'

Her words, spoken in a hushed, sex-hardened voice, bring a well-gagged gasp of intense, red-hot need to his stopped lips. Yet even now his fetishistic transformation is not complete; for, as she teases him with words of desire, she returns to the dressing table and produces a pair of red latex rubber gloves. Still smiling gently, she then slips these over his hands.

'You'll need these to serve,' she says, her gorgeous eyes seeking out his, her hands gently securing the pearl buttons built into the sides of the gloves around his thin, girlish wrists.

Then she leads him over to the mirror built into the front of the new wardrobe and once again he is facing an image of startling sissy perfection, a truly perfect vision of utter and deeply erotic submission that sends shudders of profound sexual delight through his feminised body.

'It's better than perfection, Chrissie,' Donna whispers, her hands sliding behind the layers of frou-frou petticoating to caress his red nylon-sheathed thighs.

Soon, he is returned to the living room and his other mistresses. As he curtseys before them, Helen and Anne are clearly very impressed by this latest incarnation of Chrissie and compliment Donna on her make-up and

130

dress skills. Then he is led to the kitchen and returned to the high-chair. A large bib is fitted around his befrilled neck and his hands are tied to the sides of the chair. Donna then slowly feeds him another baby food concoction, a rusk and two full bottles of the creamy milk, all of which he consumes with some desperation, the trials of the afternoon having given him a ferocious appetite. And all the time, Donna teases him with the most delightful and very exciting baby talk, adding to his exquisite sense of utter humiliation and ensuring that his sex remains in a state of almost constant discomfort.

The rest of the evening passes like a surreal hallucination. After his baby meal, he is set to work helping serve dinner to his gorgeous mistresses. Most bizarrely, Donna never bothers to slip back into the dress and spends the whole evening in her sexy underwear. Poor Chris can subsequently hardly keep his eyes off her and receives a number of very hard slaps to his stockinged thighs from both Anne and Helen to ensure his continued attention to his maidservant tasks.

At the end of the evening, he is made to kneel once again before his seated mistresses in the living room and demonstrate his considerable oral skills. For an entire hour he eagerly inspires orgasm after orgasm and, by the time the living room clock strikes 11.00 p.m., he is covered in their intimate juices and they are all very obviously exhausted.

It is left to Donna to return him to his cot, still fully dressed in the red baby maid's outfit. Once he is secured in place, she gently kisses him on the forehead and bids him sweet dreams. He stares up at her, his sissy eyes filled with appalling desperation as her splendid breasts, so tightly restrained by the basque, stare back down at him.

With a brief, slightly sad smile, she then leaves and he is soon once again plunged into darkness. His first day as Baby Chrissie is over and, as he quickly drops, utterly exhausted, into a very deep sleep, he is already looking forward to the trials and humiliations of the next day.

The rest of the week passes like the strangest, kinkiest and thus, for Chris, most erotic dream imaginable. From the Sunday of this babified week, it becomes clear that he will be required to work as well as entertain his three lovely mistresses. On the Sunday morning, he finds himself in another version of the pretty sissy baby maid's dress, this time an elaborate powder-blue version, complete with matching stockings, plastic panties, and Mary Janes. Tightly sealed in a matching bonnet, dummy-gagged, his hands freed from the mittens (but still wrapped in matching latex gloves), his dress protected by another beautiful white silk pinafore, he spends the day cleaning, ironing, washing and helping Helen cook. From the first moment of his early morning transformation to the moment when he presents himself fearfully before his mistresses after completing the post-dinner washing up, there is nothing but surprisingly hard work and strict instruction in the methods of this work from Helen, Donna and Anne.

By midday, his poor thighs and bottom are stinging from the relentless round of spankings his failings inspire, yet there is no bondage therapy and, despite Helen's promise, no breast-feeding. Indeed, the general tone of the women seems to have changed considerably and even Donna treats him with a painful indifference and administers the hardest of the spankings when he fails to follow her instructions to the letter.

Yet despite this, he once again shows that he is a gifted domestic and, with the experience of the previous two weeks behind him, is able to complete most of the tasks he is ordered to carry out.

After providing oral relief to his mistresses, he is taken upstairs by Helen and put back into the cot, quite exhausted, yet still in a state of deep, highly masochistic excitement. As she straps him tightly into the cot, he looks up at her splendid bosom and remembers the joy of suckling each large, soft breast. He moans expectantly into his fat dummy gag, yet she ignores him, and soon he is plunged back into darkness and, despite his terrible frustrations and resultant discomfort, he quickly drifts into a deep sleep.

Yet, despite the obvious repetition of his babified days, there are still a number of bizarre and highly erotic moments that note further description.

For instance, on the Monday evening, after another day of very demanding domestic labour and strict discipline, Chris finds himself subjected to an elaborate and extended photo shoot. After dinner, he is summoned from the kitchen. Expecting the now nightly pleasure of bringing his three marvellous mistresses to shattering orgasms with his expert sissy tongue, he instead finds himself at the centre of a sissy photo session supervised with some considerable gusto by the beautiful, perverse Anne.

For over an hour, using a state-of-the-art digital camera, she takes photo after photo of her she-male slave in his exquisitely sissy baby attire. The gloves are replaced by the mittens, the Mary Janes by booties. The pinafore is removed. He is bound hand and foot with white stockings, made to stand with his skirt and petticoats pulled up to reveal his matching plastic panties, nappies and stocking-tops. He is put over Helen's hosed knees, his panties lowered, his nappy removed, and then soundly spanked with a very painful hairbrush. Real tears are captured in the midst of exploding flash-lights; his poor, crimson bottom is immortalised.

This, he knows, is all part of Anne's plan to turn Baby Chrissie into a web celebrity. Earlier, during dinner, she had told the other women of the progress already made in setting up a 'Chrissie web site'. He had listened in horror, yet never once hesitated in his maidservant duties. A main part of her plan is to put a selection of photos up on the web page, and this was now quite clearly taking initial shape. Yet, despite the threat of this awfully public exposure, Chris finds himself participating in the shoot with some enthusiasm. Indeed, at one point, when tied with the stockings, he responds with a true method actor's passion to Anne's insistence that he show 'utter humiliation, fear, even sissy anger' and finds himself squealing angrily into the fat dummy gag and wriggling helplessly in his delightful baby bondage.

The next afternoon, he receives his first 'deportment and movement' lesson from the lovely, beloved Donna. After lunch, he is returned to the nursery by Helen and quickly stripped down to the cock-ring and stocking restrainer. The wig and dummy gag are removed and he is showered and rescented. He is then returned to the nursery and presented with a very sexy, very sheer pink nylon leotard and a pair of exactly matching dance tights. As he excitedly slips into this soft, teasing attire, Helen, a very wide smile on her gorgeous, dark-featured face, produces two more large pink boxes and places them on the small single bed. From inside the largest box, she takes a billowing pink lace tutu and quickly fits it around his waist. From the second box, she takes a pair of pink silk ballet slippers which, following her instructions, he proceeds to slip into.

He is then forced to sit down before the dressing table mirror and Helen carefully styles his short hair with a hairbrush before making up his face with a mild tan foundation, pale-blue eye-shadow and a pink lipstick. A layer of very strong, musk perfume is then sprayed across his body and this delightful, mincing she-male ballerina is led back down the corridor and into a room he has never seen before. The room, obviously once one of the many bedrooms, has been emptied of all furniture except a leather-backed chair. There is no carpet, but rather highly polished floor boards, and across one entire wall is a large rectangular mirror, running along which is a thin wooden beam.

Helen leaves Chris facing his reflection, insisting that he keep his hands behind his back and that he stands at a rigid attention. He obeys, of course, and spends ten uncomfortable minutes staring at his feminised sissy reflection, noticing that his restrained, tormented erection is made quite blatantly clear by the tight leotard and finding this exposure strangely exciting. And it is as he contemplates his bulging sex that Donna enters the room. Donna, dressed in a black leotard, matching nylon tights and ballet slippers, the tight second skin of the dance costume revealing her splendid, generous figure in all its deeply erotic glory.

He turns to face her and curtseys. She smiles. She is carrying a small portable CD player, which she then places on the chair.

'If you're going to become a convincing she-male, we need to make sure you can move in an appropriately feminine manner,' she says, her eyes never leaving his tortured, exposed sex. 'So each afternoon for the next five days, I'm going to help you learn how to move properly. We'll start with simple dance instruction. Some basic ballet steps and moves, practised daily, will give you grace and confidence. Then we'll move onto walking, walking in heels and then general deportment.'

He curtseys his understanding, trying to avoid staring with savage desire at her beautiful, so expertly displayed body.

In their sexy costumes, they spend the next ninety minutes practising a series of basic ballet moves to the music of Debussy and Mozart. To his surprise, he finds the dainty, ultra-feminine movements that Donna demands he perform relatively simple. Indeed, by the end of this very arousing session, he is able to carry out most of the steps and other movements very effectively, and certainly well enough to earn Donna's praise and her teasing, infuriating caresses.

'Helen's right about you being a natural,' she purrs at the end of the session, her hot hands slipping beneath the tutu and gliding over the nylon-sheathed outline of his rigid, imprisoned sex. He moans angrily and she turns a vague brush into a tortuous caress. His moan becomes a cry halfway between agony and ecstasy.

'But you're so noisy! Tomorrow, I'll make sure you're gagged – with a pair of my panties, of course. Not that this'll be a punishment for you.'

She then kisses him on the forehead and leads him back to the nursery. By 4.00 p.m., he is fully babified once again and serving afternoon tea to his mistresses, demonstrating his new feminine agility in each submissive, sissy movement. And it is during this exhibition of his new sissy skills that Anne announces that she has already managed to get the 'Baby Chrissie' website up and running and that the digital pictures snapped the day before have already been posted on the site.

'I've linked it to an adult baby web ring and we're already getting loads of hits. I'm sure Chrissie will be very popular with all her fellow sissies in no time at all. Perhaps we have a superstar in the making.'

The women laugh and Chris tries not to show his concern, mincing from mistress to mistress with a silver plate of biscuits, today's gorgeous baby dress, cream-coloured, protected by the standard and very lovely silk and lace pinafore.

'I wonder if he already has any sissy friends,' Helen asks. 'Do you have any secret sissy friends, Chrissie?'

It has been nearly a month since he last communicated with Annette. Indeed, he has not been near his computer since his enslavement by these three beauties. However, he performs an affirmative curtsey and Helen's smile broadens.

'Really,' she says, her mind clearly pondering a potential new line of sissy development. 'Do you have a particularly special sissy friend?'

Another wary curtsey follows.

'Well, I think it's only fair we get to meet this friend, don't you?'

A much slower curtsey greets this question.

'You don't seem too enthusiastic, Chrissie. We expect a bit more commitment than that!'

Chris duly performs a much deeper curtsey, making sure to expose his lovely cream plastic panties completely for his mistress.

'I think she's getting a little complacent,' Anne suddenly snaps.

'Yes, maybe she needs a lesson to liven her up,' Helen replies, her lovely brown eyes now filled with the familiar flame of sadistic cunning.

'I suggest we give the silly little girl an enema. That should lighten her step a little.'

Anne's words, delivered with a dark, cruel humour, strike into Chris's poor sissy heart like a hot knife.

'A good idea. Donna, if you wouldn't mind taking her to the nursery and we'll follow on shortly. If you could prepare the enema equipment as well, I'd be very grateful.'

Donna smiles, takes a long, knowing look at Chris and snaps a confident, 'No problem,' before getting up and leading her now wide-eyed sissy slave from the room.

As he minces along behind his gorgeous, sexy mistress, the thought of the impending enema fills the pretty, babified she-male with utter horror. After the deportment lesson, Donna has, as usual, dressed to thrill, and now, his mind reeling with fearful anticipation, he finds himself staring with paradoxically desiring eyes at her long, black hosed legs, revealed expertly by a red leather mini-skirt and red, patent leather stilettos.

137

As she quite deliberately wiggles her pert, sexy bottom in his china doll face, he moans fearfully into the fat dummy gag and tries to prevent large tears welling up in his sissy eyes.

'Don't worry, babikins,' Donna teases. 'It really isn't that bad. And it'll make you feel much better later.'

As she turns to face him, despite his fear, his eyes fix onto her shapely breasts pressing against the skin-tight nylon cocoon of her sweater. The terrible dialectic of pain and pleasure is surely never-ending.

Once in the bedroom, he is made to stand to attention by the cot as Donna proceeds to reveal some of the hidden delights of the nursery.

From beneath the bed, she takes a large black rubber mat that has been rolled into a tight tube. She places this in the centre of the room. She then tells Chris to strip naked. As he obeys, she returns to the space beneath the bed, this time producing a long silver bar with a thick black leather shackle attached to each end. She places this on the rubber mat and then strolls over to the rows of shelves built into the wall beyond the bed. As he struggles out of his cream stockings and matching plastic panties, he watches with increasing unease as Donna takes a long length of pink rubber tubing and a very large pink rubber bag from one of the shelves. She places these on the bed and then minces over to the wardrobe. From inside she takes a strange metal tripod base set on casters and places it down by her high-heeled feet. Then she produces a strangely shaped metal pole with what seems to be a large metal peg set into the top. She slots the pole into the tripod and then wheels the completed device over to the rubber mat.

By this time, poor Chris is naked except for the appalling cock-ring and its black nylon stocking partner, his tormented erection still strong and protesting painfully against the wicked metal prison.

Donna then removes his bonnet, dummy gag and wig and straightens his own hair with a comb.

'Would you like a panty-gag, Chrissie?' she asks, her lovely eyes filled with teasing arousal.

He eagerly curtseys an affirmation and Donna's smile widens.

'I'd love to put my panties in that lovely mouth but, as this is a punishment enema, I'm afraid we have to use a special ball gag.'

He is then forced to watch as she returns to the shelves and takes from one of them a very large pink rubber ball attached to two lengths of thick white leather. Yet before she returns, she dips the ball into a bowl of clear liquid resting on a lower shelf. She then brings the gag over to Chris and tells him to open his mouth as wide as possible.

As she forces the gag home he is immediately aware that the liquid is salt water. Indeed, the gag is covered in glistening salt crystals and this, plus the vast, mouth-filling size of the gag, makes for an extremely unpleasant experience, an experience significantly worsened as Donna buckles the gag tightly in place at the back of his slender neck.

Squealing in discomfort, he watches angrily as Donna proceeds to take two lengths of the now familiar black rubber cording from the shelves and use them to bind his arms very tightly behind his back at the wrists and, most painfully, at his elbows.

'There's no point in complaining, babikins,' she teases, tying the knot that forces his elbows to touch. 'You've been a naughty little sissy and it's been made clear we're determined to punish any sign of laziness.'

She then kneels down before her bound and gagged slave and takes up the strange metal bar.

'A leg-spreader,' she explains, attaching the left shackle around his girlish ankle and buckling it tightly in place. 'So spread your legs.'

With his arms bound so tightly, this is particularly difficult, but he eventually manages to stretch his legs far enough to allow Donna to fit the bar between his legs and attach the right shackle to his right ankle. Poor Chris thus finds himself with his legs forced wide and irresistibly apart, his balance precarious, a sense of terrible vulnerability gripping every inch of his tethered body. Yet this is very much only the beginning.

As soon as the leg-spreader is in place, Donna climbs to her lovely, high-heeled feet, smiles teasingly at Chris and returns to the shelves. Fighting to maintain his balance, he watches as she takes a coiled length of thin, silver chain from one of the shelves and brings it back over to him.

'This fixes your wrists to that,' she says, pointing to the ceiling.

He follows her gaze painfully upwards and grunts fearfully into the gag as he notices that a large metal ring has been fixed into the ceiling immediately above Donna's head. She makes a point of showing him that one end of the chain has a clip hook which is designed to slot into the ring, and that the other end is another length of the rubber cording.

As she ties the rubber-corded end of the chain to the cording binding his wrists, he hears distinctive and familiar laughter and turns to behold Anne and Helen standing in the doorway to the nursery. This in itself is unsurprising, but what is totally shocking is the way they are dressed. To Chris's amazement, both Anne and Helen have dressed up as nurses! Anne is dressed in a very short white rubber nurse's uniform, complete with a sexy cap and a large red cross stretched across her shapely bosom. In addition to this, she has donned seamed white nylon stockings and a pair of white patent leather, stiletto-heeled court shoes. Helen, by contrast, has dressed in a particularly alluring 'matron's uniform', a simple, dark blue cotton dress covering her ample form from her neck down to her knees, over which has been tied a white silk pinafore also decorated with a large red cross at her substantial chest. In addition, she is wearing sheer black hose, black patent leather stilettos and a nurse's cap.

As the women stroll teasingly over to their tormented, stunned slave, they congratulate Donna on her bondage expertise and then watch with wide, cruel smiles as Donna takes a chair from besides the shelves, brings it over to Chris and then takes up the slack of the long, sinister chain. She climbs onto the chair and pulls the chain up with her, reaching above her head and pulling the metal clip up to the hook. As she does so, poor Chris finds his wrists are pulled upwards and that the rest of his body is pushed downwards. Soon he is bent painfully forwards, his legs and buttocks spread wide, his arms pulled very painfully behind his back. He squeals into the ball gag and tries to pull himself upright, but the pressure between his shoulders is now tremendous, and the only way to relieve it is to stoop even further forwards.

Completely exposed to the cruel view of his wicked mistresses, Chris can only stare pathetically down at his tormented, still painfully stiff sex and wonder in terror what appalling torture awaits him. He listens as Donna steps down from the chair and moves to one side. Then Helen's beautiful, black-stockinged legs and gleaming stiletto-heeled feet suddenly step into his very restricted field of vision.

'Well, I think the patient is prepared for her treatment. You may begin, Nurse Anne.'

The first thing he feels is the rubber-gloved fingers slipping deep inside his anus to retrieve the plug, hands he knows belong to the cruel, unyielding Anne. And as the plug is slowly eased free of his backside, Helen describes the terrible truth of the impending 'operation'.

'We will start by removing the plug. Your arse will then be lined with a film of special irritant cream. This will no doubt produce a pretty ballet of wiggling and a lot of discomfort. You will then receive ten strokes of the paddle from each of us. After this you will receive the enema. Once the enema has been administered, you will be renappied and left to ponder the reasons we have seen fit to punish you so severely. You will also have to avoid spoiling yourself, a task I think you will find extremely difficult.'

Almost before Helen has stopped describing his terrible fate, fingers are again exploring his backside, but this time probing, caressing fingers that spread a sticky film over the walls of his now helplessly twitching anus.

Poor Chris squeals desperately into the uncomfortable gag as Anne applies another layer of the awful cream. Large tears of terror begin to trickle from his eyes and to drop onto the rubber mat beneath his prone, tormented form. Then he feels the heat, a warmth at first, but then hot, then very hot, then almost burning. And as the heat increases so does the itching, an itching that soon seems to have spread all over his body and which leaves him swinging his head angrily, squealing even louder into the gag and wiggling his tormented and very pretty bottom uncontrollably.

The sound of his mistresses' cruel laughter fills his tormented head as he dances helplessly before them. The women circle him; they continue to mock his extreme discomfort, then there is a strange, anticipatory silence, the awful silence before the storm, the first devastating sign of which is a sudden, hard blow to his exposed, wiggling buttocks, the furious, stinging slap of a leather-backed paddle administered to his bottom with considerable strength and enthusiasm by one of his mistresses. He has no idea which one, and as the dreadful paddling continues he quickly understands this anonymity is quite deliberate.

Soon the tears of pain are flooding from his eyes, and the wiggles that rumble over his body like earth tremors are wiggles of real pain as well as extreme discomfort. He receives a total of thirty hard, merciless whacks against his backside, each one as forceful as the last, none providing the slightest evidence of reluctance or hesitation. And by the time the paddling is complete, there is a terrible, satanic fire burning across his backside, a fire that spreads inevitably between his legs and into his imprisoned, still painfully stiff sex and quickly transforms into the fuel to power his demanding, unrelenting and deeply masochistic desire.

Then hands fall upon his upper thighs, holding his bottom still while more hands spreads his buttocks even wider apart. He moans in tightly silenced misery as a wet, cool rubber tube is slipped into his anus and then pushed deep inside him. Eventually the tube encounters resistance. His tormenter, however, is quite determined and, with a painful shove, the tube seems to erupt into the very core of his being and he squeals angrily into the huge, mouth-filling ball gag.

This is the most intimate and uncomfortable invasion of his body yet and, as he contemplates the true horror of his situation, the three gorgeous women mock him relentlessly. More tears well up in his baby girl eyes as Anne and Helen circle his prone, naked form. The terrible pain between his shoulders is now a molten metal spreading across his back and burning into the very heart of his twisted spine. Then he hears the sound of liquid being poured, an awful sound, a damning sound that he knows is the filling of the rubber enema bag.

'Try and keep still, Chrissie,' Anne teases. 'It helps the flow into your intestines.'

Then the beautiful, black nylon-sheathed legs of Helen are before him again.

'We're using soapy water to clean you out, Chrissie,' she informs him, her voice filled with cruel amusement. 'It'll take a couple of bagfuls, so I suggest patience. Once you're filled up, we'll apply a suitably absorbent nappy and leave you to ponder your fate. You should also know that if you fail to withhold the liquid for the hour you will be left alone, you'll be spending the night bound and gagged under the stairs with an anal vibrator for company.'

Poor Chris squeals useless cries for mercy as he feels the liquid flood into his bowel. The sensation is utterly appalling and is accompanied by a sudden and very violent need to go to the toilet. Yet even after the contents of the first bag have been emptied into him, he is just able to resist this urge and endure the second bag with more pained wiggles and angry squealing.

Then, after some fifteen truly dreadful minutes, the enema tube is slid from his back passage and invisible hands quickly wrap him into a very heavy, very thick nappy and secure it very tightly in place.

'Have fun, babikins.'

Anne's voice, followed by the laughter of the three women. Then the light is flicked off, plunging the crying sissy into a very familiar but no less terrifying darkness. The nursery door is then closed and locked.

Almost immediately, the intensity of the discomfort created by the irritant cream seems to increase. Chris's position is deliberately designed not just to make him easily available for intrusion and spanking, but also to make it very difficult for him to control his already considerably weakened sphincter muscle. So as much as he struggles to restrain the flood of liquid and faeces now demanding release from his bowel, he knows that, sooner rather than later, he will mess his nappy rather spectacularly, and that when he does he is sentencing himself to a very uncomfortable and kinky night locked beneath the stairs. Yet, despite all the torments he has endured in the last few hours, and to his considerable amazement, he still finds himself deeply aroused. The well of his masochism, it seems, is bottomless.

He manages to hold back the tide for maybe fifteen minutes, then, with the sweat of an intense and futile effort soaking his tortured body, he gasps helplessly into his fat, salted gag and unleashes the tidal wave. The sound and the smell are appalling. This is the deepest, darkest humiliation and, as the explosion rages, as the nappy is filled to bursting point, he feels what may well be the destruction of the very last vestige of his masculinity and any sense of self-respect or ego that might have assisted in the defence of that masculinity.

And there he remains, so tightly and painfully secured, enveloped in the stink of his own bodily functions, appallingly uncomfortable, thanks to the twisted symphony of punishments racking his sissy frame: the pain of his bondage, the torment of the salt-lined ball gag, the constant torment of the irritant cream lining his anus and his full, pungent nappy. Here he remains for at least another forty-five minutes in absolute, unforgiving darkness, begging for release, yet, most perversely, most bizarrely, at some deep, weird level, also enjoying every second of this supreme degradation.

By the time the women return, the room stinks to high heaven and their declarations of disgust, while exaggerated, are rooted firmly in a quite genuine response to their slave's helpless spoiling.

With more loud and mocking cries of outrage, the women free him from the spreader-bar and bonds and unbuckle the gag. He gasps with a profound relief as the ball gag is pulled from his mouth, but has very little time to adjust his aching body; for, as soon as he is free, he is sent to the bathroom to clean himself up and prepare for the next stage of this extended punishment.

* * *

By the time he presents himself before his mistresses half an hour later, the filthy nappy hidden in a special scented plastic bag at the bottom of the bathroom rubbish bin, reshowered and scented, he has no idea what time or what day it is. He is utterly exhausted and finding it difficult to keep his eyes open. Despite this, he is also very much aware that he is starving hungry.

He has been forced to shower with the cock-ring and stocking restrainer still in place but, despite the fact that the stocking is soaked, no notice of it is taken as he is led from the room by the women and returned downstairs to the living room.

Here he discovers new, even more kinky attire awaiting him. Anne and Helen are still dressed in the very sexy nurse's uniforms and this ensures that Chris remains painfully erect throughout this next bizarre stage of his punishment. Donna plays little part in what happens next, preferring to sit on the sofa with her long, sexy legs crossed and a wide smile lighting up her beautiful face, watching every development intently.

The first item that Anne takes from a strange pile on the coffee table in front of them is a long, pink rubber, ribbed dildo.

'This will keep you company for the night, babikins. I'm pretty sure it'll fit, more or less.'

He is then made to bend forwards and touch his toes, the memory of the pain induced by his previous bondage returning as he does so. Anne then forces his legs apart so that a rubber-gloved Helen can spread a film of Vaseline around his anal passage, her long, teasing finger inducing moans of intense pleasure. Her finger is eventually removed and then Anne very carefully eases the dildo into his arse. At first he is terrified that it will not fit and that some terrible damage will be done. But after a few painful pushes, and much to his surprise, his anus suddenly gives way and accepts virtually the whole dildo.

The pleasure of this intrusion is quite considerable and his moan very loud.

'Told you,' Anne says to Helen. 'He's wide enough already and he loves it. We should explore this, just like you said.'

His contemplation of her mysterious words is interrupted as he is pulled to his feet, forcing his thighs together and pushing the dildo even deeper into his arse. The dildo is followed by another very large nappy, which is secured with another very large silver safety pin. Then Anne uses more lengths of the sleek black-rubber-lined cording to bind his wrists and elbows tightly and painfully behind his back and to tie his ankles and knees together with equally unyielding knots. As Anne secures his knees, Donna steps up from the sofa and rather brazenly rolls up her mini-skirt over her hosed thighs.

'Use my panties,' she says, her sex-fuelled gaze never leaving Chris's wide, stunned eyes.

He continues to watch as she wiggles out of her tights and then pulls her black silk panties down over her long legs. She hands the panties to Anne, who somewhat unceremoniously stuffs them into Chris's quickly opened mouth. And once they are rammed securely home, Chris revelling once again in the powerful taste of Donna's sex, Helen takes up the familiar role of silver masking tape from the table, tears off a very long, thick strip and then spreads it firmly over Chris's now closed, very soft and sissy lips.

Tightly bound and gagged, Chris, now terribly excited, watches as Anne, a particularly wicked smile lighting up her beautiful face, then takes from the table what looks like a long white rubber bag. He continues to watch in amazement as she proceeds to roll the bag up into a wide bowl and then kneel down by Chris's feet.

'Step into the body glove,' she orders.

He obeys without question and then watches in utter astonishment as Anne begins to draw the bag up his smooth, scented body, revealing as she does so that the bag is in fact a very light, thin and very strong rubber cocoon. His mouth and nostrils filled with the lovely perfume of Donna, his eyes wide with aroused astonishment, he watches Anne carefully roll the glove up over his knees and thighs, then over his nappied waist, up over his stomach and chest, and then pull it tightly into place around his neck, thus imprisoning his sissy body in a second skin of cream-coloured latex rubber.

He whimpers into his gag, amazed at the strength of the glove, at his utter helplessness and the pleasure that is flooding through his so effectively restrained form.

'Perfect,' Helen whispers. 'Absolutely perfect.'

Donna then disappears into the kitchen, returning a few moments later with, of all things, an upright station porter's barrow painted hot pink! Poor Chris can then only watch horrified as Helen and Anne proceed to load the mummified sissy onto the barrow and Donna, aided by Helen, wheels him out of the living room and down the corridor to the small door beneath the stairs. Here, Anne produces the final terrifying item of bondage: an eyeless, latex rubber hood that exactly matches the colour and material of the ultra-tight body glove that is now so effectively imprisoning his feminine body. Chris moans fearfully into his pungent panty-gag and shakes his head angrily as Anne stretches the base of the hood wide and prepares to pull it over his head. It is Donna who steps forwards and, assisted by her very high heels, manages to hold his head still as Anne, the cruellest and darkest of smiles on her face, slowly pulls the hood down over his sweaty and terror-streaked face.

Eventually, Anne manages to pull the hood firmly down over his head and allow it to take up its natural clinging second-skin form over his face. As it does so, she carefully ensures that two air holes are positioned directly beneath his nostrils, allowing Chris a deeply disturbed, panic-stricken breathing.

Plunged into a terrible, bottomless darkness, Chris also finds that the rubber hood blocks out all sound and that he is once again lost in a vast pit of total sensory deprivation. The skin-tight body glove, combined with the cord bindings, makes any kind of movement absolutely impossible. In this mummified state he can only wait for the inevitable teasing hands that grasp his body and lift him from the trolley, his well-gagged squeals of despair and fear heard only in his terrified mind as he is then carried through the doorway of the small cupboard and carefully laid out face up on a black rubber mattress. Then he is left. He has no idea that the three women have turned off the light, shut the small door and locked it. He has no idea about the world outside this total, absolute bondage. And so he has no idea that once the door is locked, Anne takes from a pocket in her sexy nurse's uniform a small remote control device, basically a red plastic button built into a metal box, and then pushes the button down, sending a surprisingly powerful electric signal through the door and through the layer of latex and into the heart of the dildo, an electric signal that triggers a wicked internal mechanism which makes the dildo begin to vibrate deep within Chris's expertly expanded arse.

And Chris can only scream silently into the tasty panty-gag as the vibrations begin to increase, and as the waves of intense sexual pleasure once again course through his sissified, so expertly restrained body. Unable to move more than an inch in the absolute darkness, he can only endure what quickly becomes a terrible, all-pervasive pleasure. His erection is soon once again straining angrily against the metal restrainer and he is once again riding the roller coaster of pain and pleasure. Yet this torment, this awful ambivalence, is new. For it doesn't end; or, rather, its end is unknown.

This is the deepest sea of masochistic pleasure he will dive into. As the long night passes, he will forget everything except the teasing pleasure of the dildo deep in his arse and the burning, unfulfilled desire it inspires. He will travel to the black, molten heart of sex and become nothing but this sex; it will consume him and remake him. In the terrible fire of this long, lonely, agonisingly pleasurable night, the last traces of his masculinity will be destroyed forever and Christina will finally be fully alive.

Eight

By the time he is released from his mummified bondage hours later, he has descended into a hallucinatory madness of absolute sex. He has no memory of being carried from the cupboard, of being carefully stripped of the rubber body glove and hood. Visions of his three mistresses haunt his dreams. Maybe they are talking, maybe there are looks of considerable concern in their beautiful eyes. But then there is blackness, a deep, empty blackness from which he is pulled by another voice, the very sexy, yet also stern voice of Helen.

'Chrissie? Chrissie – wake up. You've been asleep for twenty-four hours, you silly little girl. Wake up immediately!'

He opens his eyes slowly, fearfully, afraid yet again that this whole wondrous adventure has been a dream. Yet here is Helen leaning over the cot, her gorgeous brown eyes betraying the slightest uncertainty. And here he is, in the cot, secured by the shackles, dressed in the sexy baby clothes, dummy-gagged, the bonnet tied tightly to his head.

How did he get here? Much later Donna will tell him that they had pulled him from the cupboard to discover a sex zombie, that once the glove and hood had been removed, he had been found in a deep, delirious sex-trance; that Donna had wanted to take him to the hospital, that Anne had disagreed, that there had been an argument. But Helen had insisted they continue as planned. Then, to their relief, he had stirred, showed signs of life. But he was still incoherent, still possessed by the sex-heat, and rambling about his desires, calling out their names. They had carried him upstairs, bathed him, calmed him down. To their amazement, he had begged to be refeminised as quickly as possible, making it quite clear that at the heart of his passion was a mad need for his complete subjugation to femininity and thus the true expression of Christina. They were amazed as he ranted about these desires, as he confessed his addiction. So they had made him up once again and put him back into the latest version of the sweet baby attire.

It had been Helen who suggested they put him back in the cot. And as soon as he had been secured, his baby girl eyes had fluttered sweetly, he had moaned weakly into his fat dummy-gag and then fallen into a deep, prolonged sleep.

Now, twenty-four hours later, he faces the lovely Helen and knows he is a changed person, that Chris is now truly lost in the mists of a memory virtually destroyed by the events of the past forty-eight hours. As he is helped from the cot by this stunning woman with her sensual brown eyes, her full, cherry-red lips and ample, shapely body, he feels an intense, almost over-whelming desire to obey her, to serve her, to submit completely and absolutely. At the same time, the sense of his own femininity is now all-pervasive. Even as he is guided to the dressing table and allowed to sit before his expertly sissified and quite beautiful reflection, he knows he has reached a point of no return: that he can never go back to being Chris, to living as a man of any kind, to work in that prison-like office and pretend to care about the stifling boredom of the administrative pro-cess.

For the rest of the week, he positively revels in his babification, demonstrating his increasing femininity to his mistresses with every gesture, every movement, every act of enthusiastic submission. Even as he is spanked, bound, gagged, as he is relentlessly humiliated, as he subjected to the constant painful presence of the cock-ring and driven to the edge of sexual madness by the teasing, the oral sex, the forced breast-suckling, the torments of the refitted anal plug, even as he endures all of this, his pleasure is absolute, his desire for more of the same powerful, unbowed, unending.

Then, suddenly, it is Saturday again, and his week of babification is over. He is taken from the cot in the very early morning by Helen and Donna and congratulated on his sissy progress. Then he is informed he will now act as their personal maidservant on a full-time basis for the next seven days. He curtseys his understanding and cannot help display his intense pleasure, yet at the back of his mind is the terrible reality of time, the fact that at the end of this next week he will be returned to the world of Chris, to the slavery of work, to the despair of his very poor masculine disguise.

Helen and Donna spend the next hour or so meticulously preparing their sissy maid, quickly stripping away his baby attire and, to his considerable relief, removing the terrible cock-ring and the soft, cruel stocking restrainer. Then he is taken to the shower and made to wash thoroughly, removing the china doll make-up and the various odours and memories of his extended and deeply bizarre babification.

Once showered and dried, the two women envelop him in a fine mist of expensive, pungent perfumes and return him to the nursery. Here he is transformed into the maid Christina, a deliberately slow and loving resurrection of the sexy she-male created by the women before his imprisonment in nappies. But this transformation is taken to a new level of magnitude, the creation not only of a she-male servant but also of an utterly convincing woman. What Donna and Helen create here is a new, genuinely feminine person. Assisted by the psychological impact of the babification, by the new personality they have forged out of an extreme act of imprisonment and mental restructuring, they are able to give Christina a unique rebirth. The new, improved Christina, as it were. Christina Mark II.

The first item in this new feminisation is a fresh restrainer. To Chris's relief, he is not to be returned to the torments of the cock-ring. Instead, Helen opens one of the dressing table drawers and takes from inside it a pink rubber sheath. She then holds the sheath before him in an almost teasing manner.

'A little less brutal than the cock-ring, Christina, but just as effective. The sheath is made of a type of latex rubber that contracts when heated. Thus the more hot blood that pours through your naughty little prick as you become excited, which seems to be most of the time, the tighter the restrainer becomes. Believe it or not, a full erection will be quite impossible. But the level of discomfort will be far less. This said, we obviously reserve the right to put you back in the cock-ring at any time.'

She hands the restrainer to Donna, who then slips it over the bulging crimson head of Chris's swelling cock and pulls it slowly down the rigid shaft. His inevitable moans bring mocking laughter and a slap to his backside from Helen. Donna then pulls the rubber restrainer down over his balls and lets it tighten almost immediately over his long-suffering genitals.

After the restrainer, he is forced to lean forwards, his legs wide apart, his hands resting on the dressing table chair. Donna then produces the long, black rubber, ribbed dildo and waves it cruelly before his now wide, startled eyes.

'Five inches,' she teases, her smile cruel and excited. 'Two inches longer than the plug.'

Helen then dons rubber gloves and carefully eases the plug from his arse. As soon as it is free, she greases his anus with more Vaseline, producing a series of long, deeply aroused moans, which are rewarded with another firm slap to his pert, girlish buttocks. And it is Donna who then slowly slips the dildo into his back passage, all the time teasing him and thus inspiring even more pleasure.

'We've been really impressed by the way you've taken to the plug, Chrissie. And when you responded so well to the previous dildo, we knew it was time to use it on a regular basis. It won't be long before you can take a real cock.'

Her closing sentence makes his heart skip with a sudden, dark dread, yet despite this he cannot deny the very real pleasure he receives from this relentless and developing anal stimulation.

Once the dildo is pushed deep inside him, he is made to rise to his feet and then ordered to step into a pair of very slight black rubber panties, which are then pulled up his long, elegant, silky smooth legs by Helen. With a strangely maternal smile and a very erotic delicacy of movement, she guides the panties up over his sheathed cock and pulls them firmly into place around his slender waist. To his amazement, he quickly becomes aware that the panties are made out of exactly the same material as the sheath. As soon as they are in place, the panties seem to shrink around his waist, pressing his tightly restrained cock against his stomach and slipping between his legs to press very tightly against the dildo.

After the panties come a pair of seamed, very sheer, silk tights. This unusual and very expensive item of hosiery is handed by Helen to Chris with a knowing smile.

'A special treat, Christina – to mark your full initiation into femininity.'

He accepts the tights with the sweetest curtsey he can manage, then sits down on the dressing room chair and begins to guide them up his lovely legs. The sensations the soft, delicate silk tights produce against the smooth skin of his long legs is virtually indescribable. He gasps with a profound, giddying pleasure as he guides the hose over his knees and then stands to carefully guide them up over his thighs.

By the time he positions the tights around his waist, tears of pleasure are welling up in his pretty eyes and Donna has returned from a visit to the wardrobe carrying a spectacular black and red leather corset with rose-patterned satin panels. Chris stares at the latest item of fetish wear with hungry eyes, eager for it to be fitted around his sissy body. This she does with a lingering gentleness, her own gorgeous body brushing against his as she leans around his torso to pull the two halves of the corset together at the centre of his back. It is as she then uses the thick, black silk ribbon laces to pull the corset painfully tight that Chris becomes aware that this corset has a very strong and utterly unyielding whalebone frame.

'A genuine antique, Christina,' Helen informs him. 'Mid-Victorian. I hope you appreciate it.'

He tries to curtsey his appreciation, but the corset is bound so tightly, the level of movement required to perform a full curtsey is impossible, and his attempts inspire mocking laughter from the two lovely women.

'It'll take a little while before you can perform a full curtsey, Chrissie,' Donna says, a loving smile lighting up her beautiful face.

The dressing continues in an atmosphere of electric sexual excitement. An expertly padded black silk bra follows the corset and Chris once again wallows in the strange, intense pleasure of false breasts. Then there is a very delicate black silk petticoat which barely reaches the tops of his thighs. This lovely, scanty item of exotic lingerie is followed by a return to the dressing table, where Donna reacquaints Chris with the beautiful face of Christina, with the impressively convincing she-male beauty he has always known, but who only Donna and Helen have been able truly to reveal.

And after the make-up comes the glorious Bettie Page wig and once more he is lost in his own startling reflection.

'I should be used to it now,' Helen mumbles. 'But she's so convincing. It's almost unbelievable.'

A moment of almost reverential silence follows before Chris is helped back to his feet and presented by Donna with the stunningly beautiful, intricate black maid's dress he had first been introduced to a few weeks before.

As he is helped into the dress, a sense of beautiful serenity washes over him. Suddenly he feels perfectly natural, at one with himself in a way that he has never felt before. Now there is no guilt, no anxiety, no fear. Christina is now so natural, so absolutely him. So absolutely *her*.

As if reading his mind, Helen announces the latest rule of the house.

'From now on, Christina, you will be regarded as a fully-fledged female. There will be no reference made to your biological sex or to your previous gender. Here, and in the company of all your mistresses, you will be *she*. You must regard yourself as such at all times. Eventually, it will become instinct.'

And who are we to argue with the glorious, regal Mistress Helen? From now on, at her command, Chris is no more. Now we are telling the story of the beautiful she-male Christina and the emphasis is most definitely on *she*.

Christina spends the rest of the morning serving Helen and Donna with a delicately mincing and deeply sub-missive enthusiasm. In five-inch spike-heeled court shoes, she totters from room to room, from task to task, cleaning, washing, serving with a cherry-lipped smile, her sissy eyes wide with masochistic pleasure, her pretty, girlish bottom wiggling teasingly beneath its layers of feminine imprisonment.

Helen and Donna are both surprisingly relaxed with their lovely charge, adopting none of the stern mannerisms of the last seven days. Indeed, they seem particularly proud of their sissy creation and Christina finds herself praised and encouraged throughout the morning. Donna is particularly pleasant towards Christina, her manner much more that of the few weeks before her slave's intricate and so successful babification. And Donna's charming, sensual manner is made even more effective by two things. First, there is her clothing: a beautiful, very short pale-blue silk dress, very fine white stockings and a pair of pale-blue stiletto heels that match the dress almost exactly. With her hair in a tight bun held in place by a sparkling diamond clip, expensive diamond stud earrings and a pearl choker necklace, she is a vision of cool sophistication, a vision that is both new and bold, a vision that makes it clear Donna is eagerly developing her role as a dominant mistress. Secondly, there is the restrainer. Unlike the cock-ring, there is little or no pain associated with the rubber sheath. At most there is a firm, restraining tight..ess that makes a full erection impossible yet, at the same time, the feel of the restrainer is strangely arousing. So, paradoxically, the more Christina is restrained, the more excited she becomes, a striking reaffirmation of the pain/pleasure dialectic, which she is sure is quite deliberate.

Helen, dressed in a long, loose black dress, very sensible shoes and black hose, appears to be indifferent to any potential effect she may have upon her lovely sissy maid. Yet, even in these rather unappealing clothes, she is still very beautiful and an object of total adoration for the gorgeous, simpering Christina.

And it is Helen who, just before lunch, summons her to the living room. Christina totters delicately from the kitchen and curtseys before her stunning mistress.

Helen smiles and appraises the sexy slave with warm, quite obviously aroused eyes.

'After lunch Donna and I will take you shopping. You need some clothes for out of doors and for visits. Also, some more undies. We also thought it would be good practice for developing your feminine persona.'

Stunned, even horrified, yet also helplessly excited, Christina curtseys her understanding and gives no sign of her inward fear.

'Now,' Helen continues. 'There is also the question of this friend you were reluctant to tell us about.'

Christina curtseys again, less surprised than curious now, prepared to tell Helen everything without a moment's hesitation.

'Tell me about her.'

So Christina quietly, politely, and somewhat nervously tells her beautiful mistress about Annette, about their e-mail relationship, about how beautiful and confident she is, about her envy and desire for this attractive, outgoing she-male who has tried so hard to bring Christina out of her shell.

'She's sounds very interesting, Christina. I want to meet her. I want her to meet us all. I take it you can arrange it?'

'I can try, mistress.'

'Good. After we've been shopping, we'll stop off at your flat and you can send her an e-mail. I suggest you get her phone number. You should also send her a photo – do you have a scanner?'

Christina painfully curtseys in the affirmative.

'We'll get a photo done in town – I know someone who'll do it quickly.'

Christina listens in amazement, but never once shows any sign of doubt or fear. This, she realises, is the next step in her development, in the realisation of her dream to become a complete she-male. How often has she dreamed of finding the courage to send the lovely Annette a photo, to develop a real friendship, even to meet her. Now this dream, like so many others, is coming true. Now she is truly stepping out of the closet!

Christina is then sent off to prepare a simple salad lunch and serve it to her two mistresses, her sissy heart pounding with joyous anticipation.

Christina eats her own salad lunch at a counter in the kitchen, her mind racing with thoughts of the impending trip and her communication with Annette.

After lunch, Donna takes the gorgeous she-male upstairs to the spare room. The nursery items have now been removed, and the room is once again a simple, somewhat Spartan guest space.

Donna helps Christina out of the maid's dress, cap and gloves, but insists that she remain in the rest of her beautiful, sexy attire. From the wardrobe, which has been emptied of all its baby wear, she takes a very pretty silver-grey blouse and a very short, matching skirt. She places the clothes on the bed and tells Christina to put them on with a sexy, slightly devious smile. As Christina slips into the blouse and the skirt with as much feminine grace as possible, Donna returns from a second visit to the wardrobe with a grey jacket that matches the skirt exactly.

The very high neck of the blouse is fitted with a wide bow, which Donna then carefully positions before helping her slave-lover into the jacket. As she secures the jacket's pearl grey buttons, their eyes meet.

'You look fantastic, Chrissie. In fact, you just keep looking better and better. And the better you look, the more I fancy you.'

Christina moans her appreciation and feels her in-flamed, frustrated sex press hungrily into the tight rubber fabric of the restrainer.

'Seeing that you've been such a good girl,' she continues, her eyes burning into Christina's, 'you can sleep with me tonight. And I'll expect you to demonstrate all your sissy sex skills.'

Poor Christina can barely manage the slightest of curtseys without losing her balance, her knees are so weakened by the erotic power of Donna's words.

'And while we're out,' she continues, slipping a hand beneath his short skirt, 'I'm going to buy you a suitably erotic nightdress.'

Christina moans with a terrible, aroused longing as Donna runs an index finger along the curved, rigid contour of her pantied, rubberised and hosed sex. Then her lover's lips are brushing against her rouged cheeks, then they are embracing, then they are locked in a long, desperate kiss. Christina's own hands seek out Donna's heaving breasts, but her mistress pushes them away and then stands back from her gorgeous she-male slave.

'Later, Chrissie. Now it's time to go down and show yourself to Helen and then we can go shopping.'

But before Donna leads Christina from the room, she makes sure the lovely she-male has a full view of herself in the wardrobe mirror. And, of course, Christina is quite astounded. This is the first time she has seen herself in non-fetish wear and the reality of the illusion, or rather the reality of Christina, is complete and undeniable, a very beautiful, incredibly sexy woman in the shortest of mini-skirts, her long, shapely legs teasingly displayed in the seamed, black silk tights and five-inch high stiletto heels.

'Every man in town will be on his knees before you, Chrissie,' Donna teases, her own eyes filled with a powerful hunger for this startling she-male beauty.

Her words fill Christina with a strange, ambivalent pleasure. The thought of men, of *a man*, wanting her, desiring her. She feels the dildo locked deep between her buttocks and cannot deny that the thought excites her, and even to allow herself this radical thought, to confess to such a reaction, is a significant indication of how much she has changed in the last seven days. I will do anything they want me to do, she thinks, even – even pleasure a man. And as she thinks this, her erection struggles that little bit harder against its far from unpleasant pink rubber prison.

Helen is obviously very impressed by Christina's new look. Yet it is Christina who finds herself the more impressed for, during her transformation, Helen has changed into a knee-length black skirt, a white blouse and a black velvet jacket, plus a pair of very high-heeled court shoes and black nylon tights. Her hair is tied in a tight bun, her lips painted a thick, blood red. She is the perfect, ample-figured dominatrix. And as Helen leads Donna and Christina out of the house to the driveway, a sense of almost unbearable erotic elation washes over the beautiful, utterly convincing she-male.

Helen opens the rear passenger door of her car and helps a mincing, nervous Christina climb into the back. As the sexy she-male does so, she finds herself struggling with the very high heels and the ultra-short mini-skirt rides up her shapely, finely hosed legs, exposing her pretty panties to full view. Poor Christina blushes furiously as Helen and Donna burst into laughter.

'You'll have to do better than that in the town, Christina,' Helen jokes, 'or the boys will be in for a very entertaining treat.'

As Christina hurriedly pulls her legs together and straightens her skirt, Donna and Helen climb into the front of the car. Helen starts the engine and slowly guides the car out onto the main road. As she does so, a sense of skin-tingling anticipation washes over the gorgeous she-male. Rather than the fear and anxiety she had expected, her 'debut' outside of the house is an intensely exciting and liberating event. Now she is very much looking forward to revealing herself in the town, to finally stepping out of the closet and into the big, wide world. She now sees that this is the only way she will ever truly become Christina.

As the car heads into the town centre, there is very little conversation. Christina finds herself staring longingly at the back of her mistresses' lovely heads and contemplating the afternoon ahead. And by the time Helen drives the car into a large multi-storey car park in the centre of town, Christina's sissy heart is pounding with a helpless she-male excitement. Now she is positively desperate to be out of the car and on the street, open to the gazes of all the other shoppers, fully exposed, yet at the same time so expertly disguised.

They park on the top floor of the crowded car park and Donna helps Christina out of the car. Unfortunately, her exit is no less revealing than her entrance, and once again poor Christina is tormented by the cruel laughter of the women. But soon they are walking across the car park. Finally, Christina is fully in the outside world. But it is not until they leave the car park and suddenly plunge into the mayhem of the Saturday afternoon shopping frenzy that the full impact of Christina's exposure crashes over her expertly feminised body like a vast wave of erotic self-realisation. Yet this is more than just the startling face of reality: this is reality heightened, reality expanded and deepened, reality accentuated almost unbearably by sex.

She takes small, dainty steps, she wiggles her barely covered bottom, her delicately hosed thighs rub together and the dildo travels deeper into her. The very convincing false breasts bounce merrily before her and she fights the urge to shout out her excitement and delight. Then there are the eyes, the eyes of the men especially. Suddenly she sees what all beautiful women must see every day of their lives: the hungry, helplessly fascinated, desiring eyes of men, eyes drinking up this gorgeous sex-pot, eyes filled with need and desperation. Yet, for Christina, there is nothing intimidating in these eyes. Indeed, it soon becomes clear that it is the men who are intimidated, that behind their desire is a very real fear of such powerful, blatant and, in some ways, unobtainable beauty. Yes, powerful beauty, the strength of this sexy, forceful exhibition. They want me, yet they fear me. And they want me because they fear me. And it is these simple, obvious thoughts that encourage her, that and the more aggressive confessions of fearful desire, the cheeky remarks, the wolf whistles, even on one occasion, a very quick and arousing pat on her shapely, hosed behind.

'You're quite a hit, Christina,' Helen teases, as they cut through the crowds.

'Do you like it, all this attention, all these sad male eyes burning into you?'

'Yes, mistress,' Christina confesses. 'I thought it would be frightening, or horrible. But it's really rather sexy.'

'Turns you on, does it?' Donna asks, her own eyes filled with desire.

'Yes, mistress. Very much.'

They arrive at the women's clothing store soon after this exchange, a large, elegant and obviously very exclusive shop that stands proudly in the centre of the main shopping complex . The two women lead their she-male slave through large, gold edge glass doors. And almost as they step through this doorway, a very plump, yet strikingly beautiful woman appears from between two long rows of dresses, her thick, strawberry blonde hair styled in a classic film star cut and gleaming under the powerful white light that fills the shop. She is dressed in a black silk suit consisting of a loose-fitting jacket and a skirt reaching down to just below her knees, a high-necked white silk blouse with a diamond broach centrepiece placed beneath its frilled collar, jet black hose and matching black patent leather, stiletto heeled court shoes. Her eyes are a stunning pale blue, her lips a sparkling blood red. As she smiles warmly at the new customers, she reveals a generous double chin and a very full, yet pleasantly chubby face.

'Helen, how nice to see you again. Anne told me you would be popping in.'

Helen smiles and Christina watches as they share a very warm embrace.

'Amanda, this is Donna, my friend, and this, as you probably know, is Christina, our maid.'

Christina blushes at Helen's description and then astounds herself by performing a deep, sexy curtsey that brings an even wider smile to Amanda's lovely mouth.

'My, my. Yes, indeed. Anne told me all about Christina, but I never expected this! She's incredible. I mean . . . she . . . he?'

Amanda stares at Christina in amazement, her mouth slowly dropping open, her eyes widening as the true extent of the she-male sinks in.

'She,' Helen corrects. 'Very definitely *she*.'

Still obviously astounded, Amanda leads the two women and Christina down a marble floored walkway that runs between row after row of beautiful and clearly very expensive dresses hanging from golden framed racks. A number of elegant, extremely well dressed women are looking through the racks, one or two attended by younger women dressed in what is obviously the store uniform: a very tight white nylon sweater, a very short black shirt, black tights and high heels.

Eventually, they reach the rear of the shop. It is here that lingerie and shoes are displayed, the shoes on a series of wooden shelves, the various items of lingerie either on showroom dummies or further golden-edged racks. Beyond the racks are a series of curtained changing rooms and a door. They go through the door and then down a long corridor. At the end of the corridor is a large office and just before the office, another door, which leads into a private changing and viewing room.

It is this room into which Amanda leads the two women and the lovely, startled she-male.

The room is perfectly oval. It is painted a soft yellow, with a sky-blue carpet, a number of striking watercolour nudes hanging at regular intervals from the curving wall, and a large, white leather sofa at its centre. Next to the sofa is a wooden, leather-backed chair and a glass-topped coffee table. Amanda asks Helen and Donna to sit on the sofa. She sits on the wooden chair. It is made clear that Christina is to remain standing.

'Anne mentioned that you were looking for quite formal attire, formal but sexy?'

As she speaks, Amanda's large, very beautiful blue eyes crawl over Christina's expertly feminised body. She is fascinated, yet also disturbed. It is clear that this is not what she was expecting, that the reality, or rather the conviction of the transformation, is much stronger than she had previously thought possible. And even as Helen is nodding in response to her question, Amanda is confessing her disturbance.

'He ... she's so very convincing, Helen. And so beautiful. How on earth did you find a man ... a ...'

'Christina had been practising before we met her. But I think it is fair to say that we have helped her realise her full potential.'

Christina curtseys her appreciation of Helen's remarks and Amanda's smile widens.

'And she is totally obedient?' Amanda asks.

'Oh, yes,' Helen responds. 'Christina is intensely masochistic, so she actually takes pleasure in her servitude. In fact, the more we humiliate her, the more excited she seems to become.'

Amanda's smile widens even further. She sits back slightly and then slowly crosses her legs, allowing the modest black silk skirt to rise up her legs to the border between her mid- and upper thigh. Despite her generous figure, Christina immediately notices that Amanda has very long, shapely legs and feels her sex expand hungrily inside its inescapable rubber prison.

'You're very lucky, Helen,' the plump blonde whispers.

'Maybe. But personally I think Christina is the lucky one.'

'Yes, perhaps she is. But I know a lot of women who would pay quite a lot to spend time with a pretty she-male slave girl.'

Helen smiles sympathetically. 'Perhaps we could arrange for Christina to spend some time with you, to help you round the shop, or maybe act as your house maid for a day. I'm sure Christina would be more than willing to demonstrate the possibilities of her servitude.'

Christina listens in amazement and watches as Amanda's smile widens even further.

'Yes, that would be very nice. I'll talk to Anne.'

There is a brief pause during which Amanda's eyes remain fixed on Christina. Then there is a knock at the door. Shaken from her trance, Amanda utters a curt 'Enter'. The door opens and a rack of clothing is pushed into the room by one of the erotically uniformed assistants, a very pretty brunette, certainly no more than eighteen years of age, and her eyes fix immediately on the stunning she-male beauty.

'Thank you, Myriam,' Amanda says, her eyes regarding the brunette in an obviously sexual manner. 'Please bring the rack into the centre, and I'd be grateful if you would stay and help Christina.'

The lovely brunette smiles shyly and whispers 'Yes, Miss Chalmers', in a thick, very sexy southern French accent.

Under Amanda's instruction, Myriam then steps forwards and begins to help Christina strip down to her sexy undies. Myriam's jet black hair is styled in a very short page boy manner. She has incredibly large, very soft brown eyes that peer up at Christina with an intense and very sexual curiosity. Her wide, sensual mouth, painted a light peach, widens into a shy smile as she begins to unbutton Christina's suit jacket and the she-male fights a gasp of pleasure, her own eyes feasting on Myriam's very large breasts pressing teasingly against the erotic material of the tight white nylon sweater and, for such a small beauty, her very long, black nylon-sheathed legs.

With Myriam's assistance, Christina spends the next two hours in an almost sublime state of intense embarrassment and wild desire. Aroused and humiliated, aroused *because* humiliated, she models every item of clothing on the rack. Skirts, blouses, dresses, jackets: a whole variety of formal yet very feminine attire

And as she models these lovely outfits for her mistresses, she listens to their conversation with an interest regularly undermined by the close proximity of the lovely Myriam. It quickly becomes clear that Amanda is Anne's lover. Not only that, but the two women live together. This information alone is enough to make Christina's eyes widen in amazement. Despite Anne's dark nature and apparent sadistic streak, the she-male has never even remotely considered the possibility that she might be a lesbian. And as she considers this new, surprising fact, she also recalls the rumours that have surrounded Katherine and Helen for so long. Most people in the office consider Katherine to be a lesbian of some sort and Helen is seen as her not so secret object of desire. But now Christina finds herself wondering if Katherine's desire is in fact rooted in some deeper knowledge of Helen's true nature.

Eventually, three separate outfits are chosen from the rack. As Myriam gathers up the clothes, Donna asks Amanda if she has any 'nightwear'.

'Something erotic,' Donna adds, her gorgeous eyes falling longingly on a highly aroused Christina.

Amanda smiles knowingly and then tells Myriam to return to the shop and find something suitable. Still stripped down to her undies, Christina is told not to dress until the gorgeous assistant returns. Meanwhile Helen rises from the leather sofa and walks over to the sexy she-male beauty.

'You're a big hit with Amanda,' she whispers, running a long, blood-red-nailed index finger over the front of her slave's pretty panties and inspiring a moan of desperate pleasure.

'Thank you, mistress,' Christina gasps.

'I think you should spend some time with her. She'll be very useful to us in the future and I want her to see the advantages of involving herself in your transformation. Do you understand?'

Christina answers with a deep, affirming curtsey.

'Good. I'll tell her you'll come over on Monday.'

As her spinning sissy mind attempts to deal with the implications of Helen's words, Myriam returns to the room carrying a large black box and hands it to Amanda.

'I think this is the sort of thing you're probably looking for,' Amanda says to Donna, placing the box at the gorgeous blonde's side.

Donna thanks her and removes the lid. From inside she takes a stunning pink silk baby-doll nightdress, which has been frilled at the short sleeves, very high neck and wide, also very short hem with thick cherry-red fur. As well as the nightdress, Donna also produces a pair of very skimpy, see-through pink panties.

Smiling broadly, she turns her lovely blue eyes onto the scantily glad, highly aroused Christina.

'Oh, I think these will do wonderfully, Amanda. Don't you agree, Chrissie?'

Christina curtseys weakly and whispers a hoarse, 'Yes, mistress.'

The women burst into laughter at this helplessly aroused response. Donna then packs the nightdress back into the box as Myriam, supervised by Amanda, packs the other clothing that Helen has chosen for her beautiful sissy slave. Helen then orders Christina to put her original clothing back on and turns to Amanda.

'You've been marvellous, as usual. I'll make sure that Christina is at your house by 8.30 a.m. sharp on Monday morning. I'm sure you'll find her very accommodating.'

Amanda thanks Helen and her gaze slowly passes over the lovely she-male, who curtsies her own thanks to this generously proportioned beauty and the lovely, petite but very shapely Myriam, whose beautiful brown eyes still betray a very powerful and deeply perverse desire.

It is well after 4.00 p.m. by the time the two women and their she-male servant leave the shop. Once outside, Christina is again overwhelmed with an intense excitement and all thoughts of her impending adventure with Amanda quickly fade.

Carrying two large, elegantly designed bags full of the sexy clothing Helen and Donna have chosen for her, Christina minces prettily behind her two mistresses, making sure to keep her legs as tightly together as possible, her steps as short as possible and thus her wiggling bottom teasingly prominent. Wolf whistles and bawdy comments follow the sexy she-male across the shopping centre and into a small photography shop located only a few hundred yards from the multi-storey car park. Christina is led inside by her two beautiful mistresses, her sissy heart once again pumping desperately with aroused anticipation.

The walls of the shop are covered in portrait photographs and very little else. Three much larger group portraits are placed on tripod stands by the front window. At the rear of the shop is tiny counter and sitting behind it is a pretty teenage girl reading a newspaper. She only looks up from the paper when Helen, standing impatiently at the counter, coughs angrily.

The girl looks up, her eyes filled with boredom .

'Yes?' she mumbles.

'We're here to see Ingrid. I'm Helen, this is Donna and this,' she says, pointing at Christina, 'is the commission I mentioned over the phone this morning.'

The girl suddenly sits bolt upright, drops the paper and begins nodding nervously, her wide eyes never leaving Christina.

'Yes. Er, sorry. I'll go and get Miss Hessler.'

She then jumps up and disappears through a curtain into the back of the shop.

Helen sighs impatiently and turns to Donna. 'Why does Ingrid work here? What a terrible dump!'

As Helen bemoans the shop, the curtain parts and, to Christina's surprise, a very tall blonde woman enters the shop, a stunning Nordic beauty with piercing ice-blue eyes and golden hair that stretches down over her broad shoulders, a woman dressed in a very tight white T-shirt and jeans which display her very voluptuous figure perfectly. She smiles at Helen and Donna and looks very carefully at Christina.

'This is . . . her?'

Her accent is heavy, German or Scandinavian, and her eyes betray a steel-hard countenance that sends a shiver of fear down Christina's sissy spine.

Helen smiles and nods. 'Ingrid, meet Christina. Christina, say hello to Mistress Ingrid.'

Christina performs a suitably deep and submissive curtsey and Ingrid bursts out laughing.

171

'Good grief!' she shouts, tossing back her golden river of hair. 'What a stunner! Where on earth did you find him or her? We can make a fortune!'

'Anne seems to agree with you.'

'Yes, she left a message. I'll ring her later.'

Poor Christina hasn't the foggiest idea what these gorgeous women are talking about. But whatever it is, she feels certain it will involve even more bizarre and ultra-kinky adventures.

'Bring her through,' Ingrid says. 'Everything is ready.'

Helen then leads Christina around the counter and through the tatty curtain. She finds herself in an ill-lit corridor that smells badly of damp. She minces slowly along behind her mistresses until they reach a large metal door near the end of the corridor. Ingrid opens the door and they are suddenly covered in a powerful white light.

'Ladies first,' Ingrid jokes, and Helen ushers Christina inside.

To her amazement, Christina almost immediately discovers herself in a very large photographic studio, a vast white-walled room housing a vast array of hi-tech photographic equipment, numerous backdrops and, in one corner, what appears to be a very large bed.

Helen seems as surprised as Christina.

'Amazing,' she says. 'And the place looks such a dump from the outside.'

Her deep, sensual voice echoes around the cavernous room, as does the collective sound of their high heels striking the concrete floor.

'The shop is a front. As seventy-five per cent of my work is of a rather intimate nature, I find it much easier to work behind the disguise of drabness and mediocrity. Now let's see what we can do with your pretty sissy, Helen.'

Ingrid then takes Christina by the hand and guides her onto a circular platform in the centre of the room.

Resting on the platform is a metal-framed stool. Christina is made to sit on the stool with her long, delicately hosed legs crossed while Ingrid takes a camera from a side table and aims it directly at the lovely she-male.

'Anne tells me she has actually started an internet site for Christina,' Ingrid says, seeking out good angles to photograph the gorgeous sissy, 'that it will eventually become a pay site, concentrating on heavy S&M. It sounds very ambitious.'

Christina listens in horror and amazement as Ingrid then takes a number of preliminary pictures.

'Yes,' Helen replies. 'Anne has been inspired. Given her connections and tastes, she seems to have discovered the perfect hobby.'

'A hobby that could make serious money,' Ingrid says, moving in very close to Christina's legs.

'If everything works out, she'll begin working full-time on the site very soon. And that's why she'll be needing your help.'

It is then that Ingrid begins to shout instructions at Christina – ways to pose, attitudes to adopt. At first Christina is terribly embarrassed by these demands, but after a few minutes finds her new feminine self is certainly far more relaxed about public 'performance' than her previous male identity. Indeed, it is almost as if the sexy attire and general 'design' of the lovely Christina requires an element of theatrical performance. Helen seems particularly interested in the way that her sissy slave quickly adapts to Ingrid's instructions and a large, satisfied, yet ultimately mysterious smile crosses her face as the she-male strikes a series of sexy, provocative poses before the wildly clicking camera lens.

The photography session lasts maybe thirty minutes and, at the end of it, Ingrid disappears into an adjacent dark room to develop the pictures she has taken of the lovely she-male. As Helen helps Christina down from the platform, she praises her obvious acting abilities.

'That was very impressive, Christina.'

Christina curtseys her gratitude.

'Would you like to try acting?'

This question confuses the she-male and her reply betrays her uncertainty.

'I don't know, mistress. If you wish me to, then of course.'

'Well, I think there's a very good chance I will want you to.'

Christina curtseys her understanding and is then ordered to stand facing a far wall with her hands behind her back while Helen inspects the studio in more detail. Eventually, Ingrid returns from the dark room carrying a collection of photographs and Christina is called over to see the pictures.

Both Helen and her sexy slave are more than impressed by the quality of the pictures, and for the first time Christina sees her true feminine persona revealed photographically. Unlike a reflection, a photograph always appears to provide a more profound insight into the truth of a physical image, and the sexy, teasing beauty that these pictures reveal fill Christina with a strange mixture of pride and desire. It is almost as if she fancies herself!

'These are excellent, Ingrid,' Helen exclaims, pulling one particularly sexy shot from the pile. 'We'll take this one with us. Bring the rest over next weekend.'

After brief goodbyes, Helen and Christina leave the studio, stagger through the dark recesses of the shop and are soon back in the car and heading to Chris's flat. And it is only as Helen helps her sexy slave into the back of the car that Christina remembers Donna.

'Donna had some other shopping to do,' Helen says, reading Christina's sudden, sad look. 'I'm sure you'll be seeing her later.'

By the time the car pulls up outside the apartment building, Christina is very nervous. While walking through the town was a surprisingly straightforward and very exciting undertaking, returning to the flat where she had lived so unhappily as Chris will be a real test. Surely someone will recognise her – surely she will be exposed!

'Don't worry, Christina,' Helen says, turning from the driver's seat to face her slave. 'You look utterly convincing. No one will recognise you. Now go upstairs and send the picture to Annette, and hurry up. I want you back here in fifteen minutes, otherwise your little rendezvous with Donna will be cancelled and you'll spend the night under the stairs.'

Genuinely appalled by this threat, Christina quickly climbs out of the car and minces into the building. The sound of her heart pounding in terror accompanies her all the way up in the lift, down the second-floor corridor and into the flat. Once inside, she rushes to the computer and turns it on. She discovers two e-mails from Annette, both sadly asking why Christina has stopped talking to her. Christina immediately types out an extremely apologetic message explaining the bizarre adventures of the past few weeks. She also scans in the picture and attaches it to the e-mail as a JPEG file. The e-mail also contains an invitation to meet as soon as possible and the promise that Annette would not only meet Christina but also her three stunning mistresses. As she presses the send button a sense of utter elation washes over her. Now all her dreams are on the verge of coming true. Not only is she now the gorgeous, sexy she-male she has always dreamed of becoming, but she is under the stern and deeply erotic care of three beautiful, dominant and endlessly kinky women. And now, she will hopefully finally get to meet her only true friend through these last deeply frustrating months, the equally beautiful she-male, Annette.

By the time Helen and Christina get back to Helen's lavish home, it is just after 6.00 p.m. Helen immediately takes her slave upstairs and helps her change back into her spectacular, ultra-sexy maid's costume. They then return downstairs, and the lovely she-male spends the next hour or so helping her regal mistress prepare dinner for three. Christina is, without a doubt, now in a state of ecstasy. As she minces sexily before her mistress, her petticoats swaying before her to reveal her silk-pantied behind and long, perfectly shaped, silk-hosed legs, her false breasts bouncing so realistically in their tight silk and nylon prison, the corset forcing her into a helplessly upright posture that insists she totter perpetually on the high, high heels, as each tiny, mincing step forces the dildo deeper into her sexy, eager arse, and as her long-imprisoned and angrily frustrated penis fights hopelessly against its sensual rubber prison, there is an almost transcendent sense of a new, much improved and much larger self. In this intricately feminised state, Chris has become not just Christina, not just a sexy she, but also a totally different being, almost as if the masculine and feminine within him/her have come together and produced a third gender.

This profound, mind-altering pleasure is made even more intense by the domestic tasks that are the practical application of her servitude. As she helps prepare food, as she washes dishes and cooking pans and as she minces so daintily between the kitchen and the dining room, she feels a totally delicious sense of utter submission. It is as if each task has been sexualised, as if the world itself has become a fetishistic sexual entity designed to drive this lovely, sissy she-male mad with desire.

Over the coming weeks, as each day of her maidservant enslavement passes, she will become obsessed with the intricacies of her duties, with ensuring that each task is performed with an exactitude that will both amuse and disturb her mistresses. And of course, one of her greatest pleasures, and also her greatest honour, will be the care of her mistresses' clothing, a task that Helen will quickly notice arouses Christina terribly, and a task the dark-eyed mistress will subsequently insist the lovely she-male spend the majority of her time undertaking: washing, drying, ironing, storing, even mending every item of Helen's clothing, from her panties and hose to her most expensive clothes and jewellery. And on top of this delight, there will be an even greater pleasure: the supreme honour of assisting her mistresses, mainly Helen, with dressing and make-up. To stand to rigid attention in her lovely uniform, a large towel at the ready as Helen steps from her steaming shower, to carefully dry and perfume her gorgeous, generous figure, then to help her dress and prepare her make-up. Then, perhaps the most erotic moment, to brush Helen's beautiful, thick, gleaming brown hair. All these tasks will be performed as if the holiest of religious rituals.

But now it is nearly 8.00 p.m., and the lovely sissy is putting the finishing touches to the dining table as the doorbell rings. Helen orders Christina to answer the door and she minces somewhat nervously from the room and down the hallway. Opening the door, she discovers Donna and Anne and performs the deepest curtsey she can manage. The women ignore their beautiful slave and walk past her into the house. Slightly hurt, especially by Donna's indifference, Christina minces after her stunning mistresses.

It is only as Christina enters the room behind the two women that she gets a reasonable view of Donna and her sissy heart sings with a terrible, sexual joy. For the lovely blonde has certainly dressed for the occasion. Her voluptuous form is sealed in a very tight black mini-dress made from latex rubber, a spectacular second skin that reveals every erotic contour of her perfect body. Indeed, the dress is so tight and figure-hugging that her long, stiff nipples are clearly defined by the rubber material. Christina's eyes widen in excited amazement and travel down the dress to her long legs, which are wrapped in ultra-sheer, black nylon, and which lead down to feet erotically imprisoned in a pair of black, patent leather, stiletto-heeled mules. She is wearing her sparkling blonde hair lose tonight and it spills over her rubberised shoulders like a lake of pure gold. Around her slender neck is a choker necklace of black pearls. Her full lips are painted a very bloody red and a hint of pale-blue eye shadow perfectly complements her stunning eyes. Poor Christina cannot resist a moan of hungry desire as she turns these eyes on Christina and smiles teasingly.

Anne is dressed in a very expensive black silk suit, a white, high-necked silk blouse and very high-heeled ankle boots, her own hair bound tightly in a very prim, strict bun. She is wearing little make-up. In her emerald eyes Christina sees a familiar cruel cunning laced with a darker sexual desire and a wave of paradoxically sexy dread washes over her perfectly sissified form.

'You both look fantastic,' Helen says, entering the room. 'You may serve the wine now, Christina.'

The lovely she-male performs another deep curtsey, making sure to display her sexy panties, and then wiggle-minces back into the kitchen, returning a few seconds later with a silver tray bearing three glasses of golden Chablis.

The women spend the next half hour chatting and drinking, and Christina totters sweetly between them, serving more wine as required. The conversation covers all the bizarre events of the day, and the gorgeous she-male cannot help but listen intently between her serving duties.

'Amanda was very impressed by Christina,' Helen says, once the women are seated.

'She told me,' Anne responds, her eyes crawling over the lovely Christina like two poisonous snakes. 'We had a long chat about what she's going to do with her on Monday.'

Christina's heart misses a beat, yet she stands perfectly still before her mistresses, having learnt well the lessons of the last few weeks.

'And do we get to know?' Helen asks, a smile spreading across her beautiful face.

'Not tonight. I want it to be a surprise for Chrissie.'

The conversation then turns to Anne's website project and Christina listens in horrified fascination as the redhead updates her comrades on progress. The 'Baby Christina' website is up and running and a huge success. There are thousands of 'hits' every day to what is at the moment a free site providing access to the numerous scanned photos of Christina taken during the previous week. Anne also reveals that she has written extensive text as Chrissie's 'webmistress' detailing the humiliations the poor she-male has endured and the plans for her on-going feminisation.

'I want the site to be a personal history of Christina,' Anne says. 'We'll start with the baby pictures and then progress onto her role as our maid and general slave. Ingrid phoned me earlier this evening and she's willing to do a whole series of photos of Christina for the site. She's really enthusiastic. Once we get the full range completed, we'll establish the pay site and post the pictures. She wants to cover every aspect: Chrissie as a maid, in other uniforms and fetish wear, Chrissie in bondage. She's also really keen to get some interactive stuff – Chrissie with her mistresses, even Chrissie with a master. She's even talking about streaming video.'

'What's that?'

'Doing video scenarios involving Chrissie and putting them on the web. She's convinced we can make a fortune.'

Even Christina, now in some mental discomfort, can hear the devious and highly imaginative machinery of Helen's brain ticking over.

'Videos?' she mumbles, taking a long sip of the wine. 'That's a very interesting idea.'

Helen then announces that a special photo session should be arranged with Ingrid as quickly as possible, only to discover that Anne has already organised 'an initial shoot' for the coming week.

The conversation continues over dinner, which Christina serves with a deeply worried sissy heart, but a keen and eager sissy body. For the most part the women ignore her, although Donna does pull the gorgeous she-male out of her pit of concern by secretly stroking her hosed thighs as she leans forwards to pour gravy over her roast beef, producing a sudden gasp of pleasure and a much-needed reminder of the treat that lies ahead.

It is after 11.00 p.m. by the time the meal is completed and Christina is left to clear the dining table and do the washing up. And it is near midnight by the time she returns to the living room to find only Donna sitting on the sofa, cross-legged, sipping contemplatively from her wine glass.

'You've really impressed everybody, Chrissie. I'm very proud of you,' she says, rising from the sofa and walking towards her lovely slave.

Christina curtseys her thanks and feels her heart pound with a terrible desire.

'Yes, you've come a very long way in the last seven days. Helen is really happy with you. And Anne, well, she's got so many special plans for you. You really are a very lucky little sissy.'

Another curtsey and Donna's smile widens.

'And me? Well, you know how I feel about you, Chrissie. This is the way I want you for ever. Just looking at you makes me wet. And I've wanted you so badly every night for the past week. And I know you've wanted me. Well, as you've been such a good girl, tonight you can have me.'

A moan of delight trickles from Christina's painted lips as Donna then leans forwards and gently kisses her on the lips.

'Let's go up to your room,' she whispers, and the poor she-male beauty nearly faints.

Christina follows Donna up to the spare room in a deep sex-trance, her cock now stretching with a mad fury against its rubber captor and screaming for release. Her eyes eat up Donna's sheer-nylon-sheathed legs and the perfect contours of her rubberised bottom as they climb the stairs. She has waited so hungrily, so desperately, for this moment, for Donna's reward, her present for Christina's patient and so painful days of restraint.

By the time they enter the bedroom, Christina is openly moaning with a deep, boiling need. Donna turns to face her sissy slave, her smile gentle, reassuring. She steps forwards and slips a hand behind the she-male's petticoats and strokes the front of her pretty, sexy silk panties.

'Dear me, Chrissie – it's like a furnace down there. I think we need to let some cool air in.'

Tears of long-denied need begin to trickle down Christina's carefully painted cheeks as Donna then proceeds very gently to lower the panties over her hosed thighs and lets them drop around her slender ankles.

'Take the pinny and the dress off,' she orders, standing back, her eyes filled with desire, her voice hoarse, sex-edged.

Christina obeys, going through the now instinctive balletic contortions that enable her to put on and remove this intricate and so sexy uniform. And soon, she is standing before Donna in only her well-stuffed bra, corset, hose and heels, her rubber-sheathed sex hidden by the very tight, deliberately flattening rubber panties. Donna removes the corset and then helps Christina to remove the bra, carefully taking the silicon-filled false breasts in her elegant hands as she does so. Then, after the sissy has kicked off her high heels,

Donna slowly rolls the fine, silk tights over Christina's long, silky smooth legs and, kneeling down, gently pulls them off her small, dainty feet.

Now, only the rubber panties are left, and it takes a considerable effort of wiggling and pulling for Christina, at Donna's command, to remove them. Indeed, by the time she has stripped down to just the tight, cruel rubber restrainer, a fine sweat of effort is covering her sissy body and she is standing weakly before the gorgeous Donna, her rampant, furious sex straining upright in its wicked rubber prison and demanding immediate release.

Donna turns from Christina and goes over to the dressing table. She takes a jar of clear gel from the table and brings it over to her slave.

'This expands the rubber and makes it easier to remove. It will be rather pleasant, so try and control yourself.'

Christina watches with fascinated, hungry eyes as Donna proceeds to daub a large blob of the gel onto her rock-hard sex and then slowly rub it into the second skin of tight rubber. As predicted, Donna's necessary caress is incredibly pleasurable, and very soon Christina is moaning loudly.

'You really are a noisy little girl, Chrissie. No wonder we have to gag you!'

Luckily, it takes only a few seconds for the gel to take effect and the rubber restrainer to expand. Donna then slips it from her slave's engorged sex and Christina releases a loud gasp of relief as she is, for the first time in many days, truly free of tight genital restraint.

Now completely naked before her most beloved mistress, Christina is sorely tempted to pounce on Donna and ravish her on the spot, a terribly regressive, deeply male urge that betrays the fundamental and inescapable nature of her deeper biological make-up, but which her training has ensured is quite controllable.

'Right. Now let's get you washed and scented.'

Christina follows Donna into the bathroom, her sex standing proudly and angrily before her like a lightning rod especially attuned to the electro-erotic vibrations emitted by her stunning mistress.

In the bathroom, the lovely Bettie Page wig is removed. Christina is then placed beneath a jet of steaming water, ensuring that every inch of make-up is washed from her face, along with the sweat the strip-tease has produced. Eventually satisfied her slave is clean, Donna then takes Christina from the shower, quickly dries her and then smoothers her sissy she-male form in a fog of powerful musk perfume. Christina is then led back to the bedroom and to the bed. Laid out on the bed is the sexy baby-doll nightdress that had been selected earlier by Amanda.

'Put it on. And the shoes. Then come down to my room – the second on the left.'

With this and a very promising smile, Donna departs, leaving Christina to ponder the nightdress and a pair of five-inch heeled, pink patent leather mules that are resting on the floor by the bed.

In a state of quite painful sexual excitement, Christina takes up the skimpy, see-through pink silk panties that accompany the baby-doll. She slips into these with a sigh of pure pleasure and wiggles them up her long, sexy legs. The delicate, diaphanous silk material feels like a thousand baby kisses against her silken skin and as she gently pulls the panties over her enraged sex, she cannot avoid a girlish squeal of uncontrollable pleasure.

It is quickly apparent that the panties are far too small to encompass the raging mass of her sex, and the engorged, purple head sticks out of the top of the panties like a giant sex flower, an effect that is surely quite deliberate. And after the skimpy panties, the lovely, deeply frustrated Christina addresses the wonderful baby-doll itself, taking up the nightdress, made from exactly the same material as the panties, with shaking hands and carefully stepping into it. Then she is falling into a whirlpool of tactile ecstasy, the gorgeous silk material enveloping her ultra-sensitive silken skin and sending electric sex shivers crashing over her sissy body.

Still reeling from the effect of the baby-doll, Christina steps elegantly into the sexy pink mules and totters from the room, wiggle-mincing down the corridor to Donna's room. Her heart pounding with girlish anticipation, she gently knocks on the door. Donna's husky, sex-edged voice tells her to come in.

A gasp of amazement is her first reaction to the glorious sight that meets her as she steps through the door. For before her is Donna, the rubber dress removed. She is standing before her slave topless, in black rubber panties, a garter belt, black nylon stockings and her own beautifully high-heeled mules, her hands on her hips, a smile of sinful intent spread across her lovely face, her long blonde hair spilling over her tanned shoulders like a fresh flow of honey-coloured lava.

'I hope you're ready to please me,' she purrs, stepping towards Christina. 'You can start by taking the rest of my clothes off.'

Moaning her need, she obeys, stripping Donna naked in a few furious, desperate minutes and then leading her to the large, silk-sheeted bed in the centre of the room. Then Donna pulls Christina down onto the bed. The two beauties roll around on the bed in a half-embrace for a few bizarre minutes; then Donna spreads her long legs wide and pushes Christina's head between them. And for the next two hours, Christina pleases and deeply pleasures her stunning mistress. First with her mouth and tongue, eagerly probing her sex and arse, teasing her stiff nipples, licking every inch of her beautiful, flawless body, covering her in kisses. Worshipping her body, serving her goddess. Then, with her sex. After being carefully sheathed in a thick, ribbed condom by her mistress (a process which inspires cries of ecstatic pleasure), Christina is finally allowed to plunge deep into her mistress. By now they are both soaked in sweat, by now the baby-doll has been ripped from her body. By now they are both naked and lost in the multiple joys of their sexy bodies. And as Christina mounts Donna, as the mistress allows the slave to ride her like a fiery-eyed blonde stallion, Donna's hands reach up and begin to tease Christina's nipples.

'Would you like breasts, Chrissie?' she gasps, as Christina begins to build a powerful, hard rhythm. 'A pair of real, ultra-sensitive whoppers?'

Christina, wildly excited, only a few moments away from a huge, volcanic eruption of an orgasm, cries a desperate, 'Yes, mistress; yes, I'd love to have breasts, the bigger the better.' And, as if to emphasise the point, her own hands then fall onto Donna's splendid bosom and begin to knead them quite roughly. Donna's response is to pinch Christina's nipples very hard and cry out as the first shock-wave of her own impending orgasm crashes across her superb body.

Then they come, within seconds of each other. The earthquake of desire, the eruption of primal need. In Christina's case, weeks of suppressed sexual hunger explode like a tidal wave crashing against the fragile brick wall of a dam. Her scream is high-pitched, insane, animal; her whole body is racked by a shudder of extreme ecstasy; silver lights explode before her tightly closed eyes. Then she has fallen into a vast black hole, a place where, momentarily, there is nothing, where she is nothing, a moment of eternity, where time and space have neither begun nor ended. And when she emerges from this strange place, she is on her back, soaked in sweat and Donna is lying against her, her head resting on her slave's chest, listening to her heart pound. And it is only a few minutes before the two of them, mistress and sissy slave, have fallen into a deep, contented sleep.

Nine

Christina is pulled from the pit of sleep by Donna just after 7.00 a.m. Within seconds they are once again in each other's arms and making a desperate, passionate love. By 8.00 a.m., Christina has been returned to her room and she shares a hot, highly erotic shower with her beautiful mistress. Once they are dried, Donna, dressed only in a very skimpy black silk dressing-gown, helps her pretty sissy slave to transform herself back into a gorgeous, utterly subservient she-male maid. And by 9.00 a.m., Christina and Donna are in the kitchen preparing breakfast, the lovely sissy tottering sweetly on her high heels, Donna, still in her dressing-gown, gently ordering her slave from task to task.

Helen and Anne come down just before 10.00 a.m. and Christina has the pleasure of serving all three, stunning women a full Sunday breakfast, her own meal of toast and a cup of black tea having been consumed earlier.

The rest of the morning is spent vacuuming, dusting and polishing. Christina performs each menial task with an enthusiasm that betrays a much deeper arousal. As she daintily minces about the house, the vision of Donna fills her every thought. The beautiful memories of her night of passion accompany every careful, elegant gesture and feminine movement. Her erect sex, now safely back in its tight rubber restrainer, struggles desperately as glowing images of Donna's stunning naked form wash via rapid sex-hallucinations across her pretty, bedazzled eyes, hallucinations that plunge Christina back into the sex world and thus the complete sexualisation of the current reality and each task she so eagerly performs.

Her feelings for Donna are now stronger than ever. As they had made love the night before, the sissy she-male knew she was hopelessly in love. Indeed, as Donna had patiently helped her slave with her make-up earlier, Christina had again declared her helpless infatuation with Donna. Donna had smiled gently and told Christina to be quiet, but there was no doubting the depth of her own feelings and her intense attraction to the she-male beauty.

After serving lunch, Christina is called before Helen and told to go upstairs and change into one of the new outfits they had purchased at Amanda's shop the day before.

'I want you to go back to your flat and check if Annette has responded to your e-mail,' she explains. 'I'm very keen to meet her.'

Christina curtseys deeply and then minces back up to her room. Within the hour she is sitting beside Helen in her car, dressed in a very sexy and very short black cotton skirt, a black nylon sweater and a black jacket, plus her normal black nylon tights and a pair of black patent leather, very high-heeled court shoes. And it is as they are crossing the city to Christina's flat that the she-male makes a very bold announcement.

'I don't want to go back to work next week, mistress. I want to stay with you, to be your maid permanently.'

Where these brave, perhaps foolish words come from, she has no idea. Helen's initial silence fills her with dread: she has spoken out of turn and is sure to be punished!

'I know, Chrissie,' Helen eventually says. 'And I understand. And I think I can make the necessary arrangements to ensure you don't go back.'

Stunned, amazed, elated, Christina finds more brave words.

'That would be so wonderful, mistress. Thank you! All I want to do is serve you in any way you wish – for ever.'

'I will talk to Katherine. Now be quiet or I will have to punish you later.'

Christina obeys, wondering just exactly how Helen can talk to Katherine, her boss, about the sissy she-male not returning to her job and thus her previous identity as the lonely, bored, frustrated Chris. She again recalls the rumours concerning Katherine's sexuality and her rather obvious interest in the lovely, regal Helen.

Unlike her previous visit to the flat, Helen insists on parking the car and accompanying her slave. Luckily, there are few people about to notice Christina, the beautiful sexy she-male, unrecognisable as Chris, and they enter the building together and travel up to his second-floor apartment. Once inside the flat, Helen orders Christina to see if Annette has responded to her previous e-mail while she carefully inspects each room.

As she logs on, Christina has no real hope that Annette can have replied so soon. Yet, to her surprise, there is a fresh message from the lovely she-male friend waiting to be read. And as Christina reads the message a smile of joy and terrible excitement lights up her pretty sissy face, for the message is as follows:

Dear Christina,
Thank you so very much for the photo! I have waited a long time and my wait has not been in vain: you are beautiful; in fact, you are incredibly beautiful! I am shocked and very, very jealous! And yes, we *must* meet. Your 'mistresses' sound a little too good to be

true, but of course I'd like to meet them too. I can come and visit next weekend, if you want. I am putting my mobile number on the bottom of this message. I'll be available most of Sunday, so why don't you ring me? I'd love to hear from you!

Annette.

Christina looks at the mobile number and feels a nervous giddiness wash over her. Then she is aware of Helen, standing directly behind her, also reading the message.

'I think you should ring her straight away, Christina. See if she can come down on Friday evening. Tell her she can spend the weekend with us at my house. Then we can show her how much better than the truth we are.'

Christina mumbles a nervous, 'Yes, mistress,' and minces over to the telephone. Her hands are shaking with fear and desire as she taps in the number of Annette's mobile. The phone seems to ring for ever, and as each ring explodes in her ear her nervousness increases. Then, a voice, a calm, relaxed, strangely feminine voice.

'Hello?'

Christina hesitates, the sound of her pounding heart filling her pretty sissy head.

'Annette?'

A pause, the sound of unsure breathing?

'Who is this, please?'

'Annette, this is Christina.'

A shorter pause, followed by a very audible sigh of relief.

'Christina. Oh, right. Sorry . . . I wasn't expecting you to ring so soon. Well, great, thanks for getting back to me. And your picture. Yeah, thanks for that. What a surprise! You look absolutely great. Who took that photo? It looked incredibly professional.'

'I'm glad you liked it,' Christina nervously responds. 'But it's not as good as yours.'

Annette laughs. 'That's rubbish. God, if I'd known how good-looking you were before, I don't know if I'd have had the guts to send you my photo.'

'Can we meet?'

A simple question, put by Christina as Helen, who is now standing over her, gives every indication of impatience. A question whose response is another pause.

'Sure,' Annette says, eventually. 'I've told you I'm free next week. Where are you?'

Christina tells her and Annette laughs again. She lives in a nearby city, only forty minutes away by car.

'Well, then,' she continues. 'Let's meet next weekend. I'll drive over to you?'

Christina is relaxing now, calmed down considerably by Annette's soft, girlish voice and laid back manner.

'That would be really good. My mistresses are also very keen to meet you.'

Laughter follows, slightly incredulous, but still friendly.

'Are you really serious? You've met three women who want you to be their maid? Sorry, Christina, but that sounds too fantastic.'

'I know. I'm not denying that. But it's true.'

At that precise moment, Helen grabs the phone from Christina.

'Annette?'

Another long pause and then a nervous, 'Yes?'

'This is Helen, Christina's mistress. I'm sure she's told you all about me. If you could come down next weekend we'd be really grateful. I assure you that Christina is not exaggerating, and that you'll find this out for yourself if you visit us.'

She then gives the phone back to Christina. 'Get her over here next Friday evening.'

When Christina goes back onto the phone, Annette expresses amazement, yet in her voice there is a distinct tone of intense sexual excitement. At Helen's insistence Christina gives Annette the address of the apartment block and they agree to meet at 7.00 p.m. the following Friday.

'I want you to spend some time with Annette, to reassure her, and then bring her over to the house about 9.00 p.m.,' Helen explains, once the phone call is over.

Christina rises from the computer and curtseys her understanding. The beautiful mistress and her lovely sissy slave then leave the flat.

For the rest of the day, she acts as maidservant to all three women, beautifully attired in her formal French maid's uniform, serving tea, cleaning, helping to prepare dinner. The pleasure she takes in this sweet subjugation is heightened by two things: Helen's assurance that she would arrange for Christina to stay as her slave permanently and the impending visit of Annette. Yet even as she anticipates meeting the lovely she-male, she also finds herself wondering why the three women, and particularly Helen, are so keen to meet her as well. Could it be that they intend to induct her as a sissy maid, that she and Christina are to serve Helen, Donna and Anne together? This thought, still a fantasy, fills Christina with joy.

After dinner, she is presented with a huge pile of ironing, the product of a weekend's washing and drying. Led by Helen into a small, windowless room off the kitchen, she finds herself standing before two large plastic baskets filled with her mistresses' clothing, an ironing board and an iron.

'This lot should take about two to three hours,' Helen says, her voice cut through with a cruel, yet sexy amusement.

Christina curtseys and is about to step forwards, her masochistic excitement clearly dimmed by the size of this task, when Helen places a hand on her shoulder.

191

'To ensure all you do is iron, you will be hobbled and gagged.'

To Christina's surprise, Helen then takes from a large pocket in her long black skirt a pair of black panties, a roll of masking tape and two lengths of the very strong black rubber cording. She kneels down by Christina's high-heeled feet and tightly binds her delicately hosed ankles and knees with the rubber cording. Once the sissy's legs have been secured, she takes up the panties and dangles them before Christina's wide eyes.

'I've had these on most of the day, Christina, so I hope you appreciate the flavour.'

Helen forces the panties deep into her slave's more than willing mouth, quickly tears off a long strip of the tape and then spreads it firmly over Christina's glistening, cherry-red lips.

Yet this is only the beginning of her domestic bondage. For once the gag is secured, Helen leans down once again and takes up a pair of previously unnoticed slender metal shackles from beneath the ironing board. The shackles are attached by a silver chain to a metal hoop fixed to the floor. Helen locks the shackles around Christina's wrists.

'There's enough give to allow you to take clothes from the basket and place them on the board, and to manipulate the iron,' Helen informs her now horrified slave. 'The corset will make it virtually impossible for you to bend forwards far enough to remove the gag, but you will be able, if somewhat painfully, to squat down and take the clothing from the basket. Donna will come back at eleven to check on your progress. If you haven't finished by then, you'll be spanked, hog-tied and left in here for the night.'

With this delicious, teasing threat, Helen then leaves Christina hobbled, shackled, tightly panty-gagged and facing the ironing board and the two huge piles of washing.

It is only as she considers the task ahead that she notices that there is a large clothes rack directly to her left loaded with coat hangers and, beneath the rack, another large white plastic basket. It quickly becomes apparent that the lovely, tethered and gagged sissy is expected not just to iron the two huge piles of clothing, but to fold or hang them as appropriate!

Breathing heavily through flaring nostrils, she hops forwards slowly and painfully squats down to take the first item of clothing from the basket: a very sheer, semi-transparent white silk blouse that she recognises as belonging to Helen.

It takes her nearly ten minutes to iron the blouse and then hop two paces to the left to slip it over a hanger. By the time she has managed to do this, she is covered in sweat and gasping into her fat, pungent gag, the musky taste of Helen filling her stuffed mouth and, despite her discomfort, ensuring that her rubber imprisoned sex remains hard and deeply frustrated.

She labours desperately for over two hours, managing in this time to complete only one basket. And by the time the door is unlocked and Donna slips into the small cupboard-like room, poor Christina is only just beginning the second, her body soaked in sweat, her hosed legs aching terribly, tears of discomfort and desperation flooding from her pretty, girlish eyes.

'We had a bet how far you'd get,' Donna mocks. 'I thought you'd have nearly finished. But perhaps I think too highly of you, Chrissie. Anne got nearest. And she, of course, was the most pessimistic.'

Christina watches in painful anticipation as Donna removes the shackles and then disconnects the iron and folds up the ironing board, creating a narrow floor space. She then orders her slave to bend over and touch her toes. After hours of deportment training, Christina can now perform this physical feat with very little effort, her body shivering with fear as her petticoats and tiny skirt are raised up her nylon-sheathed thighs to offer her tightly pantied buttocks for inspection and torment.

Donna then makes a point of walking around Christina to show her a long, thick leather strap.

'A present from Amanda.'

Poor Christina's tightly muffled squeals of fear and her desperately shaking head produce a sharp laugh from her gorgeous, beloved mistress.

'Pain and pleasure, Chrissie,' she teases. 'That's what it's all about.'

Donna then disappears back behind the quivering she-male and there is a long, terrifying pause broken only by the sound of Christina's muffled pleas for mercy. Then there is fire, a terrible, blinding fire that rips into her buttocks and floods across her sissified form. She screams uselessly into the perfumed panty-gag and the force of this first brutal cut of the strap causes her to hop desperately forwards. Then a second blow, then a third. All together, six hard, mercilessly cuts of the strap that leave huge tears of pain pouring from Christina's eyes, squeals of outraged discomfort fighting to escape her so expertly gagged mouth and a terrible, inescapable fire eating up her shapely, sissified buttocks.

Then she is being pulled to her feet and her arms are being forced behind her back. She moans hopelessly as her wrists and elbows are then bound tightly together with more lengths of the unyielding black rubber cording.

'Do you still love me, Chrissie?' Donna asks, her voice filled with a strange, almost tormented excitement.

Despite her pain and the intensity of her punishment, Christina nods her head and attempts a curtsey of affirmation. Yes, she still loves Donna. In fact, as Donna forces her to kneel on the cold, concrete floor and then carefully lowers her bound form face down onto this floor, Christina loves her with an even greater power. Face down, her buttocks aflame, her body racked with the torments of the past two or so hours, she cannot help but accept that the more Donna dominates and humiliates her, the more the gorgeous, deeply masochistic she-male loves her.

Donna then uses a final length of the rubber cording to bind her tethered ankles to her trussed wrists, forcing her into such a severe hog-tie that the tips of her stiletto heels are forced painfully into the palms of her hands.

Then a pair of black-hosed legs fill Christina's severely restricted vision. Then, a pair of black panties fall down these legs. Donna then steps out of her panties and picks them up from the floor.

'I thought it would be nice to leave you with a little reminder of me, as you've got a rather long and uncomfortable night ahead.'

Donna then leans down and stretches the panties over Christina's head in such a way that the soaked gusset is forced directly over her nose. The powerful sex-smell of Donna thus mingles with the tastes of Helen and Christina squeals with a mad, masochistic pleasure into the panty-gag, wiggling her sexy, roasted bottom and bound, hosed ankles desperately.

'See you in the morning,' Donna purrs, stepping out of Christina's field of vision.

Christina moans fearfully as Donna disappears. Then she is plunged into an all too familiar yet still terrifying and absolute darkness as the light is flicked off and the door closed and locked.

Trussed, gagged, her body aching all over, the heat in her buttocks now pouring between her legs and into her rubberised sex, Christina is once again cast adrift on a sea of intense, perverse and ultimately deeply enjoyable ultra-bondage. Despite the pain and the discomfort, she struggles with a real, almost crazed pleasure in her sissy bonds and moans hungrily into her savoury gag. The

195

smells and tastes of her mistresses fill her mind, the darkness inspires a vast array of sex hallucinations. Utterly enslaved, she is in her own glowing, erotic heaven. A heaven built on pain, pleasure and the absolute reality of unending submission to three beautiful women, one of whom she loves with a passion that grows ever more powerful as she is forced by this glorious woman to play each new game of intricate and delightful suffering.

As predicted by Donna, the night is long and hard. And by the time Helen comes to retrieve her exhausted, battered slave, it is a full eight hours later. Still in her flimsy nightgown, the lovely, plump mistress flicks on the light of the small room to find poor Christina still tied tightly in place, her gag still held firm by the thick silver masking tape. The sissy has passed in and out of consciousness, and slept for maybe an hour at most. The rest of the time she has endured cold, hard darkness and the increased numbness of her tethered body. Yet even as the sexy Helen unties her charge, Christina is helplessly aroused. Her erection has been fighting its restrainer with a warrior's tenacity all night long and, as Helen leans down to pull Donna's panties from her head, Christina's bloodshot, tired eyes are filled with the heavenly image of Helen's very large, rosy breasts barely concealed by the flimsy pink silk material of the nightdress. She moans with a fierce, desperate excitement as her bonds are loosened and the life floods back into her hands and feet. Soon, she is back up on her high-heeled feet, facing her mistress, the tape gag the only remnant of her tight bondage ordeal.

'You stink, Christina,' Helen announces. 'Go upstairs and shower immediately. I expect to see you in the living room, fully bathed, perfumed, made-up and dressed in one hour. You'll find a fresh maid's dress and accessories in your room.'

Christina curtseys somewhat shakily and then minces from the cupboard/room, still devastated by the incredible vision of Helen in her nightdress.

And, as commanded, she returns to her room, strips, removes the gag and virtually staggers into the shower. Yet less than an hour later she is curtseying deeply before her mistress, fully made-up, her wig combed through and sculpted back into its Bettie Page beauty, displaying a new maid's uniform of spectacular red silk, complete with a cream pinafore, white lace petticoating, seamed red nylon tights, red patent leather stiletto heels, red rubber gloves and a dainty red silk and lace maid's cap. A vision of crimson loveliness that Mistress Helen applauds.

'A rather miraculous transformation, Christina. Well done,' Helen says, her genuine admiration apparent in a warm smile.

Dressed in a formal business suit of black silk, black silk hose and high heels, Helen is, as usual, a vision of perfect dominant womanhood.

'You will find a bowl of cereal and some milk in the kitchen. You have ten minutes to eat your breakfast. Then we are going over to Anne and Amanda's house.'

Christina is startled by this announcement. She had expected to be taken to Anne and Amanda's home at some point, but not dressed in her maid's finery!

'I'll take you over in the car,' Helen continues.

Christina curtseys her somewhat shocked understanding and minces into the kitchen. Less than twenty minutes later she is sitting rather nervously in the back seat of Helen's car, being driven by her divine mistress to Anne and Amanda's house.

The two women live is a surprisingly large detached dwelling, located in a posh neighbourhood on the very edge of the city. The journey takes nearly forty minutes, and poor Christina spends most of this time submerged in a sea of appalling embarrassment, dressed as she is in the wildly erotic, intricate French maid's uniform and exposed to the eyes of any passer-by or motorist.

Helen parks the car in the driveway of Anne's house and leads her sexy slave to the large white wooden door. Christina is terrified that she will be spotted, but the road around the house appears more or less deserted.

Helen rings the doorbell and they wait, Christina's sissy heart pounding with very nervous anticipation. The door is opened by Amanda and Christina feels a sudden wave of very powerful sexual excitement wash over her at the sight of the very beautiful woman. This is because Amanda is dressed in a just above knee-length black cotton skirt, black hose and a pair of very high-heeled courts shoes, together with a very tight black nylon sweater, her beautiful blonde hair freed from its previous intricate fifties movie star styling and now exploding over her shoulders in a golden water-fall. Strangely, this very plump woman looks absolutely fantastic in this tight black outfit. It is almost as if she is possessed by a strange, very powerful sex force, a halo of incredible desirability which makes Christina's rubberised sex twitch almost uncontrollably.

'She looks absolutely marvellous, Helen,' Amanda says, her cool, piercing blue eyes holding the stunned sissy in an almost hypnotic gaze. 'I really am very impressed.'

Helen smiles modestly. 'Yes, she's quite something. And she's yours for the day. I'll be back around 6.00 p.m.'

Helen then slaps Christina's finely hosed thighs and the lovely sissy minces into the house past a smiling Amanda.

Inside, the house is light, clean and very elegantly decorated. A long corridor runs through the centre of the ground floor, a number of doors leading off the left side, a steep, thickly carpeted stairway to the right. To

198

Christina's surprise, the walls are decorated with numerous portraits, all nudes, all very beautiful and very plump women, and most copies of classic Renaissance works.

Amanda leads a now very nervous Christina into the huge Victorian-style living room and very gently tells her to stand to attention with her hands behind her back.

'You really are quite delightful,' Amanda purrs, her gorgeous blue eyes eating up her pretty sissy charge, her very powerful perfume washing over Christina like a breeze of desire.

Christina curtseys her thanks and awaits her first instruction.

'Helen is so lucky to have found you. I've always dreamed of having a maid, although a she-male . . . well, that certainly never crossed my mind. But looking at you . . . I think Myriam can learn a great deal from you, Chrissie.'

Christina finds the reference to the pretty French girl very mysterious, but quickly performs another deep curtsey of gratitude.

Then Amanda begins to circle Christina, her eyes burning with curiosity.

'The dress is very lovely, Chrissie. Anne tells me that Helen has had all kinds of sexy sissy outfits made for you and that you're addicted to them. Is that true, do you like your feminisation that much? You may talk.'

'Yes, mistress. I love being feminised. I want nothing more than to serve all women as their pretty she-male slave.'

Amanda laughs and claps her hands together. 'Dear me, you say that with such enthusiasm! How wonderful! Well, you can certainly serve me all day, but I would like to make one or two small amendments for my own amusement. So to start, I want you to follow me upstairs. '

Amanda then leads Christina from the living room and up the stairs. Christina finds that she cannot take her eyes off of Amanda's very large, but still shapely backside and her long black-hosed legs, that she is intensely attracted to this very pretty, ample woman, and is filled with an electrical sex-anticipation regarding her proposed amendments.

Eventually, she is led into a large, beautifully decorated bedroom. At the centre of the room is a huge oval bed covered in white silk sheets. Beside this, the only furniture is a bedside table, a dressing table and a single full-length mirror fixed to a beautifully carved wooden frame and stand. Just beyond the mirror is another door.

Amanda tells Christina to stand to attention before the bed. The she-male obeys and watches as Amanda goes over to the door by the mirror and pulls it open to reveal a large, walk-in closet filled with rows of beautiful feminine attire and, to Christina's absolute amazement, the tightly bound and gagged form of Myriam! As the door opens, a powerful light automatically switches on to expose the petite French girl face down on the floor of the closet, her arms pinned behind her back at her wrists and elbows with black silk stockings and lashed to her similarly trussed ankles by a black leather belt. A huge pink rubber ball gag fills her mouth and tears of despair flood from her bloodshot eyes, eyes which squint against the sudden explosion of light.

Dressed in a white basque, white-seamed stockings and white patent leather stilettos, the poor gallic beauty squeals angrily into her gag, her terror-streaked eyes briefly meeting Christina's with a pathetic begging look. Her struggles have caused her large, firm breasts to burst out of the basque's bra cups and Christina can only respond to her hapless gaze with a look of stunned desire.

Amanda ignores her bound employee, stepping over her squealing, wiggling form with a quite deliberate indifference, and takes a large cardboard box from beside her struggling form. She then returns to the bedroom after closing the closet door behind her.

'I'm afraid Myriam was rather naughty last night and will be spending the day in the closet. I was hoping you could get to know her a little better, but that will have to wait for another day. Now, I want you to bend over on the bed, face down.'

Amazed, appalled and deeply confused, Christina still manages to obey without a second of hesitation.

'Anne tells me that you have a very accommodating arse, Chrissie,' the plump beauty whispers, placing the box on the bed and then pulling up the she-male's pretty petticoats and quickly lowering her panties, tights and then the rubber panties.

She slips a hand between the she-male's buttocks and seeks out the dildo positioned so deeply and erotically in her backside.

'Well, I think it's time we made it a little more accommodating.'

Christina moans as the dildo is then pulled free.

'I understand Helen is determined that you will be able to take a real cock, and she's asked me to make sure you get a new, bigger dildo today. Of course, I'm only too happy to help. But I thought it silly to mess about with a gradual increase. Best to go straight to the point.'

The frightened she-male watches as her new mistress takes from inside the box a jar of clear gel and a long, thick, hot pink vibrator. Poor Christina's eyes widen in horror: surely this monster will never fit in her backside!

'Anne bought this for me when we first met. She used to use it on me every night. Eight inches of pure ecstasy. And I'm sure you'll agree.'

Then a well-greased finger is exploring her already widened arse and the lovely sissy is soon moaning loudly with an intense pleasure. Then there is the kiss of cold plastic against the entrance to her arse. Almost instinctively, Christina relaxes to allow the vibrator inside. Yet it quickly becomes apparent that this intruder is much larger than anything the gorgeous she-male has previously experienced and her moans of pleasure soon turn to squeals of some discomfort as Amanda continues to push the vibrator deep into her back passage.

'Just relax a little more and I'm sure it'll go in,' Amanda says, increasing the pressure.

But relaxation is the farthest thing from poor Christina's mind! She feels as if she is being split in two and her squeals of discomfort quickly becomes cries of pain.

'Please, mistress,' she cries. 'It hurts. It's too big!'

In response, Amanda pushes even harder. Then something very odd happens. Christina feels her anus suddenly expand and almost suck up the vibrator. With a strange, sickly ease the wicked device is then forced home. Suddenly, she feels like a huge rubber pole has been pushed into her very gut and her buttocks have been permanently prised apart. There is a gaping hole in her that has been filled to bursting point by an impossible and fiendish torture toy!

As she struggles with this strange, worrying sensation, Amanda slowly helps Christina back to her feet. As she does so, Christina feels the massive intruder push even further into her arse and tears of panic begin to trickle from her baby girl eyes.

'Don't worry,' Amanda whispers, her voice full of a deep sexual excitement. 'It's just the last bit of physical resistance. It'll feel strange at first, but there'll be no permanent physical damage done.'

Christina tries to stifle her tears. Amanda then helps Christina back into the rubber panties, tights and delicate silk panties and straightens her sexy maid's costume.

'Right', Amanda says, her eyes consuming the she-male beauty. 'Now for the gag.'

Then, to Christina's further distress, Amanda takes from the box what initially appears to be another vibrator, yet closer inspection reveals that it is in fact a large, rubber penis gag attached to two lengths of thick black leather!

'Open wide!' Amanda snaps.

Christina obeys and Amanda forces the long, ribbed gag deep into the helpless sissy's pretty mouth.

The rounded tip of the gag is pushed firmly up against the back of Christina's mouth and then strapped tightly into place. Her tongue is completely flattened by the gag and any sound, even the tiniest squeal, is subsequently made impossible. Also, there is the terrible, utterly humiliating sense of having a huge rubber cock rammed tightly into her mouth. Yet this is not all, for once the gag is strapped in place, it quickly becomes apparent that, at some point very recently, it has been inserted in a very intimate female place.

'The gag will be uncomfortable at first, Chrissie,' Amanda says, a teasing smile lighting up her face. 'But you'll need to get used to it. Also, look at it as good practice for the real thing. And I hope you like the taste: I was using it on Myriam's cunt last night.'

As Christina struggles to come to terms with the gag, Amanda returns to the box and takes from within it a small pair of black leather shackles joined by a very thin, short silver chain. As Amanda kneels down to attach the shackles to Christina's slender, hosed ankles, the trembling, highly aroused she-male notices that each shackle is fitted with a row of tiny bells. Once these belled shackles have been attached, Amanda then produces a second set, almost identical, but with an even shorter connecting chain. These she fits just below the lovely she-males nylon-sheathed knees. Yet even this is not the end of the shackling, for another set is soon being fitted to her wrists. Then, finally, a longer length of silver chain is produced, which is fitted with a small self-locking hook at each end. This is fitted to the connecting chain running between the knee shackles and the connecting chain between the wrist shackles.

'There,' Amanda says, obviously satisfied that her she-male slave is adequately secured. 'All ready for a morning's sissy labour.'

Like a member of some bizarre she-male chain gang, poor Christina is then led from the room, shuffle-mincing behind the stunningly ample form of Amanda, the huge vibrator throbbing sensually in her arse, the vast penis gag ensuring an absolute silence, her lovely eyes wide with fear and arousal, each tiny, high-heeled step accompanied by a symphony of delightfully tink-ling bells. And it is in this strange state that she is set to work by Amanda. First, to clean the ground floor, to wash up a huge pile of dirty plates in the kitchen, to polish, to dust. Then to work on the upstairs, cleaning the toilet and bathroom, hoovering, dusting and polish-ing in each of the four bedrooms. A hard, continual graft made ten times more difficult by the gag and the shackles and the constant intrusive presence of the large, hard vibrator. Four hours of intense sissy labour, often carefully observed by Amanda. Not just observed, but also examined. It is almost as if Christina is being put to the test for some mysterious, no doubt deeply perverse reason. Yet the lovely she-male has been very well trained and, despite the difficulties imposed on her, she performs her tasks with a striking sissy enthusiasm and style, and the gorgeous Amanda is clearly very impressed.

Then, at precisely 12.30pm, she is led back to the original bedroom, unshackled, freed of the dreadful gag and then helped to undress. She is very quickly stripped down to her rubber restrainer and then taken back down to the corridor to the bathroom. Here, carefully supervised by the ample blonde, she is placed under a steaming hot shower and made to wash herself thoroughly with scented soap. She is then dried, powdered and perfumed and taken back to Amanda's bedroom, placed before the dressing table mirror and once again very carefully made up.

Despite the bizarre torments of the morning, Christina has remained continually and quite violently erect. The plump blonde beauty exudes a very powerful sexual energy and her beautiful, sparkling blue eyes are filled with a wicked erotic electricity. As Amanda applies the finishing touches to her slave's make-up, Christina finds herself staring with intoxicated desire at the beautiful blonde's very large breasts. Momentarily, sweet memories of suckling Helen return and she wonders what it would be like to worship these substantial, impressive melons.

Satisfied that her charge is suitably decorated, Amanda returns to the closet. Once again, the tethered, tightly gagged figure of poor Myriam is displayed, her struggles now considerably lessened, her muffled protests weak, sad, exhausted. As Amanda carefully steps over her, Christina wonders once again what on earth is going on in this house. It would seem that Myriam is, in some way, a slave to Amanda in the same way that Christina is to her three mistresses. This bizarre truth fills the kinky she-male with a deep arousal and for a moment she envies the lovely French girl's tight, inescapable bondage.

'I suppose you're wondering about Myriam,' Amanda says, closing the closet door and returning holding a large collection of particularly unusual clothing. 'She started off in this country as an exchange student. I took her on as a temp at the store over a year ago. She was rather hard up and needed the work quite desperately. Then I offered her a room, for all the wrong reasons. It didn't take long for things to develop. She was eighteen, rather impressionable. Amazingly, a virgin. Then we became lovers. Or rather, Anne and I shared her. One thing led to another. She willingly joined in our little power games. Then the games became reality and she was very happy. So now she's more or less my sex slave. And despite appearances, she loves every second of it.'

Christina struggles to take in this amazing tale as Amanda lays the collection of clothing out on the bed. The poor she-male's eyes then widen in a mixture of horror and amazement as the nature of the costume becomes apparent. For before her is a very fine white satin blouse with thickly befrilled and puffed up sleeves, a very high, equally befrilled neck and a band of wavy satin frilling that runs straight up the middle and within which are located a row of large, silver-grey pearl buttons. Next to this astonishing sissy blouse is a beautiful black velvet jacket with very large red buttons shaped in the form of roses. It too is covered in lacy frilling at the sleeves, hem and neck. Then, next to the jacket, there is a large pair of Victorian-style child's short trousers, also made of black velvet and also covered in lace frills at the waist and the base of the short legs. Finally, there is a pair of very fine, self-supporting black silk stockings.

'As Myriam is rather indisposed at the moment, I need a replacement in the shoe section this afternoon. I think you'll make a rather appropriate replacement, Chrissie. I also thought it would be amusing to dress you up for the occasion. I'm sure my customers will be very impressed.'

And so, under Amanda's instruction and in a state of terrible trepidation, Christina begins to put on this highly embarrassing, very intricate 'Little Lord Flaunteroy' costume. First, slipping expertly into the long, sheer and very sexy black silk stockings, which ensure that she remains very firmly and desperately erect. Then, she is helped into the gorgeous white satin blouse. As she secures the row of buttons running right up to the very top of the frilled neck, a terrible, deeply masochistic sense of sissy surrender overwhelms her: suddenly, the idea of being exposed in public in this sissy attire is not so terrible; indeed, as she is helped into the short trousers, whose befrilled legs only just reach the tops of her stockinged knees, fear has well and truly been replaced by a terrible, kinky arousal, an arousal whose result is made strikingly obvious by the design of the trousers, which are very tight and zipless and, without any panties, reveal the true extent of her excitement for all to see. Yet Amanda seems indifferent to this blatant exposure and concentrates on helping her slave into the jacket and then carefully buttoning it up to the edge of the blouse's wildly befrilled neck.

'My, you look gorgeous, Chrissie!'

Christina has little chance to respond before Amanda takes a black shoebox from beneath the bed and produces a pair of truly stunning shoes. Made of black patent leather, they are essentially very pretty Mary Janes, yet each is fitted with a four-inch high stiletto heel and a lovely diamond butterfly buckle. Christina is made to sit on the bed. Amanda kneels down before her and then carefully slips the shoes over the sissy's delicately stockinged feet. Yet even this is not the end of this new sissification. For as soon as the shoes are secured, Christina is made to rise to her feet and follow her amply formed, ultra-sexy mistress back to the dressing table. Here, a spectacular wig of long blonde 'bang' style curls is produced and carefully fitted over her own very short hair. Then, a broad, perverse smile lighting up her lovely face, Amanda carefully applies two rouge circles to the sissy's cheeks and a new layer of blood-red lipstick to Christina's helplessly pouting, very full lips.

'Perfect,' Amanda purrs. 'Absolutely perfect.'

Poor Christina stares at her reflection in absolute horror and is even more appalled when Amanda helps the sissy to her feet and then makes her stand before the full-length mirror. Without the feminine padding, Christina appears little more than a very feminine young man, a disturbingly pretty youth lost halfway between male and female, but whose biological sex is made glaringly obvious by the very tight black velvet trousers. Yet it is not just the bizarre spectacle that Amanda has created that fills poor Christina with dread: there is the awful fact that she is to be paraded in this condition before a series of strange women in a public place, a humiliation made perhaps more severe than anything she has experienced so far. And as huge baby tears well up in her lovely eyes, Amanda bursts out laughing.

'Oh, yes, marvellous – the final sissy touch! Well, not the final touch, actually.'

As the tears trickle down her sissy cheeks, Christina can only watch fearfully as Amanda then opens a small silver box resting on the dressing table and takes from within it a very large baby's dummy, a dummy that is terrifyingly familiar: the phallic-shaped dummy gag that had been her constant companion during the first seven days of the induction week!

The poor sissy is soon begging for mercy, but this only increases Amanda's laughter and soon Christina's mouth is once again tightly filled and the dummy gag's ribbons have been tied tightly in place at the back of her slender, pretty neck.

'Yes. That's it. Now, put your hands behind your back.'

Christina obeys, now bleakly resigned to this new humiliation, her eyes wide, tear stained, and beholding her strange reflection with a sense of ultimate doom. And as Amanda tightly ties her wrists behind her back with a black nylon stocking, forcing her chest out and making her already blatant erection even more apparent, the sissy realises that, despite all this awful embarrassment, this quite evil psychological torture, she is more excited than ever.

* * *

Amanda drives to her shop with Christina travelling in the back seat, her hands and feet bound with stockings, her mouth filled with the humiliating dummy gag. Despite the strange, even disturbing spectacle that she makes, no one seems to notice the tethered sissy and, even though Christina spends the journey terrified that she will be spotted or that the car will be stopped, they arrive outside the service entrance to the shop without incident.

Moaning fearfully into the gag, Christina's feet are untied and she is then gently helped from the car and led into the rear of the shop. She is soon once again in the corridor leading to the main display area and then back in the private viewing room. Here, Amanda unties her wrists and carefully removes the gag.

'You will cover the shoe section between 2.00 p.m. and 4.00 p.m. Lucy, my senior assistant will oversee your work. I have also arranged a private fitting for a friend at 4.00 p.m.'

Christina curtseys her understanding, relieved that she is to be spared the awful torment of spending the afternoon dummy-gagged. Then the door to the private room opens and a tall, willowy blonde enters the room, a broad smile on her face, her eyes eating up the bizarre spectacle that is Christina with a sly enthusiasm which turns to titters of cruel entertainment when her eyes finally reach the kinky vision of the poor she-male's tightly restrained and quite deliberately displayed sex.

'Lucy, meet Christina. You will supervise her until Lady Ashcroft arrives.'

Lucy, her golden hair tied in a tight bun and clad in the sexy shop uniform of tight white sweater, very short cotton skirt, black hose and heels, snaps a confident 'Yes, Miss Chalmers', and then takes Christina by the hand.

'This way, Christina.'

Staring with pleading eyes at a smiling Amanda, Christina is then led from the room, wiggle-mincing in her heeled Mary Janes, her sex swinging from side to side in the teasing velvet trousers.

'My, you are a pretty little thing,' Lucy coos, as they return to the long corridor. 'But perhaps not so little?'

Christina blushes and Lucy bursts out laughing.

'And I love your outfit. You look so cute! When you came in the other day, none of us could believe you were a boy. But now, well, there's really no denying that fact!'

Then they walk out into the rear of the main display area and a wall of blank, sickening fear washes over the helpless she-male. Christina stops dead and gasps in horror. Lucy laughs and pulls the terrified she-male forwards.

'Don't be silly, Christina. There's nothing to be afraid of!'

Poor Christina is then forcibly led to the section of the display floor specialising in ladies' shoes. Four large racks, each with six shelves loaded with a vast variety of elegant, expensive ladies' footwear, form a quadrangle, at the centre of which is a number of leather-backed fitting stools. Luckily, there is nobody in the shoe section and Christina finds herself relaxing only very slightly as she is led to the stools.

'If you work in the shoe section, you spend most of your time on your knees. But I'm sure you'll like that!'

Christina fights to listen as Lucy explains far too quickly how each set of shelves hold a certain variety of footwear and within each set how there are various sub-varieties. As she explains, Lucy makes a point of bending over to retrieve a lovely, patent leather boot from a bottom shelve, causing her short skirt to ride up her legs and reveal dark stocking tops followed by very shapely thighs and a black silk-pantied bottom. This quite deliberate display is designed purely to excite the hapless she-male and thus to enrage her already very prominent erection even further. And she is still in a state of some considerable sexual distress when a very attractive middle-aged lady suddenly appears and asks for assistance. In response, Lucy spins around, a broad, helpful smile on her face and points directly at Christina.

'Of course, madam. I'm sure Chrissie will be more than pleased to serve you.'

As Lucy then quickly disappears, her gentle laughter bells of doom in the she-male's sissy ears, poor Christina turns to face the lady and instinctively performs a deep curtsey.

It is only as the woman gasps in amazement that Christina has the courage to face her fully. Surely, she thinks, the woman will complain, the police will be called. But by the time their eyes meet, the woman is smiling broadly, her eyes filled with cruel humour and something else: desire.

'Well, well. Another one of Amanda's little pranks, I assume. And what a particularly lovely one!'

The woman is maybe fifty, dressed in a long black dress, an expensive fur coat and very high heels. Her steel grey hair is bound into a very tight bun with a diamond clasp. Her piercing green eyes remind Christina of Anne, yet there is more humour here, and thus more humanity.

'And you are?'

'Christina, mistress,' the she-male meekly replies, performing another helplessly deep curtsey. 'How can I serve you?'

The woman's cherry-red lips widen. 'Oh, I can think of quite a few ways, actually. But you can start by showing me some shoes. I'm particularly interested in your heeled boots.'

As she speaks, she points a long, red-nailed finger at a rack of very elegant leather boots directly opposite. Christina curtseys and wiggle-minces over to the rack, making sure that the woman is treated to a sexy display of her bouncing and, because of the tightness of the trousers (and the fact he is wearing no underwear), very clearly defined buttocks, two ripe plums in a soft velvet sack.

Keeping her knees tightly together, she bends forwards and selects two types of particularly high-heeled boot, one cut from brown leather with a strange but very attractive flower patterning, the other a stiletto-heeled, black patent leather boot with a pin-pointed, silver-capped toe. Knowing that the woman is feasting her eyes on her now very obviously displayed bottom, Christina performs a naughty little wiggle, straightens up and then returns, her very stiff, very angry sex straining both against the tight rubber restrainer and the taut velvet fabric of the kinky trousers.

The woman now seems quite overcome with arousal and allows herself to be gently led to a fitting stool. Once she has sat down, her eyes glazed yet still fixed firmly on this gorgeous, sexy sissy, Christina elegantly kneels by her feet and bends to slip off her high-heeled court shoes, a familiar she-male confidence washing over her, a deeply enlivening sense of her own feminine charms that brushes the fear and humiliation to one side.

The woman is wearing black hose and her cherry-painted toes are clearly visible through the erotic film of sheer black nylon. Christina recalls her adventures at the feet of her three mistresses and her erection struggles a little more desperately.

'I think you'll like these, mistress,' Christina purrs, slipping the brown boot over the woman's shapely foot.

The woman stares down at the boot now gracing her left foot and smiles weakly. 'Yes, it's nice. Can I try the other one?'

Subdued because overwhelmed, excited, and now confused, the woman watches astonished as Christina then slips the boot from her foot, making sure that her fingers glide over her hosed calves as she does so. She then fits the patent leather boot with an equally erotic care and the slightest moan of pleasure escapes from the woman's lips.

'Who are you?' she asks, trying her hardest to concentrate on the foot.

'I am the personal maid of some friends of mistress Amanda, mistress.'

'Maid? But you are . . . I mean, you're male?'

'Yes, mistress. But "she-male" would be a more accurate description.'

'Indeed . . .'

Then Lucy appears, a huge smile still glued to her very beautiful face. 'Mrs Jarvis, how nice to see you again. Is Christina performing adequately?'

The woman, Mrs Jarvis, looks up, startled, dragged from a distinctly erotic day dream. 'Yes, of course. She . . . he's very attentive. Where on earth did you find . . . him?'

'Perhaps you would like to talk to the owner?'

'Yes. I certainly would. And I'll take both these pairs.'

Christina smiles sweetly, replaces Mrs Jarvis's original shoes and, at Lucy's command, hands her the boots.

By the time Lucy has packed the boots and supervised their sale, Christina is already at the hosed feet of another amazed woman.

The next two hours are, despite Christina's initial horror of exposure in the bizarre costume, quite delightful and very exciting. She is surprised by how busy the shoe section becomes, but the pleasure she takes in serving a succession of mainly older women, all of whom seem to know Amanda, and tending to their finely hosed feet, is a very intense one.

Then, at just before 4.00 p.m., Lucy leads the lovely sissy back to the private viewing room. Here she is presented to Amanda and a strikingly regal woman in her early fifties. Very tall, with stunning, very long blonde hair, dressed in an elegant powder-blue suit consisting of a tight, silver button jacket and a pencil skirt reaching down to white hosed ankles, together with a white silk blouse and matching powder-blue leather court shoes, she is both an image of distinct feminine beauty and considerable authority. Her cool, crystal blue eyes behold Christina with a mixture of disdain and curiosity and as the sissy performs a deep curtsey, she unleashes a whip crack laugh of contempt.

'Good grief, Amanda, what on earth is this?' she exclaims, her voice rich, deep, aristocratic, and deeply sexual.

'Meet Christina, Lady Ashcroft. Helen's she-male maidservant and general slave.'

'Helen? Yes, that doesn't surprise me one little bit. Where did she manage to dig him up?'

'Believe it or not, he used to be her boss.'

Another brutal, mocking laugh follows. 'Oh, I believe it . . . I certainly do believe it.'

It is only as Christina stands fearfully before this impressive woman, her eyes angled demurely at the lovely powder-blue shoes, that she realises she is standing before Lady Emily Ashcroft, the ex-Cabinet minister and now prominent Tory peer. Helen and Amanda, it seems, keep particularly rich company.

'Well,' Lady Ashcroft says, 'what have you got for me?'

Amanda smiles and offers Lady Ashcroft a seat on the sofa. The beautiful, steely-eyed woman slowly, gracefully lowers herself onto the sofa, her eyes never leaving Christina and, more importantly, Christina's uncontrollable and helplessly exposed erection.

Amanda stands back to reveal a mobile shelving unit consisting of three racks. On each of the racks is a pair of beautiful shoes: a pair of stiletto-heeled, cream silk covered mules; a pair of stiletto-heeled ankle boots with spectacular diamond buckles and black silk ribbon lacing; and a pair of very high-heeled court shoes made from blood-red patent leather.

At Amanda's instruction, Christina takes the cream coloured silk stilettos from the top rack and then gracefully kneels down by Lady Ashcroft. Placing the new shoes by her feet, she then carefully removes the powder-blue court shoes, delicately and somewhat covertly caressing Lady Ashcroft, white nylon-sheathed feet as she does so. A slight shiver of pleasure runs through the gorgeous aristocrat.

'You have very delicate hands, Christina.'

'Thank you, mistress.'

Christina then gently guides Lady Ashcroft's feet into the powder-blue shoes. The lovely peer stretches out her legs and admires the shoes. For the first time a look of genuine human warmth crosses her beautiful face.

'Very nice, Amanda. Yes, I like these a lot.'

Over the next thirty minutes, Christina helps Lady Ashcroft into all of the shoes, an increasingly erotic process, more due to the subtle caresses of Christina than the fetishistic pleasure produced by the shoes. But by the end of the fitting, Lady Ashcroft is clearly very happy and agrees to purchase all three pairs. Unfortunately, as Christina is refitting her original shoes, the she-male's finger becomes caught in the instep of the left shoe and as she struggles to pull it free, her nail scratches the older woman's foot and ladders her hose. Noticing this, Amanda steps forward, apologising profusely and drags Christina to her feet.

'Oh, you silly girl!' she scolds. 'Now look what you've done!'

Christina tries to apologise, but a sudden sharp slap to her velvet imprisoned buttocks immediately induces a painful silence.

Lady Ashcroft then stands up and faces the now very frightened she-male.

'That was very naughty, Christina. I think a spanking is in order.'

'Of course, Lady Ashcroft,' Amanda snaps. 'I'll see to it at once.'

'No. No, I will see to it. Please prepare her and then I will deliver the spanking personally.'

As she speaks, her eyes burn into poor, helplessly sexy Christina. The she-male curtseys and feels a sense of dreadful masochistic arousal wash over her.

Almost curtseying herself, Amanda drags Christina over to the mobile rack. On the top shelf is a small wooden box containing the dummy gag and the two stockings. Within seconds, Christina's mouth is once again very tightly and perversely stopped and her wrists and ankles are tautly bound. She is then made to hop back to Lady Ashcroft and, despite her bondage, perform a deep, apologetic curtsey.

'You look very sexy tied and gagged, Christina. If I were your mistress, you'd be gagged all the time.'

Her words, hoarsely spoken, betray the extent of her attraction and arousal. Then, to Christina's utter amazement, the stunning woman unzips her skirt and lets it fall to the floor, revealing a pair of very shapely legs sheathed in white nylon tights.

'I'll be able to control her better without the skirt,' Lady Ashcroft informs Amanda, who has already knelt down and picked up the skirt as if it were a holy relic.

Lady Ashcroft then sits back down on the sofa, leans forward, takes Christina by the waist and pulls the lovely, terribly excited she-male over her long, hosed legs. Resting helplessly in the peer's warm, deep lap, her erection pressing deeply into the older woman's thighs, she is then soundly spanked, receiving twelve hard, firm blows to her backside, a series of very committed blows that leave the poor sissy sobbing into her fat, phallic dummy gag and large girlish tears spilling from her pretty eyes.

Still sobbing, she is then pulled to her feet by Amanda and made to curtsey her thanks for the spanking. Lady Ashcroft rises, takes the skirt from Amanda and steps back into it.

'You have a very sweet bottom, Christina. I take it your mistresses spank you regularly?'

Christina, now feeling the familiar spread of the spanking's heat from her bottom to her stiff, rubberised sex, curtseys in the affirmative.

'Yes, of course. Helen knows what she is doing.'

Then their eyes meet and Christina feels a sense of utter, high erotic helplessness.

'I will want to see much more of you, Christina.'

Amanda then smiles broadly. 'I'm sure that will be possible, Lady Ashcroft, especially if we get my proposed business venture off the ground; with your help, of course.'

Lady Ashcroft smiles and nods. 'Yes. Well, I've looked at the business plan you provided and I'm impressed. And if the others are as good as Christina . . . well, I'm sure we can reach an understanding.'

Confused by this strange coda to the afternoon, Christina curtseys once more before Lady Ashcroft as Lucy enters the room and removes the mobile rack, the young girl's pretty eyes beholding the bound and gagged form of sissy Christina with great amusement.

Lady Ashcroft then turns to face Christina directly, her eyes quite glazed by sexual excitement. 'I'll see you soon, Christina.'

Another curtsey follows, then Amanda leads her very eminent customer from the oval room. Poor Christina must then stand, bound and dummy gagged, for nearly half an hour, her mind racing, her sex burning into her velvet-clad form, desperately trying to make sense of what has just happened.

Amanda eventually returns with a very large smile on her face.

'Excellent!' she exclaims. 'Everything went exactly to plan. Helen and Anne were certainly right about you, Chrissie: you're the key to a new life for us all!'

Puzzled and even frightened by these strange words, the gorgeous she-male, her bottom burning sweetly, her sex infuriated, can only watch helplessly as her feet are untied. She is then led from the room, back to the rear entrance and to Amanda's car. Soon, she will be returned to Helen, but in the back of the car, still tightly bound and gagged, all she can think of is the arctic beauty of Lady Ashcroft and her obscure references to a very unclear future.

PART THREE
A New Life

Ten

The next few days pass in a whirl of work and sexual excitement. The more bizarre punishments and adventures previously experienced are replaced by a return to the routine of servitude and education. From 6.00 a.m. to 10.00 p.m. each day, Christina eagerly performs an apparently never-ending array of household duties and undergoes further training in her domestic role and in the various erotic trappings of sissy femininity. Each morning is spent undertaking mainly unsupervised duties such as cleaning and washing and more ironing, although not in the rather harsh conditions of the previous Sunday evening. Each afternoon is spent in a trance of delight as she undergoes movement and deportment training with Donna. And each evening she minces prettily before her mistresses in her finest and sexiest maid's outfits, so eager to serve and please in any way. Although she is often spanked, especially by Helen, there are no more strange bondage ordeals. This is partly due, Christina is sure, to the absence of Anne, who has returned to work, but is also very busy transforming Christina's website into a full-blown commercial venture. And then at night, there is the simple ecstasy of sharing Donna's bed and expressing her deep, perhaps bottomless love for the blonde beauty through a passionate and prolonged love-making that leaves both of them exhausted, yet even more obsessed with each other.

And Friday comes so very quickly. Then Christina is faced with the imminent arrival of Annette. She spends the Friday afternoon with Donna choosing a suitably sexy outfit in which to meet her fellow she-male. Helen is also very keen that Christina look 'appropriately alluring' and insists she inspect the lovely sissy once a costume has been selected and fitted. So, at just before 6.00 p.m., Christina wiggle-minces into the living room behind Donna to present herself to Helen. She is wearing a very short pink skirt, a white silk blouse, a matching pink jacket, together with very sheer white nylon tights and pink patent leather, stiletto-heeled mules. The black Bettie Page wig has been replaced by a thick, very curly 'Monroe-style' blonde wig and her lips have been painted a pink that matches exactly the skirt and shoes.

'You're the essence of sissy femininity,' Helen says, her eyes filled with a profound triumph. 'You have fulfilled all our hopes.'

Christina curtseys her thanks.

'Poor Annette won't know what hit her,' Donna says. 'She'll be over here begging us to turn her into a maid.'

Christina's look of concern weakens Helen's smile.

'There's no need to be concerned, Christina. We're not going to replace you. But we do want a second sissy to help you. We have some very ambitious plans for you, Chrissie, but we can't achieve them without a little more she-male support. Therefore, I've decided to interview Annette and see if she will make a suitable companion for you and a second maidservant and general slave for us.'

Christina listens in utter astonishment, but makes sure merely to curtsey her understanding before the two gorgeous mistresses. Helen's plans fill the sissy with both trepidation and a deep, disturbing excitement.

Suddenly, she realises that she is being used to lure Annette into an elaborate trap, that she is bait to capture the beautiful she-male and condemn her to a life of ultra-feminised sissy slavery. Yet the more this simple fact sinks home, the more appealing and arousing it becomes. To share her delightful servitude with Annette: yes, that would be simply wonderful.

At exactly 6.30 p.m., Christina, now filled with a sexually tinged nervous anticipation, is led from the house and into Helen's car. Driven across the city by Helen, she stares down at her long, white-nylon-sheathed legs and feels her sex strain against its tight rubber prison. All her dreams are coming truer than she could ever have imagined; everything is finally working out for her. She is in a state of bliss.

'Oh, I forgot to tell you,' Helen says, turning briefly to her slave. 'I've sorted out the situation at work. You're now on sick leave but, providing my contact can get around the personnel paperwork, you should be able to resign without notice on medical grounds within the month. So you won't have to go back.'

A smile of utter joy lights up Christina's pretty face. 'Oh, thank you, mistress!' she exclaims.

Helen smiles and nods. 'You should know that I intend to resign as well, to concentrate on developing your potential. Anne has already submitted her resignation and, once she has worked out her period of notice, she will work full-time on the website. Donna is still considering her position.'

Christina takes in these revelations with a servile nod, but soon her mind is racing with their implications for her very sissy future. Yet at the back of these almost delirious ponderings is a question: how on earth did Helen, a relatively low-grade clerical assistant, manage to arrange for Christina (as Chris) to develop an illness that circumvented the personnel regulations of her (his) employer?

They arrive at the apartment building a few minutes before 7.00 p.m. As Christina elegantly steps from the car, Helen reminds her that she expects the two she-males to be at the house by no later than 9.00 p.m. Christina whispers a nervous, 'Yes, mistress,' and begins to mince towards the building. As Helen's car pulls away, a soft, vaguely familiar voice calls her name. Christina turns and finds herself facing Annette. She is dressed in a long black coat that is open to reveal a tight white sweater, a black leather skirt, and very sexy, long legs sheathed in black nylon which are resting on black leather stiletto-heeled mules. Her red hair bound in a tight bun, she is a striking image of sophisticated womanhood, her pretty blue eyes wide with trepidation and excitement, her cherry-red lips curved into a slight, nervous smile.

'Annette?' Christina responds, stunned by this sudden, beautiful manifestation.

The two she-males behold each other in a shocked, highly erotic silence.

'Yes, it's me,' Annette eventually says. 'I thought it was you, even with the blonde wig. I recognised your legs. You look fantastic, even better than the photograph.'

Christina smiles. 'Thanks. You look great, too. I love the coat.'

After this, there is another short, painful silence as the sissies nervously size each other up.

'Well, let's go up to my flat and talk,' Christina says, leading Annette into the main entrance.

In the lift, going up to Christina's apartment, there is a terrible, electric silence, the she-males' eyes never meeting, but both of them studying the other's sexy form intently. Then, her voice cutting through the dreadful sexual static filling the lift, Annette speaks.

'You're so beautiful, Christina. I can't believe it.'

Her voice is filled with sex, with desire, with a hoarse, brutal arousal. They have been together only five minutes and already Christina is nearly overwhelmed by an intense, yet deeply ambivalent desire for this she-male beauty. She had never thought this would happen, especially so quickly.

'So are you,' Christina stutters. 'To be quite honest, I'm shocked. I didn't think this would happen.'

'What?'

'That we'd be . . . well . . .'

'Turned on . . . by each other?'

Christina nods weakly, feeling her heart pound furiously in her head and her sex stretch angrily against the rubber restrainer. The lift door opens and she nearly falls out into the corridor.

She fumbles with the door key and eventually they mince into the flat. Christina leads Annette through to the living room. Here she helps the gorgeous she-male to slip out of her coat, revelling in her powerful musky perfume as she does so. Annette sits down, crossing her long, black-nylon-sheathed legs. Poor Christina can only stare in astonishment as the black leather skirt rides up her shapely thighs to reveal hints of stocking-tops.

'Would you like a drink? I have a bottle of white wine, somewhere.'

Annette smiles and nods, her eyes now fixed on Christina's own legs.

Christina hangs the coat up, digs the bottle of wine out of the fridge and returns to the living room. She places the bottle on a glass-topped coffee table and returns to the kitchen for a corkscrew and glasses, very much aware that as she turns away from Annette, the other sissy's eyes are drinking up her perfectly feminised, ultra-sexy body.

Eventually, Christina sits down opposite Annette and the two beautiful she-males sip nervously at their glasses of chilled wine, their eyes now connecting and betraying the true depth of a very mutual attraction.

225

'I've never done this before,' Christina confesses. 'Met with another . . . cross-dresser.'

'I've been out for nearly two years now,' Annette replies, clearly relieved that Christina is trying to break through the sex-tension surrounding them. 'It was difficult at first, but the desire was too great too resist. I just had to do it. I joined a club, met some others. Then, I found I could pass quite easily, and soon I was going out all the time. But, I have to say, in all the time I've been "out", I've never met someone as convincing as you.'

Christina blushes and looks down at the floor, mumbling a coy, 'Thank you.' When she looks up, Annette is staring straight at her, her smile filled with desire.

'I have been with other TVs,' Annette says. 'Sexually, I mean. I can see that's what you're thinking.'

Christina swallows hard, her heart in her mouth, words trapped by fear and desire. All she can do is nod.

'Have you any experience that way?' Annette then asks.

Christina shakes her head slowly as Annette's smile widens and she rises from the chair. The lovely redheaded sissy kneels before Christina and places her hands on her new friend's delicately hosed knees.

'We can have a lot of fun tonight. And you don't have to worry, I'll show you what to do.'

As the lovely she-male whispers her teasing words to Christina, her hands slip under the pink skirt towards the matching silk panties hidden beneath. Christina gasps and parts her legs slightly, her sex now furiously fighting the rubber restrainer. But then she remembers Helen's words, the purpose of this evening, the construction of her sissy future. She closes her legs and gently pushes Annette's hands away.

'You're very sexy, Annette. And I do feel very attracted to you, but I have to be back at Mistress Helen's by nine, with you.'

Annette raises her eyebrows and sits back on the heels of her feet.

'You're serious about this mistress business, aren't you? It sounds totally unbelievable to me, Christina. A wish-fulfilment fantasy. I thought it was just a game to get me down here. That once we got to know each other, you'd let me be your mistress and then a little later we could swap roles.'

'No, it's not a fantasy. It's real. You heard Helen's voice. Anyway, just look at me. Do you think I did this on my own? It's better than a fantasy, Annette – it's the most erotic reality imaginable. It's all your fantaseys times ten. I'm utterly serious.'

Surprised by the force of Christina's response, Annette elegantly stands up and returns to her chair.

'So you have three mistresses. You're their servant, their maid. This woman who spoke to me on the phone – Helen – she's the head mistress. And you work at her house. It sounds incredible.'

'There are four mistresses, now. Maybe more. And it is incredible. But it's also true. If you come with me, you'll find out.'

'I don't know, Chris. I really don't. Look at it from my point of view. Really, I hardly know you. This might be a plot of some kind. Some weird sex thing.'

The doubt in Annette's eyes is very real. Christina can see it will be very difficult to get her to come to meet Helen. Then, a simple means of helping to convince Annette pops into her mind. Now *she* slips out of her chair and kneels before the sexy redhead, placing her hands on Annette's black-nylon-sheathed knees.

'If you come with me, I promise I'll make all your dreams come true. We'll go to the house. You don't have to come in. If you want to come back, fine. And even then, I promise I'll do whatever you want, willingly. Just come to the house.'

227

As she talks, she slowly slips her hands beneath Annette's skirt and begins gently to caress her stocking-tops. As she does this, and as she whispers her promises, the other she-male moans slightly, her eyes close, she begins to slip down into the chair. Then Christina removes her hands.

'Well?' she asks.

Annette looks at her and smiles. 'OK. Let's go.'

They finish the wine quickly and then leave the building. Annette leads Christina to a nearby car park. She steps up to a beautiful, brand-new, silver Jaguar sports car and Christina gasps in amazement.

'This is yours? What did you do . . . rob a bank?'

'Sort of. I work for a bank. Or rather, an international banking house.'

Annette opens the passenger door and helps Christina inside. The lovely she-male finds herself sinking into plush grey leather seats and nearly moans with pleasure.

Annette climbs into the driver's seat and starts the motor.

'Banking must pay well,' Christina says, her eyes eating up Annette's gorgeous legs.

'I do OK. But I'd give it up tomorrow if the right offer came along.'

They arrive outside Helen's house twenty minutes later. The journey has been tense, with little conversation. It is now clear that Annette is very wary of coming to the house and still questions Christina's motives. It is just before 9.00 p.m. Annette pulls the car into the large driveway, clearly impressed by the huge, plush residence.

She then turns off the motor and faces Christina.

'Even if I don't go in, you'll make love to me tonight?' she asks, her hungry eyes betraying the true depth of her desire.

Christina smiles and, suddenly very confident, leans forwards and takes Annette's face in her hands. Then she kisses her, a long, hard, passionate kiss that leaves Annette flushed, aroused and gasping for breath.

'If you come inside, that's just a taste of what to expect. That and the realisation of all the fantasies we've discussed on the Net.'

Annette follows Christina to the door in a trance and is still staring into a sex-shocked oblivion when Helen opens the door. Christina immediately performs a very deep curtsey.

'This is Annette, mistress.'

Shaken from her trance by the appearance of the stunning, regal Helen, Annette smiles nervously.

'I'm glad you could come, Annette.'

Helen ushers the two she-males into the hallway and then leads them into the living room. Here they discover Anne and Donna waiting by the fireplace, chatting and drinking wine.

'Ladies,' Helen announces, 'meet Christina's friend, Annette.'

As Christina instinctively curtseys before the two mistresses, Anne and Donna turn to greet Annette, who is staring at the two women like an amazed astronaut coming across two beautiful extra-terrestrials.

'Hello, Annette,' Donna says, stepping forwards, her eyes filled with a strange mixture of friendliness and jealousy. 'It's nice to meet you after everything we've been told by Chrissie. Please take a seat. Chrissie, get Annette a glass of wine.'

Christina curtseys and, taking the bottle and a glass from the coffee table, carefully pours a drink for her new she-male friend.

Annette, smiling nervously, takes the glass with a shaking hand and then takes a very long sip of the expensive French white wine.

'You're very pretty,' Anne says, her eyes filled with something more than the usual mixture of cruelty and contempt. 'Much prettier than Chrissie told us you were. I think she's a little jealous of you.'

Annette laughs nervously and stares up at the tall, emerald-eyed redhead. Tonight, Anne is dressed in a short white-and-black checked skirt, a tight white sweater, black tights and high heels, her beautiful red hair spilling over her shoulders. She looks fantastic and Annette is clearly very impressed.

'Christina is very b-beautiful, too,' Annette stutters, trying not to stare hungrily at Anne's gorgeous, perfectly shaped legs.

'You like Christina?' Helen asks, joining the group now surrounding Annette.

'Yes, very much. I'm amazed by how convincing she is.'

'We've put a lot of work into her,' Helen replies. 'And she's also quite naturally talented.'

'And she really works as your maid?'

Helen smiles. 'Oh, yes. We've trained her to serve us in any way we see fit. She is completely submissive and obeys us without question. Indeed, it's very obvious she enjoys her servitude. I suspect masochism is a trait of most transvestites. Are you a masochist, Annette?'

A sudden, brutal question, a bolt of fire out of a blue sky of civility that causes poor Annette to choke on her wine and break into a brief fit of coughing.

'Perhaps I phrased the question poorly,' Helen continues, moving closer to Annette. 'Do you like the idea of being dominated, by women, by rather good-looking women? Isn't this a fantasy you share with Chrissie?'

Annette, now surrounded, looks at Helen, then at Donna and finally at Anne. She continues to stare at Anne as she whispers a very hoarse, 'Yes, it is.'

'I'm sure you'll look very sexy in a maid's uniform,' Anne purrs, holding Annette in her cobra-like gaze.

'Would you like that?' Helen asks. 'To join Christina and become one of our maids? Just for the weekend, to start with – to see if you like it. Then, well, we can think about the future later.'

Christina watches, fascinated, as fear and doubt slip from Annette's face like a worn skin, to be replaced with a very powerful arousal.

'I . . . Yes, I would,' Annette mumbles after a while.

'Good,' Helen snaps. 'We rather hoped you would. And I think there's no time like the present. So maybe Anne could take Annette upstairs and get her suitably attired?'

Anne smiles and nods. 'Of course, Helen. Come on, Annette, follow me.'

Christina watches Annette rise from the sofa and allow the cruel dominatrix to take her gently by the hand and then lead her from the room.

'She's marvellous!' Helen exclaims, as soon as Annette has gone. 'Even better than I expected. And so easy to control.'

'Anne seems to like her,' Donna says, a slight edge cutting through her normally relaxed voice.

'Yes, I didn't expect that. I thought I'd have to dress her.'

'And she's not the only one who likes her,' Donna continues, turning to Christina.

The sissy maid blushes, but does not respond.

'I suggest you take Chrissie up and get her ready as well,' Helen says to Donna. 'Then we can see what they look like together. Use the white uniform tonight.'

And so Christina is led from the room by Donna, up the stairs and into the spare bedroom. Dressed in a tight black sweater and a black rubber mini-skirt, black tights and high heels, Donna is a sleek, sexy beauty, and Christina's mad hunger for her is quickly revived.

Once in the bedroom, Donna orders Christina to strip down to her restrainer as quickly as possible. As the she-male obeys, Donna returns to the apparently

231

bottomless wardrobe and begins to take from it the items that will make up this evening's costume.

'You seem very attracted to Annette,' Donna says, placing a large pile of white lingerie on the bed.

'Yes, mistress,' Christina replies, knowing that only a truthful response will satisfy Donna.

'Well, that's hardly surprising – she's beautiful.'

'Yes, mistress.'

'And I can see she really fancies you. Which is actually a good thing, what we've been planning for, really. Especially Helen. But I can't help feeling a bit jealous. I can't help saying that to you, Chrissie.'

Christina is amazed by this response.

'Jealous, mistress? Why? Surely you know how much I love you. Love and desire you.'

A slight smile crosses Donna's face and she turns to face Christina. 'Yes, I do know. And I will go along with Helen's plans, because Annette is going to be very important for your development. But that doesn't mean I'll enjoy it, and it does mean I might be a little harder on you.'

Now naked, Christina curtseys her understanding, although what exactly Donna does mean is more than a bit of a mystery.

Over the next thirty minutes, Donna helps Christina to dress in a striking white maid's uniform. Every item of clothing is an exactly matching snow-white: lace-frilled rubber 'foundation' panties, a leather corset, white, seamed silk tights, white silk panties, an expertly padded silk bra, a beautiful silk maid's dress, a silk pinafore, and a pair of white patent leather court shoes with striking five-inch high heels. The blonde wig is kept in place and her make-up is carefully touched up. A pair of white silk gloves are slipped over her hands and then she is allowed to see the finished product in the wardrobe mirror. And what she beholds is a heavenly vision, a maid angel, the sexiest, sweetest image of

232

she-male submission imaginable, one that brings a gasp of deep, narcissistic pleasure from her lovely sissy mouth.

It is just after ten by the time Christina is returned to the living room. She wiggle-minces into the room and curtseys deeply before Helen, who is sitting on the sofa drinking another glass of wine. Helen smiles and sits up.

'My, my,' she whispers. 'What a pretty little angel.'

Christina smiles and performs another curtsey, this time making sure that her lovely silk panties are fully displayed for Helen's amusement.

'I think we need more wine, Christina. Go to the kitchen and prepare a fresh bottle and glasses.'

Christina curtseys and totters sweetly into the kitchen. By the time she returns with a silver tray laden with a bottle and three fresh glasses, Anne has brought a transformed Annette down to join them.

Upon seeing Annette, the poor sissy maid has difficulty preventing a gasp of amazement and dropping the tray. For before her is an even more striking vision of ultra-feminine submission. Annette has been dressed in a uniform that is exactly the same in every detail to the one that Christina is so happily wearing, except that hers is totally pink: pink pinafore, pink dress, pink seamed tights, pink high heels. Her red hair has been untied and is spilling over her slender shoulders, and a dainty pink maid's cap has been positioned on the top of this thick, glossy mass.

It is quite obvious that Annette is deeply aroused and as her eyes meet Christina's they communicate a profound ecstasy. Yet even in the heat of this erotic distraction, Annette manages a rather excellent and very deep curtsey that ensures all the women and Christina get a very good view of her befrilled pink silk panties.

'Wonderful,' Helen says, stepping up to Annette and taking her soft, dimpled chin in her hands. 'Simply wonderful.'

'She's obviously had her share of male lovers,' Anne says. 'Her arse is wider than Chrissie's. It took the full-size dildo with very little resistance. Although she wasn't too impressed by the restrainer.'

The women laugh as Annette blushes. Then Helen steps up to the new sissy maid.

'You will stay here until Monday morning. During the weekend, you will act as our maid and obey us and your fellow mistresses without question. You will assist Christina under our instruction. Do you understand?'

Annette curtseys once more, her excited eyes cast modestly to the floor.

The two sissy maids spend the next two hours serving their mistresses. Annette is an elegant and eager slave and spends most of her time mincing around Anne. The wicked, beautiful redhead treats Annette like a tame cat, idly stroking her silken thighs while chatting to Donna and Helen, holding up her glass when it requires refilling with an arrogant indifference that only serves to inflame Annette even more. But then, perhaps inevitably, Annette makes a mistake, spilling a tiny drop of wine on the sofa, and she quickly finds herself dragged across Anne's long legs and her panty-imprisoned bottom is the victim of a particularly sound, relentless spanking. Yet despite the obvious pain this causes her and the tears that soon pour from her lovely green eyes, intense excitement surrounds her body like a burning halo. And, once returned to her high-heeled feet, she serves Anne with an even greater enthusiasm.

And it is well after midnight when the women eventually decide to retire. Helen quite blatantly takes Anne's hand and leads her from the room, Annette's eyes widening in jealous amazement as she does so.

'Donna, I'm sure you won't mind putting the sissies to bed. Then maybe you'd like to join us?'

Now it is Christina's turn to feel the bitter bite of jealousy.

'Now you know how I feel,' Donna whispers to Christina, before ordering the two gorgeous she-males up to Christina's room.

Once in the room, Christina is ordered to strip Annette down to her freshly restrained sex. Christina eagerly obeys, taking a deep, burning pleasure in slowly undressing the redheaded she-male, whose desperate breathing and moans of pleasure betray the depth of her own sissy arousal.

Eventually, Christina has stripped Annette down to her tights and the rubber panties beneath, and it is only as she slowly begins to roll the tights over the panties that the true extent of Annette's paradoxical manhood becomes clear.

Donna, who has been watching the undressing with amused, undoubtedly aroused eyes, steps forwards for a closer look, ordering Christina to stand clear. She then pulls the tights down to the sissy's slender ankles and, with one eager tug, hauls the panties down to her knees, a sharp intake of breath following the revelation of Annette's tightly restrained sex.

'Bloody hell,' she gasps.

Poor Christina's eyes have widened with a mixture of shock, jealousy and arousal, for Annette's sex is extremely impressive, at least ten stunning, very erect inches that have pulled the rubber restrainer to the very edge of its capacity. Annette blushes furiously and then squeals like a little girl as Donna takes this substantial cock in her hands and studies it like a scientist beholding a new, mutant species.

'This'll keep you entertained,' Donna says to a very confused Christina.

Then, to Annette's extreme excitement and Christina's dismay, Donna, after applying the expansion gel, gently eases the restrainer off the huge, engorged sex.

'Go to the dressing table and look in the top drawer,' she says to Christina. 'You'll find two stockings and two cock-rings. Bring them here.'

Curtseying deeply, the she-male minces over to the dressing table and retrieves the rings and stockings. She then stands by Donna, hands held out, as her lover and mistress takes one of the soft, scented black nylon stockings and slowly slips it over the head of Annette's striking sex.

Poor Annette cries out with a familiar mixture of frustration and pleasure as the stocking is pulled into place, her knees visibly buckling under the tremendous weight of her arousal. And as soon as the stocking is positioned, she takes one of the awful double cock-rings and carefully snaps it into place. Cries of pleasure become moans of pain. The rings are actually too narrow for Annette's thick, long sex and have to be forced together, thus biting deeply into the lovely she-male's most tender flesh.

Despite her obvious discomfort, Annette remains in a state of wild arousal and watches with sex-maddened eyes as Donna strolls over to the wardrobe, returning with two very familiar baby-doll nightdresses, two pairs of matching nylon stockings and two pairs of matching silk panties. Like the maid's outfits, one baby-doll is pink and one is white, and it is the pink one, together with the panties and the stockings, that Donna then insists Annette put on.

As Annette struggles with the baby-doll, Donna helps Christina to strip down to her own fiendish rubber restrainer. As she does so, her hands glide teasingly across the sissy's silky smooth body.

'If you're going to sleep together, I'm afraid you'll have to be restrained. And there's no telling what you'll get up to if you're not tightly bound and gagged.'

Poor Christina moans with a terrible excitement as Donna then spreads expansion gell over her rubberised cock and then eases off the restrainer, only to replace it very quickly with the scented stocking and the dreadful, painful cock-ring. And once Christina is suitably restrained, her eyes nearly watering with the discomfort of the fiendish ring, she is ordered into the white baby-doll and the accompanying stockings and panties.

In a few minutes, the two lovely she-males are standing before Donna, their hands behind their backs, looking extremely sexy in the semi-transparent baby-dolls and sheer, self-supporting nylon stockings. A smile of cruel pleasure on her face, Donna then returns to the dressing table to retrieve numerous lengths of the black rubber cording, a roll of silver masking tape and two more pairs of panties, both black, both made from very fine silk.

She places the weapons of bondage on the bed and takes up the panties.

'Open wide, girls. A pair of Helen's and a pair of mine. Both worn today. It's a pity we didn't know Anne was going to take such a shine to you, Annette, otherwise I'd have found a pair of hers.'

Donna then stuffs the first pair of panties into Annette's wide-open mouth. From the look of trance-like excitement in her gleaming green eyes, it is clear that she is enjoying every second of her servitude intensely, and the sight of this beautiful she-male being tightly gagged only adds to Christina's own already consider-able arousal.

And once the panties have been forced home, Donna tears off a long, thick strip of the tape and spreads it firmly across Annette's pretty, soft lips, sealing the panties in place and making any protest against her bondage utterly impossible.

Christina continues to watch as Donna then binds Annette's arms behind her back at her wrists and elbows and then leads the beautiful, moaning sissy over to the bed. She pulls back the silken sheets and then helps Annette to lie face down. Once Annette has been positioned on the bed, Donna takes up two more lengths of the rubber cording and tightly binds her finely stockinged ankles and knees. She then uses a third length of cording to bind Annette's ankles to her wrists and thus secure her in a very tight and strict hog-tie that produces a moan-cum-squeal of deeply masochistic pleasure from the lovely sissy.

As Annette struggles helplessly on the bed, Donna returns to Christina and begins to prepare her slave lover for bed. As she forces the panty gag deep into Christina's mouth, their eyes meet and the gorgeous sissy sees once again the fires of a powerful jealousy. It is clear that Donna is determined to make her suffer tonight, yet the more she tries to punish her sissy slave, the more her sissy slave will love her. And both of them know this.

Soon Christina is gagged and her arms are lashed tightly behind her back. Then she is led over to the relatively narrow single bed. Donna carefully pushes Annette over to the left side of the bed, ensuring that she is subsequently left balancing precariously on the edge. Christina is then helped to lie face down in the space that has been created. Yet even this space is too narrow, and Christina finds herself pushed tightly up against Annette, yet at the same time positioned right on the very edge of the bed.

As Donna secures Christina's legs and then the hog-tie, she teases the two lovely sissies terribly.

'I'm afraid there isn't much room, so I suggest you don't try to arouse each other by moving about. Just to make sure you don't fall off the bed and hurt yourselves, I'm going to tie you together.'

She then proceeds to tie a further length of the rubber cording to the middle of the cord binding Christina's wrists to her ankles and then pull this length over to the cord binding Annette's wrists to her ankles, thus pulling the sissies tightly together. She then ties this extra cord in a very tight knot.

'This way, you should both be able to act as counterbalances against falling off the bed,' Donna explains, stepping back to admire her latest living bondage sculpture. 'But if you struggle too much, one will fall and drag the other one with her. So beware.'

Donna then takes up the large white silk sheet and lays it gently over the two sissies.

'Sleep tight, girls,' Donna teases, smiling broadly before turning towards the door.

As she reaches the doorway, she flicks off the light and plunges them both into a darkness that is made complete as she shuts and locks the door.

Pressed so tightly together, yet both struggling to maintain a precarious balance, the two sissies have been placed in a deliberately tortuous position. As they fight to keep their balance, they rub up against each other repeatedly, thus only managing to excite themselves even more. This in turn causes their already stiff sexes to expand and meet the painful and relentless opposition of the fiendish metal cock-rings. Yet even in this strange, uncomfortable state, the two she-males are still wildly excited, and they are soon both releasing a series of high-pitched baby girl squeals of pleasure into their fat, pungent panty-gags.

That night there is little sleep. Yet there is plenty of the strange, dark and very deep-rooted pleasure that both sissies find in the rituals of domination, submission and ultra-bondage. In their delicate, sexy costumes, so firmly panty-gagged, so securely bound, they rest so closely to each other, revelling in the sexed-up body heat of the other beneath the soft, silk sheet. Yet this is only the beginning of their relationship, and both know now that they are on the verge of a truly ecstatic and deeply feminine future.

Eleven

The two sissies are not freed from their erotic bondage until nearly 9.00 a.m. the next morning. Aching, tired and still terribly excited, they are made to strip naked by Donna and Anne. The cock-rings and stockings are slowly removed and then they are made to share a long, hot shower, their freed, straining sexes rubbing together as they struggle to wash their sissified bodies in the confined space.

Their eyes meet as their most intimate regions collide.

'It would be easier if we washed each other,' Annette whispers.

Christina smiles nervously and nods. Annette takes her bar of pink, heavily scented soap and begins to create a thick lather in her lovely hands. She then gently massages the suds into her fellow slave's silky chest. Christina responds by soaping Annette's thighs, her face momentarily brushing against the redhead's furious, stiff sex as she leans down.

Annette is a natural redhead who wears her lovely hair long both in her feminine guise and as Alan, her male persona – previously revealed to Christina in their e-mail correspondence. Already aware that the mistresses insist that Christina wear wigs, Annette carefully washes what little natural hair Christina has with an expensive female shampoo.

By the time Anne orders them both back to the bedroom, the two sissies are thoroughly cleansed and even more excited. After drying each other off carefully, they wiggle-mince back into the bedroom to be met by Donna, Anne and also by Helen.

'We've decided to have a little party tonight, girls,' Helen announces, 'and you will act as maids to the guests for the evening. The house will need to be thoroughly cleaned and you'll both be required to help with all the other preparations. Anne has also organised a photo shoot for this afternoon with Ingrid. So there's a very busy day ahead.'

Helen and Anne leave Donna to help dress Christina and Annette in the elegant, sexy maids' costumes to which they had been introduced the night before, including the less severe rubber restrainers. While Donna provides general supervision, she is keen to ensure that the two sissies help each other dress, and the pleasure the she-males gain from this co-operative transformation is quite considerable. They help each other with guiding hose up silken legs, with binding corset laces, with clipping bras into place, with buttoning up elaborate maids' dresses, with tying pinafore ribbons in fat, sissy bows, with clipping dainty maids' caps into place; every gesture performed with an exaggerated feminine grace, every gesture a form of sissy love-making.

Then they are ready, Christina in white, Annette in pink, two spectacular and utterly convincing she-male beauties, two gorgeous sissy slaves eager to do the bidding of their mistresses.

The rest of the morning is spent thoroughly cleaning each room in the large, elegant house. Under Christina's general instruction, Annette proves a willing and competent trainee. Unfortunately, Christina is constantly distracted from her instruction by the striking beauty and natural femininity of her charge, by the sight of her petticoat-laden maid's dress riding up her long, pink-hosed legs as she bends over to perform some menial task, by a flash of her beautiful green eyes or a sexy pout of her soft cherry-red lips. As they work from room to room, Christina's physical attraction to this gorgeous she-male beauty, initiated in her flat, developed in the heat of their all-night ordeal of tight sissy bondage, is consolidated in the effort of their domestic servitude.

By lunchtime, the house is even more pristine than the day before, positively sparkling under the impact of the constant round of cleaning undertaken by Christina and now by Christina with her new, sexy assistant. They serve a simple sandwich lunch to Helen alone (Donna and Anne having gone out). Helen watches every move the two sissies make and the way any excuse is always found for their sweetly feminised bodies to rub 'accidentally' together.

'Are you enjoying being with Annette, Christina?' Helen suddenly asks.

Christina hesitates, looking over to her lovely sissy companion before answering. 'Yes, mistress. Very much.'

'Are you attracted to her . . . sexually?'

A longer pause follows this question. 'Yes, mistress.'

'Donna is rather jealous, you know.'

Christina curtseys, but does not respond.

'But she understands what we are doing, that certain sacrifices have to be made. So she won't reject you, although I think you'll find her a slightly harder task mistress from now on.'

Christina curtseys once again.

'As I mentioned earlier,' the gorgeous, regal mistress continues, 'later this afternoon there will be a special photo session organised by Anne. It will take place in the spare room and Ingrid will be assisting. I also understand she will be bringing a friend. I have agreed that you can be released from your duties for three hours, between 2.00 p.m. and 5.00 p.m. Now, I want you to return to your room for the next twenty minutes or so and you will be called when required.'

The two sissies curtsey deeply and then wiggle-mince from the room, up the stairs to the spare room. Once alone, there is a deep silence framed by the static electricity of sexual desire. The two she-males face each other, they consume each other with hungry, stunned gazes. Then Annette speaks, her voice a hoarse, deeply aroused whisper.

'Oh, God, Christina. I can't believe it: everything you said was true! And it's so incredibly sexy. Last night was simply a dream. I've never been so turned on! And you look so wonderful. And when you told Helen that you were attracted to me! And the restrainer . . . my God, it's so kinky, so sexy. It just makes me want to . . .'

Her voice trails off.

'What?' Christina says, her own state of arousal all too obvious. 'Tell me what it makes you want to do.'

'To make love to you,' Annette whispers, her eyes widening, her tongue crossing her cherry-red lips slowly, teasingly.

Poor Christina sways nervously in her lovely high heels and feels her own rigid sex strain angrily against its tight, wicked rubber prison.

'You said you would,' Annette continues. 'If I came here with you.'

Perhaps surprisingly, it is Christina who then steps forwards and takes Annette's face in her hands and then gently yet passionately kisses the sexy, nervous and very excited redhead. Then they are lost in each other, locked in a tight, desperate embrace, their hot, wet mouths pressed tightly together, their hands slipping beneath their sweet, dainty petticoats and seeking out hosed, tightly panty clad, rubber-imprisoned sexes.

They totter towards the bed. Christina is amazed by the power of her sexual excitement and by her eagerness to make love to her beautiful she-male friend. Yet just as they are about to fall together onto the small, single bed that had been such a deeply erotic prison for them both, they hear voices in the corridor. Suddenly terrified, they rapidly part and stand to pretty sissy attention. Then Helen enters the room, followed by Anne, the stunning, ice-blonde Ingrid and, to Christina's surprise, a tall, handsome black man carrying a large black leather travelling bag

The sissies curtsey deeply, both making an almost helpless point of showing off their delicately hosed thighs and pretty, befrilled silk panties.

'Meet Christina and Annette,' Helen says, turning to the man.

He is dressed in a very tight pair of black leather trousers and a sleeveless black cotton T-shirt. His broad, muscular arms and firm, flawless torso betray a highly trained, athletic build. Strangely, he beholds the two she-males with a relaxed, yet clearly impressed gaze and a rather warm smile.

'Ladies,' he says in a soft, deep American accent.

The two sissies respond to his greeting with another deep curtsey and his smile widens.

'Annette, Christina,' Helen says. 'Meet Bentley. He's a friend of Ingrid's, and he's very kindly agreed to help us out with the photo shoot. Bentley is a professional master, who caters for men and women with a submissive streak. A bit of an expert, I understand.'

Ingrid is carrying a black leather hold-all and is already taking from it a very expensive Japanese camera.

'We're going to do a bondage shoot,' Anne explains, as Ingrid begins to test the light in the room. 'Basically, a damsels in distress scenario. This will make up the first pay gallery for the website: Sissy Maids in Bondage, Part One. We've already seen that Chrissie has rather impressive acting skills, and this will be a good opportunity for Annette to show us her abilities.'

As Anne explains the logic behind the shoot, Helen finds a chair in a corner and sits down to watch.

Bentley then opens his bag and takes from within it a thick roll of red masking tape and a long coil of thin white rope. Annette's eyes widen with a mixture of horror and excitement and she looks from Bentley to Anne, her concern all too apparent.

'Don't worry, Annette,' Anne says, her tone surprisingly gentle. 'Bentley knows what he's doing. He won't hurt you unless you want him to.'

'We'll start off with Christina being captured,' Ingrid says, moving around the two sissies with the camera. 'A simple scene. Christina is working, then Bentley the burglar sneaks in and overpowers her. She is tightly bound and gagged and put onto the bed. Then he is interrupted by Annette, who soon finds herself joining her pretty companion. Then Bentley decides to have some fun with his captives, stripping them down to their undies one at a time and then tying them together on the floor, before robbing the house.'

Annette watches in amazement as Christina is thrust before Ingrid's camera and immediately begins to pretend to be making the bed. After a few minutes the striking figure of Bentley enters the range of Ingrid's camera. Christina has been filled with a strange, deeply masochistic excitement ever since the nature of the scenario has been explained. As she pretends, rather convincingly, to be concentrating on straightening the covers of the bed, Bentley slips behind her and then, in one quick, balletic gesture, slips a large, elegant hand over the sissy's pretty, red-lipped mouth. Suddenly locked tightly in Bentley's relentless embrace, his hot, hard body pressed tightly against hers, Christina feels a delicious sense of helplessness, and almost swoons in his grip, but at the same time she is very much aware of her role as a damsel in distress and begins to struggle vainly in Bentley's powerful grasp and squeal fearfully into his

245

huge hand. This hand is suddenly replaced by a pair of white, heavily scented panties, which are pushed deep into the sissy's willing mouth. Ingrid is now standing directly in front of Christina and the camera is clicking away insanely. Christina widens her eyes and produces a very convincing look of sheer terror, squealing helplessly. Then a thick strip of red masking tape is spread over her lips and she is completely silenced. Next, she is pushed forwards onto the bed and her arms her forced behind her back. As she struggles, her petticoats and skirt rise up her hosed thighs to expose her panty-sealed bottom. Then, to her shock and deep, deep pleasure Bentley, holding her wrists together with one hand, begins to gently caress Christina's exposed bottom.

'My, my,' he whispers to her, 'you really are a sexy little sissy, Chrissie. We really do need to get to know each other much better.'

And as he teases her, the camera captures every melodramatic, intensely erotic moment.

Then her wrists tightly are lashed together with the rope, followed by her elbows. Soon she has been dragged across the bed and her ankles and knees have also been tightly bound. Finally, a longer length of the rope is used to tether her ankles to her wrists and leave her in the tightest, firmest hog-tie she has yet experienced. She tries to fight the bonds and squeals fearfully into the fat panty-gag; she rolls precariously from side to side, she revels in her role as the sissy maid captured and tethered by this handsome, sinister man.

Then it is Annette's turn. As Christina's struggles are so convincing, Annette is ordered by Anne to enter the scene, to pretend to interrupt Bentley's wicked work. Suddenly, the pink maid is also locked in the man's powerful, unyielding grasp, her mouth sealed by his huge hand. Suddenly she too is squealing and struggling. In a delightful moment, she is pulled off her feet and carried across the room to the bed, her heeled legs wiggling helplessly, to join her helpless sissy sister in bondage, Ingrid following every movement, taking hundreds of pictures.

As Annette is bound and gagged in exactly the same manner as Christina, her eyes widen with mock fear, her arousal not very effectively concealed, Christina's eyes wander over to Helen, sitting very still in the corner, her own eyes never leaving this kinky spectacle, her excitement mixed with a cool, careful calculation.

Then Annette joins Christina. Both are carefully positioned across the width of the bed, their lovely heads resting over the edge. Side by side once again, they are forced to look down at the floor as Bentley towers over them, his leather-clad crotch only inches from their sissy faces.

'Great, fantastic. I'm sure I've got loads of excellent shots,' Ingrid says.

'I suggest we retire for tea,' Helen responds, her voice cool, amused, perhaps aroused. 'Let's say a thirty-minute break, then we can start on part two.'

'What about the young ladies?' Bentley asks, his soft voice betraying a genuine concern.

'Leave them there,' Anne says. 'They love being tied up together.'

And so the two lovely sissies are once again left on the bed, bound, gagged, both in a state of severe sexual arousal. And here they stay for some forty minutes, moaning helplessly into their inescapable gags, struggling against the expertly secured bonds with no hope of or wish for escape, both eagerly awaiting the return of the dashing, powerful figure of Bentley.

Despite her intense arousal, Christina finds herself slightly tormented by guilt. The implications of the effect Bentley and Annette have had on her are obvious: a deep vein of homosexual desire has surfaced with the full expression of her masochistic femininity. Yet her desire for Donna, indeed for all her mistresses, is still burning strongly. So it is now clear that Christina is a fully bisexual transvestite, something that she may have known for much longer than she now cares to admit. And while this revelation brings some guilt, it is a guilt that is totally overwhelmed by the power of her desires and the intense pleasure they are bringing her.

By the time the mistresses and Bentley return, the two she-males are writhing with an almost uncontrollable masochistic pleasure. As Ingrid takes up her camera once more and Helen retakes her seat, Bentley leans down by his two captives and smiles at them.

'Are you ready for some more fun, girls?' he asks.

The two sissies nod their heads and squeal furiously into their panty gags, their legs and heels pulling and pushing against their tight bonds with a furious, desperate sexual need.

Bentley then begins to untie the two she-males, eventually leading them both, still tightly gagged, to the centre of the room.

'Take off your pinafores, dresses and bras,' Anne orders as Bentley regards them with amusement and a very real hint of arousal, his eyes particularly attracted to the quivering form of Christina, who finds herself staring up at him with shy, girlish eyes filled with a burning desire.

The she-males strip as instructed as Bentley takes more lengths of rope from the leather bag.

'Now, I want to see fear,' Ingrid says, once again beginning to snap picture after picture. 'You have been stripped and revealed to be sissy she-males. What will this dark stranger do to you? My God, he's tying us up again! What is going to happen? Please don't hurt us, we'll do anything . . . *anything*.'

Ingrid's dramatic direction provides suitable inspiration and soon the two lovely she-males are squealing fearfully into their tight, inescapable gags as Bentley begins to rebind their arms and legs. Within a few minutes, their arms are bound behind their backs at the wrists and elbows, as are their feet at their finely hosed ankles and knees. Swaying on their high heels, they wiggle and moan and then squeal with fear as Bentley gently guides Christina down onto her knees and then rocks her carefully onto her stomach. He then sets about resecuring the extremely tight, severe hog-tie and, once satisfied that the she-male has no chance of any kind of significant movement, tips her onto her side, all the while Ingrid's camera clicking furiously above her. Christina watches in mock horror as Bentley then pulls Annette down to join her on the floor, and soon the two she-males are tightly hog-tied, resting on their sides and facing each other.

It is then that Bentley leans over Christina and begins to caress her thighs and panty-kissed bottom.

'You're very beautiful, Christina. I'm not too sure I can control myself much longer.'

Christina squeals with sissy pleasure that quickly turns into aroused shock as the gorgeous black man slips his hands into the waistband of her silk panties and then slowly eases them down to her bound, hosed knees. Then he carefully unrolls her tights and begins to slip down the black rubber panties that make up the first layer of sissy restraint. As he gently guides the panties over her buttocks and hips, Christina's rigid, rubber-cocooned sex suddenly pops out. The sissy squeals with embarrassment into her scented gag, her excitement now almost unbearable. Soon the rubber panties have joined the tights and silk panties and Christina is watching as Bentley repeats this forced removal of underwear on the lovely, moaning, writhing Annette. Then Annette's very long and rock-hard sex, also tightly rubberised, is revealed and Bentley lets out of whistle of amazement.

'Zowie!' he jokes. 'Anne certainly is one lucky lady.'

As their sexes are exposed, Ingrid moves in very closely with the camera. The two sissies respond by writing with mock fear and outrage, their terror-streaked eyes beautifully capturing the essence of bound and gagged damsels in some considerable distress. Yet their bondage ordeal is only just beginning, for Bentley has now produced the roll of red masking tape again and crouched back down over the sissies. Using his free hand he carefully pushes Christina towards Annette until their sexes are actually touching. Then, to the she-males' genuine horror, he tears a very long strip of the wide tape from the roll and proceeds to wrap it very delicately, yet tightly around the two rubberised sexes, thus binding the two she-males very securely and intimately together. The two sissies squeal with a new, wild pleasure as another length of tape is torn free of the roll and added to their sexes, and soon their rock-hard cocks are sealed from base to tip with thick red tape.

So intimately bound together, the she-males' struggles begin to take on a new, highly erotic form. Squeals turn to moans of pleasure as the bizarre reality of this odd bondage hits home. So tightly bound cock to cock, even the slightest movement forces their sexes to rub together in a very exciting way, effectively causing them to masturbate each other in their tight sissy bondage.

Smiling, Bentley leans forwards and pats both she-males on their exposed backsides, then he brings his head down very close to Christina's.

'Donna tells me you've got a very clever tongue, Chrissie, and a pretty arsehole. I intend to find out for myself after the party.'

Their eyes meet and poor Christina manages to force a stunned moan of deeply pleasurable apprehension from her fat panty gag.

Ingrid packs up the camera and Helen comes over to get a closer look at her bound and gagged slaves.

'They look so sweet,' Helen says to Ingrid.

'Yes, Bentley has a way with bondage,' Ingrid replies.

250

'Let's go and have a drink and talk about some other plans I have.'

The three women and Bentley then leave the room and Christina and Annette are left on the floor, trussed together by their sexes, squirming with a terrible pleasure in their tight, intricate bondage. Their eyes meet as they struggle and all each sissy can see is an aching, animal passion and a desire for it never to end.

The two sissies struggle passionately for nearly an hour, their eyes fixed upon each other's bound, wriggling body, before Donna returns to the room. Dressed in a powder-blue silk suit consisting of a jacket and very short skirt, plus a semi-transparent white silk blouse, cream tights and powder-blue patent leather stiletto-heeled mules, she is a vision of dominant beauty. A huge smile lights up her face as she beholds the two tethered sissies.

'Dear me, what's happened here, then? A visit from young Mr Bentley, I think.'

Leaning down, she spends maybe ten minutes figuring out how to untie Annette, then very carefully peels away the tape binding the two she-males' bulging, aching cocks together. Once freed, Annette is left to untie her sissy companion, who is clearly hurt that she was not the first to be released.

'Don't give me that sad little girl look, Chrissie,' Donna snaps. 'Bentley has told me about how horny you were around him. You little slut. Well, you can be as horny as you like tonight, because Helen has given you to him for the weekend. I've already told him about your oral skills, so I'm sure he'll find plenty for that pretty sissy mouth to do.'

As soon as Christina is free, Donna insists they both strip down to their restrainers and then return to the shower. Here, under her strict supervision, they are made to wash and scent each other and then, once dried,

251

they are returned to the elegant wooden dressing table, made to make each other up and then given fresh underwear. Within a surprisingly short time, they are both fully and very expertly made-up and perfumed. Donna then presents them with fresh rubber panties and two pairs of white nylon tights decorated with a striking silk lace pattern. The sissies slip into the tights with a sense of delighted expectation, already aware that they will have a very special costume for the impending party.

The tights are followed by two white rubber mini-corsets which Donna insists they secure as tightly as possible. These are followed by something quite surprising: pink satin, lace-befrilled Victorian-style bloomers, whose long, elasticated legs stretch down to the upper edges of their hosed knees. They are then given the two familiar silk bras, both very firmly and realistically padded. Next come two gorgeous pink silk camisoles, again heavily frilled with expensive white lace, which they are made to pull over their heads and stretch tightly over their feminised torsos and down to the waist bands of their bloomers. Yet this is merely the warm-up for the main attraction. For as the two sissies excitedly position the camisoles, Donna takes from the apparently bottomless wardrobe two spectacular dresses. They are also made of pink satin, but are covered in rows of darker pink silk and lace-intertwined frills that run in hoops around the dress from the very high neck down to the wide, yet quite short skirt. Donna hands the dresses to the she-males and watches with a smile of satisfaction as the sissies, wide-eyed with arousal, help each other into them.

The dresses, which are secured by a long row of white pearl buttons that run from the base of the torso section to the top of the high, befrilled neck, are a surprisingly tight and revealing fit, their wide, petticoat-laden skirts only just reaching the tops of their bloomer-covered thighs. It is only as the dresses are buttoned into position that the sissies notice that they are designed with a much longer rear section, which stretches down to cover their bottoms, thighs, and upper rear legs. And as Donna returns to the wardrobe, it is Christina who realises the dresses are in fact elaborate Austrian 'milk-maid' costumes, a realisation that is confirmed as Donna produces two wide-brimmed cream-coloured straw hats, hanging from each of which are two lengths of thick silk ribbon. Yet before the hats are fitted, she places them on the bed and helps Christina into her gorgeous Bettie Page wig.

'You look incredibly sexy, Chrissie. Bentley will be so pleased with you,' Donna teases.

Then, from Christina, a moment of madness. 'But I still love you, mistress.'

There is a brief silence, Donna's beautiful blue eyes momentarily filled with a strange mixture of anger and hurt.

'I know,' she says, finally. 'And if you truly love me, you'll do anything Bentley wants. He is a very import-ant part of your training. If you're going to be a proper sissy maid, you must be able to pleasure both men and women.'

Christina curtseys. 'Of course, mistress. But I will never want to serve anyone as much as you.'

Then the briefest of smiles. 'We can talk another day. Now put this on before I gag and spank you.'

Obeying without hesitation, Christina carefully rests the hat on her bewigged head and then Donna ties the two lengths of pink silk ribbon in a fat bow beneath her sweetly dimpled chin.

Annette is helped into her hat and Donna then leads the two lovely sissies to the bed. Here she reveals two pink shoe boxes, both of which contain a pair of spectacular ankle boots with five-inch stiletto heels, covered in a skin of white silk and with pink silk ribbon laces and a striking butterfly-shaped diamond buckle. The sissies help each other into the shoes while Donna returns to the wardrobe to retrieve two pairs of very beautiful white glace gloves. Once the sissies have secured their elaborate, sexy footwear, Donna stretches the gloves tightly over each hand and then secures them with a row of tiny silver buttons running along each wrist.

The she-males are then allowed to parade before the full-length mirror, once again marvelling in the shocking authenticity of their transformations and admiring the pretty, ultra-feminine clothing they have been forced to wear.

'The guests will start arriving at seven,' Donna says. 'I want you to go downstairs and present yourselves to Helen. She will tell you what to do.'

Christina and Annette curtsey sweetly and mince in the lovely boots from the room. As they walk out into the corridor Annette whispers to Christina.

'This is a dream, Chrissie. I never want it to end! Will you ask Mistress Helen if I can stay here, with you and . . .?'

'And?' Christina asks, a coy smile crossing her lovely face.

'And Mistress Anne. She's . . . very special. She did things that . . . that made me feel so . . . good. I want to be her slave. I want to stay and be her absolute slave.'

'If I get a chance, I'll ask Mistress Helen. But I'm sure she'll want you to stay. And you know I want you to stay. They want us to be together.'

Then Annette takes one of Christina's gloved hands in her own and they hesitate at the top of the stairs, facing each other with wide, ultra-sexed eyes.

'I want you, too, Chrissie. So badly. But in a different way to Mistress Anne. I want . . . I want to be your lover and her slave. When we're tied up together. God . . . it's so sexy. And the restrainer, and the dildo. God, the dildo! Every step is heaven, every step is like making love with a man!'

'Or a she-male?'

'Yes! It's like I hope it will be with us . . . eventually.'

Christina leans forwards and places a gentle kiss on Annette's lips. Then the two sissies carefully mince down the steps to the living room to confront an utterly shocking sight.

At first, Christina thinks a third she-male has been brought along to the party; for before them is a tall, very shapely figure dressed in a black satin French maid's costume, her back turned to the two she-males, her head bowed, as she stands before Helen and a smiling, or rather smirking, Anne. The dress is particularly short, with a very wide skirt attached to which is a thick ocean of very fine white lace petticoating. She has very long, curving legs sheathed in black silk, seamed stockings, legs that lead down to feet imprisoned in a pair of spectacularly high heeled, black patent leather court shoes. Over the sexy maid's dress is the standard pinafore of white silk secured by silk ribbons tied in a very fat bow at the base of her spine. And over her short brown hair is a dainty maid's cap.

Confused, the sissies curtsey in the doorway and await their instructions. And it is Helen who first notices them, Helen who stops her conversation with Anne and who then gestures for the two lovely she-males to come forwards.

'You both look very beautiful,' she says, her smile hiding some deeper, stranger meaning. 'I'm sure you'll both be shining examples to Katherine.'

And it is then that the third maid turns to face them and that Christina's sexy mouth drops open in amazement. For standing before her is Katherine Grainger, once Chris's disliked, plain and mean boss, now revealed as a beautiful, sexy woman in a particularly stunning French maid's costume. Katherine's face, expertly and heavily made-up, with blood-red lips, rouged cheeks and even a sexy beauty spot, betrays no recognition of Christina, but her acute humiliation is all too obvious.

'Katherine has decided to come and join our growing staff of domestic slaves. It turns out that her interest in me is rather stronger than I thought, and that she's quite prepared to do anything I tell her. That includes becoming my slave and falsifying medical evidence to ensure your resignation can be processed without returning to work.'

It is only as Helen exposes Katherine's misbehaviour that the new slave finally understands who Christina actually is. Her own dark brown eyes widen in amazement; a very slight smile crosses her face.

'Chris? This is Chris?' she says, clearly amazed.

Helen laughs loudly. 'Yes, it's Chris. But we call her Christina now, and you've got a very great deal to learn from her ... including when to keep your mouth shut. Anne, can you get the gag, please?'

A look of terror suddenly crosses Katherine's face and she turns to Helen.

'No, please ... not that again. I'm sorry, mistress. It's just the shock ... I mean –'

The slap to her face is hard and fast and Katherine totters backward in shock. Anne then steps forwards and forces a very large, red rubber ball gag into Katherine's mouth and buckles it tightly into place.

'You'll wear that for the rest of the evening. You can also expect a sound thrashing and some very tight bondage when we go up to my room later.'

Huge tears of despair begin to trickle from Katherine's eyes and Christina now fights a cruel smile of her own.

As Christina and Annette are set to work, Katherine is made to stand in the middle of the room. Her hands are tied behind her back, then her ankles and knees are

also tightly secured. Reduced to a spectacle of humiliation and utter subjugation, she is to spend the rest of the
evening as a visual amusement for the guests, an
amusement made even more entertaining as Anne
subsequently steps forwards and hangs a white cardboard
sign around her slender, pale neck. Printed on the sign in
large red letters are the words PLEASE SPANK ME. A long
leather paddle, attached to a silken cord leash, is then
carefully tied around the unfortunate slave girl's waist in
such a way that there is just enough slack for the paddle
to be picked up and applied to her befrilled bottom.

As Katherine sways helplessly, tears pouring from her
eyes, Christina helps Helen set out a buffet of finger
snacks on the dining table.

'I want you to train Katherine, Chrissie,' Helen says.
'She has already submitted her own letter of resignation,
although she will have to work her notice. She will be
here most evenings and every weekend from next week.
You will have complete control over her, including the
right to punish her as you see fit. I suggest you take full
advantage of this power.'

Christina curtseys deeply before the gorgeous, majestic mistress.

'As you may have noticed, Bentley is rather taken by
you,' Helen continues. 'In order to ensure his continued
co-operation, I have given you to him for the weekend.
Donna is a bit annoyed, but it's all too clear you're
madly in love with her and she can see the entertainment
value of your bisexuality. Anyway, you will spend the
night with Bentley and do whatever he tells you.'

Again, Christina curtseys deeply. Helen smiles gently
then returns to talk to Anne. A few minutes later Donna
walks into the room, followed by Amanda and Lady
Emily Ashcroft. The beautiful, very plump blonde
mistress is dressed in a striking black silk trouser suit
and a pair of very high-heeled boots. Her hair exploding
over her broad shoulders, she looks every inch the

perfect dominatrix. Lady Ashcroft is dressed in a black, sequinned evening dress and a pair of very high-heeled mules. And as the two beauties step into the room, Christina notices that both women are holding leashes attached to silver chains, chains which lead back to two particularly pretty pets. For tottering along behind them are Myriam and Lucy, thick black leather collars attached to their slender necks (to which the chains are firmly attached), dressed in matching red and black maid's dresses (yet with Myriam wearing sheer nylon black stockings and Lucy wearing red silk, seamed stockings), both with their wrists lashed tightly behind their backs, both fitted with mouth-filling, blood-red rubber ball gags and both wearing impossibly high-heeled court shoes that match their stockings. The two tethered girls appear both angry and terribly excited, with Lucy particularly annoyed, her tear-stained eyes wide with both fury and a helpless sexual excitement.

Helen makes a point of introducing the two women to the tethered Katherine and there is much laughter and teasing at the maid's expense, while the two other female slaves wiggle and moan in the back-ground.

Christina watches in amazement as Lady Ashcroft then slips the paddle from around Katherine's neck and forces the squealing, crying woman to bend forwards, causing her pretty petticoats to ride up her long, hosed legs to reveal a white silk panty-clad and very shapely behind. As poor Katherine cries uselessly into her fat rubber ball gag, the sexy peer then proceeds to administer a very sound spanking with the paddle, applying at least twelve hard slaps before pulling the unfortunate woman upright.

'Does it turn you on?'

The voice of Bentley, directly behind her. She spins around to face the tall, handsome man and performs a very deep curtsey.

'Well,' he continues. 'Does it?'

'Yes . . . very much,' Christina whispers, her eyes cast shyly down at her feet.

'Yes, what?' he says, a slight annoyance in his deep, firm voice.

Christina hesitates, slightly confused, then understands.

'Yes, master,' she says.

Then his hand slips under her sissy chin and guides it up towards him. She is instantly lost in his dark, almost hypnotic gaze.

'Would you like me to spank you?'

The poor sissy nearly collapses in the sex-heat of this bizarre, electric moment.

'Yes, master,' she gasps.

His smile broadens. 'You look perfectly divine, by the way. The milkmaid costume was my idea. There are lots of other costumes I have in mind for you, as well. Now get me a drink.'

She curtseys again and minces into the kitchen, dizzy with the power of her arousal, stunned by her general reaction to this strange, beautiful man.

As she serves him a glass of golden Chablis, more guests begin to arrive, all female, mostly people she has never seen before. Friends of Helen, friends of Anne and Donna, friends of Amanda and Lady Ashcroft. By 7.30 p.m., there are maybe thirty people, all chatting, all desperate to meet the slave maids, she-male and female.

Listening to Amanda as she introduces Myriam and Lucy to the new guests, it quickly becomes apparent that the reason they appear so agitated is that both have been fitted with fully active vibrators in their sexes and their arses.

'The girls were somewhat surprised when I told then that they were to be trained as "for hire" maids,' Amanda explains. 'So I thought a nice big gag and some sexual distraction would make their display a little easier.'

The poor girls are relentlessly teased and fondled by many of the women guests, and the sounds of their muffled whimpers of despair are intercut with squeals of pain from poor Katherine as guest after guest applies the leather paddle to her shapely behind.

It is nearly 9.30 p.m. by the time Helen steps into the middle of the room and gently taps a spoon against her glass. The guests immediately fall silent.

'First,' she says, 'let me thank you for coming tonight. You've now met the she-males, Christina and Annette, and the female slaves, Katherine, Lucy and Myriam. And I can see you've all been very impressed. As you have seen, our two she-male maids are particularly gifted servants. They are able to provide a wide range of domestic services around the house. They are also experienced sex slaves and are always eager to demonstrate a variety of oral skills. The real girls are a new addition. All are currently being broken in, but they will join the domestic staff on a full-time basis within the month. For those of you who prefer the company of women, I'm sure we will eventually be able to offer three fully trained female submissives who are more than willing to meet your every need.'

Christina listens in confusion: it is almost as if Helen is advertising their services!

'And that brings me to the reason for our little gathering. Tonight, I can officially announce the establishment of our domestic cleaning company: the Sissy Maids. A partnership between Amanda and myself, with generous start up finance from Lady Ashcroft, we will offer an exclusive, specialised service for the discerning lady in need of domestic assistance and related personal services. For a reasonable price, we can provide you with a fully trained, submissive maid, either she-male or real girl, for one eight-hour period once a week. She will clean, wash, iron and also meet your more intimate requirements. Hard-working, utterly submissive and expert in all household duties, she will provide the highest level of service.'

As Helen continues, a feeling of amazement overwhelms Christina. Suddenly everything begins to make sense. She has been used; after being quite deliberately selected, she has been developed and is now being sold as a commodity to make money for these beautiful, quite cunning mistresses. They have taken advantage of her she-male desires to start a potentially very lucrative internet site and now a cleaning business! This was why Helen was so keen to meet Annette; this was why Katherine, Lucy and Myriam have been brought along. These clever, gorgeous women have turned the sadomasochistic desires of their slave lovers into private enterprise!

It is then that she feels Annette at her side.

'We're being sold into slavery,' she whispers, her hand brushing up against Christina's bloomered thigh.

'Yes,' Christina whispers, her eyes glazed over with shock.

'She knew I would stay. Anne knew.'

'They know none of us will ever leave. They know we love our servitude.'

'And they know we'll love becoming domestic servants for even more women. They know we are prisoners of our desires.'

This secret discussion is interrupted by clapping. Helen then cuts through the crowd, which is now seeking out Anne to place initial 'orders' for the sissy maids.

'I take it you approve of my plans?' she says, beholding the two lovely she-males with stern, sexy eyes.

They both curtsey.

'Yes, of course you do. Annette needs a little more training over the next few weeks, but you can watch as we, together with Christina's help, prepare the real girls.'

More curtseys follow.

'This is going to be a big change for both of you,' Helen continues. 'We will insist that you give up all aspects of your former life. Your jobs, your homes, your friends. Everything. You will sell your property and all your male possessions. You will transfer the proceeds from these sales into my company bank account, along with any savings or other monies. This will be used to finance your ongoing feminisation and to reimburse me for the considerable cost of your development so far. You will come to us with nothing but your desire. You will work for Sissy Maids four days a week, Monday to Thursday. On Friday you will be required to act in a series of videos we are developing as an extension of Anne's website. There is a massive market for internet pornography, especially of the transvestite and sado-masochistic variety. We intend to establish a video library of TV Bondage scenarios and also a sub-catalogue of straight and lesbian bondage stories featuring Katherine, Lucy and Myriam. We will stream extracts on the website and sell the full videos via a mail order service. Ingrid and Bentley will be instrumental in helping to expand this side of our business interests.

'At weekends, you will be allowed to spend time with your personal mistresses, Christina with Donna, Annette with Anne. We have also agreed that Christina can spend every other Sunday with Bentley at his home. The Sissy Maids will officially open at the beginning of next month. We will begin the first video shoot at the end of next week.'

The two lovely sissies stare at Helen in utter amazement.

'I take it you agree to the terms I have laid out?'

Without a second's hesitation, they both perform deep, eager curtseys.

'Good. Now, Annette, Anne wishes to speak to you. And Christina, I believe Bentley is waiting for you in one of the guest rooms.'

As Annette minces away into the crowd, Helen takes Christina to one side.

'You have come a very long way in a very short time, Christina. I'm very proud of you.'

Christina smiles and curtseys.

'But you should know that I wish to make even more fundamental changes to you. I have consulted a leading plastic surgeon concerning cosmetic surgery and breast implants. I intend for both you and Annette to be physically transformed into living sissy dolls, the only remaining evidence of your true sex being your genitalia. If all goes well, you will soon have forty-inch breasts and a sex-bomb body designed purely for pleasure. I will talk to Annette later, but I need to know now that you will co-operate with this transformation.'

Stunned, Christina stares up at Helen as if at a divinity and then whispers a muted, 'I understand, mistress.'

'But do you understand, Christina? *Truly?*'

'You can do anything to me, mistress. Anything.'

'Good. *Very good.* Now go and take care of Bentley.'

Christina curtseys and wiggle-minces from the room, her sissy mind spinning with the incredible revelations of the last two hours. Eventually, she finds herself standing outside the door of the room where Bentley is staying. It is now nearly 10.30 p.m. and the lovely she-male knows she has a long and exciting night ahead of her. She knocks nervously on the door and Bentley's soft voice responds.

'Come in, Christina.'

She opens the door and steps into the room, her heart pounding in her sissy head, her sex burning into its tight rubber prison, her buttocks pushing down hard on the rubber phallus positioned deep in her anus.

Bentley is sitting on the bed, wearing only a pair of black cotton underpants. His hard, muscular body is a shock and a delight to the mesmerised sissy; so is the huge erection clearly visible through the underpants as he climbs from the bed and walks towards her.

She curtseys before him and a warm smile spreads across his handsome face.

'You look stunning, Chrissie. I can't believe you were ever a man.'

He then takes Christina by the hand and leads her to the large double bed. He sits her on the bed and then takes her face in his large, elegant hands. He then leans forwards and places a soft, gentle kiss on her quivering sissy lips and she falls into his powerful arms.

He guides her back onto the bed and carefully removes the straw hat, allowing her long, thick hair to fall over the silk pillows. She watches with helpless fascination as he then kneels over her and pulls down his underpants to reveal a huge, stiff, very dark sex, a symbol of profound masculine power that sends a shockwave of submissive pleasure through her lovely form.

'Turn over, Chrissie,' he orders.

She turns onto her stomach and his hands wrap around her waist. Then she is being pulled up onto her hosed knees so that her bottom is presented directly to his rampant sex. She moans with pleasure as she feels his gentle hands work down the bloomers, then the tights, then the rubber pants. She wiggles her shapely naked bottom and gasps as his hand disappears between her buttocks and then slowly, lovingly pulls the phallus from deep within her anus. Then he parts her legs. After a brief pause, she feels a greased finger slip into her anus and begin to lubricate its velvet walls. She squeals with pleasure and wiggles her sexy bottom even more desperately. He then removes the finger and it is quickly replaced with the tip of his rock-hard cock. At his command, she tries to relax. Then he begins to push gently into her. Instinctively, she parts her legs further to accept his substantial sex. And very soon, it is slipping deep within her and she is moaning with a quite savage, wordless pleasure. Amazingly, at least three-quarters of his full length manages to enter her back-side, a testimony to the effectiveness of the other anal intruders that have filled her arse over the past weeks. Then he begins to pump, to set up a soft, easy rhythm, to fuck this sexy she-male.

Moans increase in volume. Moans slowly become cries, and soon Bentley's own pleasure is being very vocally expressed. His hands grip her slender hips and he is soon driving hard into her. She loves every divine second of it.

When he comes, it is as if she has been given an enema of lava, his hot spunk quickly filling her arse with a brutal, percussive power. Yet even this is intensely pleasurable, and as his screams of pleasure fill the room, she pushes her arse harder against his cock. Then, spent, he withdraws from her and falls onto the bed. Almost immediately, she turns around and kneels down by his prone form. He stares at her in amazement as she then leans forwards and begins to lick the remaining tears of come from the head of his circumcised cock. The taste of the come, salty, hot, fills her with a strange arousal, an effect similar to that inspired by the taste of Helen and Donna's most intimate regions and garments. And as she licks his cock clean, Bentley moans softly and begins to stiffen once again. As he returns to a fully erect state, she opens her mouth wide and lowers it over his cock, taking its impressive length deep into her mouth until the engorged head is pressing against the back of her throat. Then, using her tongue and lips, she begins to tease him back towards orgasm. His hands reach out for her head. He leans back and releases a low, hungry moan of pleasure. She feels him expand still further in her mouth, feels the central vein of his sex throb. Then his back arches and he pulls her head down hard on his sex. She feels his cock stab even deeper into her mouth. Then a powerful jet of hot come is crashing against the back of her throat, a jet she instinctively begins to swallow. As he bucks and cries out, she fights to keep his sex in her mouth and to consume the jet of thick come, ensuring that she drinks every last tasty drop and then siphons off the few drops still lingering around the fat, bulging head with her expert tongue. Then she too pulls away and collapses onto the bed beside Bentley, overwhelmed with an intense, deeply feminine sexual pleasure, her sense of delicious sissy submission complete.

Eventually, Bentley pulls himself up and kneels beside the exhausted, sated she-male.

'Everything Helen said is true, Chrissie,' he gasps, his eyes betraying both arousal and surprise. 'But even more so. You're amazing! That's possibly the best blow-job I've ever had!'

Looking up at Bentley's muscular frame with wide, baby girl eyes, Christina smiles. 'Thank you, master.'

Bentley then leans forwards and kisses the gorgeous she-male, a long, intensely passionate kiss that produces a loud, girlish moan of pleasure.

Then he very gently and carefully begins to undress her, kissing each newly exposed part of her body as he does so, and soon she is naked on the bed before him, the tight rubber restrainer the only remaining item of body covering.

'In a way,' he says, running a long finger over Christina's rigid, rubberised sex, 'it's a shame that you have to be restrained.'

Christina moans helplessly and arches her back as Bentley continues to tease her restrained sex.

'Oh please, master – please let me come,' she moans.

Bentley smiles. 'No, not yet. Now bend over.'

In the next hour, Bentley fucks Christina twice more and insists she pleasure him orally a further three times. His incredible sexual stamina amazes her, and as she falls back onto the bed after bringing him to his sixth orgasm, the room is spinning and she is slipping into an exhausted, bottomless blackness.

A desperate, muffled moaning wakes her. Her eyes flutter open. She is still in the guest room, still on her back. The room appears empty, but there is still the sound of the moaning. She sits up. She is still naked. Then, she notices that the restrainer has been removed and her sex stands before her, fiercely erect and quite desperate, a burning tower of rigid flesh.

Then she turns towards the muffled moans and finds herself staring at Annette. Annette on the floor, dressed in a pink baby-doll, with matching self-supporting and seamed stockings. Annette face down, her arms bound tightly behind her back at the wrists and elbows with white stockings, her knees and ankles tied likewise. Her mouth sealed with red masking tape, her cheeks bulging with some hidden and very fat gag. Her eyes wide with desire and desperation, now staring angrily and hungrily at Christina. Then the trussed she-male rolls onto her side, to reveal she is wearing no panties, and that the rubber restrainer has also been removed from her sex. In its place is a very sheer white stocking, pulled tightly over its furious length and tied in place with a pink silk ribbon around her balls. Unrestrained, bound, gagged, she is a tightly trussed present for Christina, a fact made quite clear by the fact that around her neck is another cardboard sign, similar to the one that had been tied around Katherine's neck, reading, SPANK ME FUCK ME.

Christina, her own sissy eyes wide with amazement, her own freed sex now so very, very hard, climbs nervously from the bed and kneels down before the squealing, wiggling Annette.

'Well,' Christina whispers, 'what a pretty package.'

Annette squeals even louder and shakes her tightly sheathed sex at her she-male mentor and would-be lover.

Christina then leans forwards to pull the tape from Annette's mouth, but the lovely sissy shakes her head furiously.

'You want to stay gagged?'

Annette's eyes widen further and she nods her head hopefully. Christina smiles tenderly and then sets about helping the lovely, tethered she-male to sit up, then very carefully she helps Annette to her bound feet. Guided by Christina, Annette hops to the bed where she is gently helped to sit down. Christina kneels down before her and begins to untie the ribbon binding the stocking sheath in place. Annette squeals with a desperate sex-fury into her gag, tears of intense physical pleasure now trickling from her eyes. It is clear she will come any second. Then, in a simple, sharp gesture, Christina pulls the stocking from Annette's maddened sex and slips it into her mouth. Annette wiggles with an almost insane pleasure, her squeals now constant and very high-pitched. Christina grips Annette's thighs to hold her in place while she licks and sucks on the redhead's large, sleek sex.

Then Annette comes, an eruption far more powerful than Bentley's, a vast explosion of desire that fills Christina's mouth with thick, white come, which she drinks like the sweet sex-honey it most surely is. As Annette comes, she bucks and wriggles and squeals and Christina fights to hold her in place. Then, after a seeming eternity, Annette relaxes and the flow of come ceases. Christina leans back, gasping for breath, and Annette collapses back onto the bed.

Now it is Christina's turn to experience the pleasure of orgasm. Annette's come trickling down her chin, she climbs onto the bed and turns Annette over onto her tummy. She then pulls Annette up onto her knees, leaving her buttocks helplessly and beautifully presented. Throwing back the short hem of the baby-doll, Christina then administers twelve very hard slaps to the she-male's sexy bottom, quickly turning it a very dark shade of red. After the spanking, Annette squeals with a heady mix of pain and pleasure, shaking her crimson arse as if begging for more. Christina unties her ankles and knees, then spreads her legs wide apart, pushing Annette's face deep into the silken covers of the bed. As she suspected, the large dildo has been removed from Annette's anus and a dark tunnel of love awaits her exploration.

She then carefully slips her cock between Annette's legs. The redhead releases a series of desperate, excited and extremely well-gagged squeals as Christina then pushes deep inside her. Soon, she has managed to slip her entire sex inside her captive lover and is establishing a slow, sexy rhythm. In response, Annette pushes her buttocks back against the probing cock to maximise her own pleasure.

It takes only a few minutes for Christina to explode inside Annette, her screams of pleasure as she comes almost rocking the walls of the guest room. A blinding, almost cosmic light of pleasure washes over her; every muscle in her body tightens. Then spent, freed of the physical urge that so dominates her sissy life, she relaxes and falls back onto the bed once again, a river of thick come trickling out of Annette's well-stretched arse and down her shapely she-male thighs.

Annette purrs like a large, sexy panther and rolls onto her side, her own sex once again rock-hard. Christina turns her head to stare at Annette, then she leans over and quickly tears the strip of tape from her lips to discover a pair of Anne's black silk panties rammed deep inside her mouth. After pulling the panties from her mouth, Christina places a soft, teasing kiss on the bound she-male's velvet lips.

'That was wonderful,' she whispers. 'I can't wait to do it again. But this time, you suck me off.'

Annette smiles and nods.

'It seems such a shame,' Christina then says, taking Annette's large, hard cock in her girlish hands. 'To keep this restrained.'

'Mistress Anne has insisted that I be permanently restrained. Tonight is a special treat and, if I behave myself, she might let me go unrestrained for one night a month, when we will be allowed to make love,' Annette responds, a look of serene acceptance washing over her lovely face.

'You like her that much?'

'Yes. But it's not just like. I can't explain it. The first time I saw her, it was something like love. But more than that. She's the woman I've always wanted to be with. The perfect, all-powerful mistress. I worship her. But it won't come between us. Anne's very, very keen that we – you and I – remain lovers. The plan is for us to share this room permanently on week-nights. But we will be bound and gagged and fitted with the fattest vibrators imaginable. It's so sexy. Just thinking about it drives me wild.'

Christina smiles, also terribly excited by the thought, yet also remembering that she will be allowed release at weekends in the loving arms of Donna and Bentley. She then sets about untying Annette's hands and feet.

She wakes to daylight. Annette has gone and Donna is standing over her.

'Come on, sleepy head. It's nearly ten.'

Christina nods, mumbles a confused, 'Yes, mistress,' and climbs off the bed, soon standing to attention, after performing a deep, sissy curtsey.

Donna is dressed in a tight white sweater, a knee-length black skirt, black hose and high-heeled mules. Her lovely blonde hair is tied in a very tight, stern bun.

'We're going over to my house for a few days. To give you a break, before we start training the real girls and preparing you for your new career. But a working break, I'm afraid: there's lots of cleaning, washing and ironing to do around the house. Plus there's my body to take care of. I also want to introduce you to Lesley, my daughter. She's heard so much about you, and I think she'll rather like having a sissy maid to do her bidding. I think you'll find a seventeen-year-old girl can be a very harsh task mistress.'

Elated, Christina curtseys eagerly.

'Now get in the shower. I want you out here in fifteen minutes. Then I'll make you up and get you dressed. I thought one of the outfits we bought at Amanda's to start off with. But as soon as we get to the house, it's straight into a maid's dress. I've had a very special one made for your introduction to Lesley.'

Christina curtseys again, overwhelmed by shock and desire and wiggle-minces to the shower, her sissy heart pounding with sheer joy. As she slips beneath the hot shower, as she soaps her silken, sissy body, a body soon to be blessed with large breasts and wide, shapely hips, as her sex strains, knowing it will soon be tightly sealed once again an unyielding rubber prison and buried in the soft folds of silk, nylon, lace and satin, she feels a sense of complete peace. All her dreams have been made reality. She is to become a professional sissy maid, a web fetish model, a dream image of forced feminisation whose every breath is the glorification of the ultra-feminine and the affirmation of an absolute dedication to serving womankind in the softest of sissy fabrics and the tightest of bondage. She is surely in heaven, a glorious, unending and relentlessly exciting silken slavery.

Epilogue

The wedding was held in Helen's house, nearly three months after she had announced the formation of the Sissy Maids. The service, conducted by a local Registrar close to Lady Ashcroft, and a regular customer, was a relatively modest affair attended by only the close-knit group of women who had come together to form the Sissy Maids and its sister internet company, Christina's Silken Slavery. As well as these women, there was one man and there were the slaves, three female, two she-male, four acting as bridesmaids, and one playing the role of the bride.

The women gasped with surprise and admiration as Christina was led into the room by Bentley. Her beautiful, intricately made up face was hidden behind a scented veil, a face with very large, baby blue eyes and the sweetest, sexiest pink petal lips, a stunning doll's face produced by her own natural beauty and a series of carefully planned visits to a leading cosmetic surgeon. An incredible white satin wedding dress covered her stunning figure, a dress with a very tight bodice section decorated in pink silk roses that led down to an open front section of white rubber which revealed the longest, sexiest of legs sheathed in cream silk tights and, perhaps most amazingly, her stiff sex held in a white nylon codpiece attached to the white rubber front panel by a length of pink satin ribbon. Sown into the silk tights was a pattern of beautiful roses that seemed to climb up her legs from her feet, which were clad in gorgeous white silk-covered ankle boots with amazing six-inch stiletto heels, to the very edge of the rubber front piece. The tight bodice section of the dress was deliberately design-ed to show off her full, generous bosom, a bosom she had only recently come to terms with. Two delightful, forty-inch breasts, testaments to the genius of plastic surgery, now filled her deceptively gentle silk brassiere, and as she minced forward they bounced gently before her. The breasts, the work on her face, her wider, sexier hips and the delightfully high-pitched baby girl's voice that was now her permanent companion were the most visible testaments to the changes she had been subject to in the last three months. Yet there were also unseen changes, such as the hormone therapy that had left her in a state of constant sexual excitement, thus continually erect, endlessly desiring and always desperate for the intricate feminisation, humiliation, bondage and sexual slavery that were her daily lot.

As she followed the temporary aisle between the two sets of seats filled with the few special guests, the train of the dress, a long sheet of shimmering white silk that led from the rear of the bodice like a vast fetishistic tail, poured out behind her, a train held by two of the four bridesmaids, Annette and Katherine.

They, like Lucy and Myriam, were dressed in very short pink silk dresses that barely reached the tops of their thighs, pink nylon tights and pink patent leather court shoes with testing five-inch heels. They too were veiled. The tight dresses revealed their full, sexy figures perfectly, including Annette's also recently added forty-two-inch chest. The veils only partially hid the fact that each of the bridesmaids' mouths were filled to bursting point by huge pink rubber ball gags, while deep within their arses were six-inch vibrators that were sending waves of almost unbearable pleasure coursing through their scented, silken bodies.

Bentley led the lovely she-male bride to the Registrar, a portly, stern women in her late fifties. Christina had spent the night with her handsome master and her bottom was still smarting from the hair brush spanking he had given her earlier that morning, just before she had been dressed by Helen and Amanda, a spanking given and received out of a genuine erotic love.

Standing beside the Registrar was Donna, and next to Donna was Helen. Donna dressed in a blue silk trouser suit, a cream blouse and blue leather court shoes. Donna with her hair in a very tight bun and with a loving smile lighting up her beautiful face. Donna, the lovely, happy and very proud groom.

Christina nervously took her place next to Donna. The couple then faced each other, their eyes filled with love and desire, before turning towards the Registrar. In a few minutes they would be married, in a few minutes the final dream would be made reality and reality itself would be the most perfect, boundless fantasy. As tears of joy trickled down Christina's softly rouged cheeks, as the gagged bridesmaids moaned their own joy behind her, as the seated guests, including Anne, Amanda, Lesley (Donna's beautiful teenage daughter, another particularly stern and inventive mistress) and Lady Ashcroft (Christina's most regular and demanding customer) looked on with their own encouraging smiles, the lovely she-male knew her life was complete, that she had everything she could ever want and much, much more.

NEXUS NEW BOOKS

To be published in August

SATAN'S SLUT
Aishling Morgan

Aishling Morgan returns to the sleepy, mysterious environment of seaside Devon, explored in *Deep Blue*. Someone has been performing the Black Mass in an old, abandoned chapel at Stanton Rocks. The local priest, Tom Pridough, is convinced it was Nich Mordaunt, local high-profile pagan, and his friend, the stunning brunette Juliana. Tired of the churchman's confusion of diabolism with his own nature-worship, Nich too sets out to find out who is responsible, and all three become embroiled in a weird and perverse world of sex-magick beyond their darkest imagination.

ISBN 0 352 33720 6

BARE BEHIND
Penny Birch

Penny Birch is currently the filthiest little minx on the Nexus list, with thirteen titles already published by Nexus. All are equally full of messy, kinky fun and, frankly, no other erotic writer has ever captured the internal thrills afforded by the perverse and shameful humiliations her characters undergo! In *Bare Behind*, Penny discovers that a friend of her family, also on the fetish scene, may know more about her private passions than is good! In the search for him, she encounters the pop band Madman Klien, and she must submit to their most perverse desires if she is to find her quarry!

ISBN 0 352 33721 4

MEMOIRS OF A CORNISH GOVERNESS
Yolanda Celbridge

Accepting a position as Governess in the household of the eccentric, port-loving Lord and Lady Whimble, the young and ripely formed Miss Constance soon finds her niche giving special lessons to the local gentlemen, including the vicar! Administering unique attention to their unusual requests, she performs her duties with glee. Employing all manner of Victorian instruments of correction, not least Mr Izzard's box of hygienic but curious bathroom accessories, Constance is destined to have a very rewarding career. A Nexus Classic.

ISBN 0 352 33722 2

To be published in September

BELLE SUBMISSION
Yolanda Celbridge

Domineering Trina Guelph is intrigued at her new corporate mission – to run the quaint Louisiana island of New Arras, a female academy with a code of flagellant eighteenth-century French discipline, to train submissive, sultry southern belles. She suffers serial misunderstandings as she is imprisoned as a spy, then the subject of court intrigues and battles for domination, waged with the lash and the tawse. Throughout her ordeal, Trina quivers under strict discipline until she accepts her true nature, as a submissive belle. As long as Trina is around, the dominant men of the South are sure to rise again and again.

ISBN 0 352 33728 1

NEW EROTICA 6
Various

The sixth volume of the very best of erotic writing from Nexus. *New Erotica 6* is a selection of ten of the horniest and most bizarre scenes from Nexus novels published over the last two years. Also included are two brand new, previously unpublished stories from Penny Birch and Aishling Morgan. All in all, that's twelve reasons why Nexus remains the market leader in fetish fiction.

ISBN 0 352 337 51 6

THE GOVERNESS AT ST AGATHA'S
Yolanda Celbridge

Having taken up residence as the principal of St Agatha's Academy for Young Ladies, the elegant and perverse Miss Constance de Comynge is determined to make her establishment the envy of all others. The most beautiful and lascivious of her students join the select 'swish' club where they learn the art of administering and receiving a variety of invigorating punishments. Their passion for discipline soon finds favour with a number of gentlemen in the locale. A Nexus Classic.

ISBN 0 352 33729 X

If you would like more information about Nexus titles, please visit our website at www.nexus-books.co.uk, or send a stamped addressed envelope to:
Nexus, Thames Wharf Studios,
Rainville Road, London W6 9HA

Nexus

NEXUS BACKLIST

This information is correct at time of printing. For up-to-date information, please visit our website at www.nexus-books.co.uk

All books are priced at £5.99 unless another price is given.

Nexus books with a contemporary setting

ACCIDENTS WILL HAPPEN	Lucy Golden ISBN 0 352 33596 3	☐
ANGEL	Lindsay Gordon ISBN 0 352 33590 4	☐
BEAST	Wendy Swanscombe ISBN 0 352 33649 8	☐
THE BLACK FLAME	Lisette Ashton ISBN 0 352 33668 4	☐
THE BLACK MASQUE	Lisette Ashton ISBN 0 352 33372 3	☐
BROUGHT TO HEEL	Arabella Knight ISBN 0 352 33508 4	☐
CAGED!	Yolanda Celbridge ISBN 0 352 33650 1	☐
CANDY IN CAPTIVITY	Arabella Knight ISBN 0 352 33495 9	☐
CAPTIVES OF THE PRIVATE HOUSE	Esme Ombreux ISBN 0 352 33619 6	☐
DANCE OF SUBMISSION	Lisette Ashton ISBN 0 352 33450 9	☐
DIRTY LAUNDRY £6.99	Penny Birch ISBN 0 352 33680 3	☐
DISCIPLES OF SHAME	Stephanie Calvin ISBN 0 352 33343 X	☐

Period

CONFESSION OF AN ENGLISH SLAVE	Yolanda Celbridge ISBN 0 352 33433 9	☐
THE MASTER OF CASTLELEIGH	Jacqueline Bellevois ISBN 0 352 32644 7	☐
PURITY	Aishling Morgan ISBN 0 352 33510 6	☐

Samplers and collections

NEW EROTICA 3	Various ISBN 0 352 33142 9	☐
NEW EROTICA 5	Various ISBN 0 352 33540 8	☐
EROTICON 1	Various ISBN 0 352 33593 9	☐
EROTICON 2	Various ISBN 0 352 33594 7	☐
EROTICON 3	Various ISBN 0 352 33597 1	☐
EROTICON 4	Various ISBN 0 352 33602 1	☐
THE NEXUS LETTERS	Various ISBN 0 352 33621 8	☐

Nexus Classics

A new imprint dedicated to putting the finest works of erotic fiction back in print.

AGONY AUNT	G. C. Scott ISBN 0 352 33353 7	☐
BAD PENNY	Penny Birch ISBN 0 352 33661 7	☐
BRAT £6.99	Penny Birch ISBN 0 352 33674 9	☐
DARK DELIGHTS £6.99	Maria del Rey ISBN 0 352 33667 6	☐
DARK DESIRES	Maria del Rey ISBN 0 352 33648 X	☐
DIFFERENT STROKES	Sarah Veitch ISBN 0 352 33531 9	☐

------ ✂ ----------------------------

Please send me the books I have ticked above.

Name   ....

Address ....

         ....

         ....

         .... Post code....................

Send to: **Cash Sales, Nexus Books, Thames Wharf Studios, Rainville Road, London W6 9HA**

US customers: for prices and details of how to order books for delivery by mail, call 1-800-343-4499.

Please enclose a cheque or postal order, made payable to **Nexus Books Ltd**, to the value of the books you have ordered plus postage and packing costs as follows:
    UK and BFPO – £1.00 for the first book, 50p for each subsequent book.
    Overseas (including Republic of Ireland) – £2.00 for the first book, £1.00 for each subsequent book.

If you would prefer to pay by VISA, ACCESS/MASTERCARD, AMEX, DINERS CLUB or SWITCH, please write your card number and expiry date here:

....

Please allow up to 28 days for delivery.

Signature ....

Our privacy policy.

We will not disclose information you supply us to any other parties. We will not disclose any information which identifies you personally to any person without your express consent.

From time to time we may send out information about Nexus books and special offers. Please tick here if you do *not* wish to receive Nexus information.   ☐

------ ✂ ----------------------------